dress up

joel skelton

Dreamspinner Press

Published by
Dreamspinner Press
4760 Preston Road
Suite 244-149
Frisco, TX 75034
http://www.dreamspinnerpress.com/

Dress Up

Cover Art by Catt Ford

ISBN: 978-1-61581-662-0

Printed in the United States of America
First Edition
November, 2010

eBook edition available
eBook ISBN: 978-1-61581-663-7

Dress Up is passionately dedicated
to my wonderful friend, Ann Hinnenkamp.

An award-winning author,
Ann treated my effort as if it were her own,
and for that I am truly grateful.

Thanks to my pals Deonne and Jackie for slogging through early drafts and not hating me for stealing away valuable time from their lives. A huge thank you to my patient, sweet partner, Patrick, who I know wishes he had a dollar for every time his innocent inquiry or comment was batted down with, "Not now! I'm writing!" I love you, P!

Chapter 1

"LANA MELVILLE."

"Lana Melville?"

"Yep. Lana Melville."

With a loud snap, Wyatt's Italian-leathered sole began to tap rapidly on the hardwood floor. Tap, tap, tap went the shoe until both feet intertwined like a pretzel. The energy, deprived of an outlet, shot up the lean, muscular legs to a washboard stomach. Stalling just long enough to cause as much indigestion as possible in its short life, the toxic mass continued up through the sculpted chest and past a pair of broad shoulders, where it was forced to tightly compress before furiously funneling its way through bulging neck veins, causing a brief shortage of air. Pausing momentarily to gain energy and rush color into the handsome face, the entire ball of frustrated tension exploded out of his mouth in a volcanic spray of warm spittle.

"Are you out of your fucking mind, Murphy?" Wyatt screamed at the phone console in such an exasperated state his eyes watered. "I fucking can't teach tits to dance! They have no legs! It's impossible... tits dancing. It's fucking impossible!"

Wyatt ended the call by slapping the console so hard he sent it hurtling across his massive desk. A flurry of dust particles jettisoned high into the air. Panting, he bounced over to the large bay window that overlooked the park. Too wound up to stay in one spot, he stomped between the window and his desk.

That was a scary thought. Damn it all, Murphy! I can't allow those West Coast, tabloid-hungry no-talents to start calling the shots this early in the game. The minute we relinquish control of our baby, the quicker we get saddled with our own version of The Wiz.

He stopped moving for a second while his body weathered another violent, angry tremor. Shaking off the memory of the Diana Ross casting nightmare, he continued to pace back and forth. As he began to calm, the enormity of the situation came crashing down. His shoulders slumped. A dark cloud of insecurity gnawed away at his usually strong and unyielding determination. In their eagerness to conquer the world, he and Murphy might have made a very wrong decision. Perhaps exposing *Dress Up*—their wildly successful musical take on the world of fashion, set during New York's madcap fashion week—to the world outside Broadway was an idea best left unexplored. *Dress Up* was his toy, and he found it hard to share.

Stalled in front of the expansive window, he stared out at the park and its infinite shades of green. Minutes passed, and eventually his breathing steadied itself. The extraordinary tenth-floor view never failed to give him pleasure. Central Park, the famous oasis of calm nestled in the heart of Manhattan, stretched out before him. Wyatt's eyes followed a hungry hawk swooping and circling high in the air in hopes of a mid-morning meal. Above the tree line, the hawk made several lazy, large circles before dive-bombing down into the vast, green jungle.

His focus shifted to one of the large walkways leading into the park. Two men, approaching from opposite directions, collided into each other's arms. Wyatt's shoulders slumped even lower as he watched the lovers break from their embrace and move into a passionate kiss.

How long had they been together? A year... two years... one week?

Even from a distance, their passion was palpable. Strong and hungry. Was their sex as passionate as the kiss he had just watched? Were they reacquainting themselves after only being separated for a few unbearable hours? Wyatt nurtured an image of the two lovers tangled underneath the warm, soft blankets of the bed they shared. He sympathized with the reluctance with which they untangled themselves.

He imagined their nakedness as they emerged from the rumpled bedcovers, their bodies steaming and tainted with the scent of hot sex. He envied the lovers as they strolled down the tree-covered pathway into the heart of the park. He felt, at once, empty and sad. Perhaps it was the call to Murphy that left him vulnerable to such feelings. After all, there was a time, not so long ago, when those lovers could have been them. To date, Murphy Smith had been his first and only real love. He longed to be in the park, walking hand in hand with someone special, someone he loved. He longed to have someone love him back. A love he could trust. Today, more than ever before, Wyatt felt terribly alone.

Realizing his right cheek had been pressed up against the glass while observing the two men below, Wyatt took a step back and looked straight down to the street. Every other car was yellow as taxi after taxi hustled their anxious contents to their respective destinations.

A figure in a dark coat caught his eye. There was something familiar about the man, but he couldn't quite place what it was. Wyatt watched as the person in the dark coat ran across the street and then, to his profound horror, turned into the soft morning sun. *Oh my God!* It was Jason Lambert. Wyatt clenched his stomach with both hands as he watched the arrogant prick walk briskly toward the entrance to the park.

"Lambert! You sorry-ass conniving piece of runny shit," Wyatt screamed at the window.

Feeling his heart begin to race, Wyatt forced himself to take several deep, even breaths. The last thing he wanted was to allow Lambert another victory. Ever since their nasty split, Wyatt had begun to experience panic attacks. In addition to the embarrassment Lambert had caused him, when it became clear to Wyatt the only reason Lambert was acting the part of a lover was to secure financial backing for a pet project by misappropriating Wyatt's name and reputation, Lambert had left, as a legacy to their time together, these awful, debilitating disruptions to Wyatt's otherwise predictable life.

Lambert was scum in its purest form. A master opportunist who had bamboozled Wyatt into thinking he had found the love of his life. And for a short time, Wyatt believed this. It never once occurred to him Lambert's intentions might not be what they appeared to be. Despite the warning signs, which Murphy had called to his attention on more than one occasion, Wyatt had let his almost-impenetrable guard down and allowed himself to fall for this asshole.

He forced himself to watch Lambert head into the park. Before he was completely out of sight, Wyatt wished every vile disfigurement on Lambert he could think of. A huge goiter, shingles, elephantiasis of the testicles—which, come to think of it, on Lambert wouldn't necessarily be a bad thing.

"Your nuts were tiny!" Wyatt shouted out.

If only one of Wyatt's wishes caused this slimeball even the slightest bit of discomfort, it would at least be something. He'd take what he could get. Staring out at the horizon, a feeling of emptiness overwhelmed him.

Take deep breaths! Take slow, deep breaths. Do not let him win!

A series of annoying beeps announced an incoming call, snapping him out of his spell and bringing him away from the window. Without even looking down at his caller ID, he knew it was Murphy getting back to him. Murphy couldn't tolerate any friction between them. Neither could he. If Murphy hadn't gotten into the habit of calling back right away, Wyatt would certainly call, no matter how frustrated or angry he had been or, in this case, how sad and depressed he felt about his life. Although he was the one with the shortest fuse, Murphy never held it against him. Wyatt still loved Murphy with all his heart. He benefited greatly from his ex-lover's undying friendship, calm demeanor, and keen business sense. He understood the value of their relationship and cherished it above all others.

"Hey," the familiar voice chirped.

"Hey," Wyatt answered into the air, barely above a whisper."We're not doing very well, are we?" Murphy asked knowingly.

"I'm a mess." Wyatt struggled to keep his emotions in check. "I don't think I can do this.... It's just coming at the worst time. The very worst time, Murphy."

"Buddy, I'm so sorry. You and I... we'll get through this. I promise. You're not alone in this one, Wy. It's you and me, like always. I know this isn't the entire reason you're so blue right now, but try and forget about the Lana thing. I'm putting together a list of casting alternatives I can pitch in place of her."

That was the great thing about Murphy. He always came back from a disagreement with an idea that worked, Wyatt thought as he listened patiently.

Breath in, breath out.

"There's a boatload of talent these guys out here haven't even considered," Murphy continued. "I'll e-mail the list to you this afternoon or early tomorrow. Once you've had a chance to look it over, you can give me a call to discuss. I've got some good ideas, I think. Sometimes I have to be reminded what is negotiable and what isn't. Sorry for ruffling your feathers."

"I'm really trying to be flexible, Murph, but it's hard for me… you know."

It was true. Wyatt was trying. He really was. He knew going into this it wasn't going to be easy. Transferring *Dress Up* to the screen couldn't compare to how he was used to working in New York. He and Murphy were the new kids moving into a well-established neighborhood of movie geniuses and fierce sharks. They hoped that, between the two of them, they would be able to tell the good guys from the bad.

"E-mail me the list and I'll look it over. I need a singer-dancer who can own the part. And… I have to remember no matter who we choose for the lead, the show is the star and we can't lose track of that."

There, he had verbalized one of the biggest challenges they faced: how to bring *Dress Up* to film and keep the integrity of the piece. The script itself was strong, and Wyatt would have to admit if they were forced, it could weather substantial alterations. Hopefully, they would stay in control. That was the plan.

"I understand, Wy. Sometimes I let these guys out here get the best of me. I have to remember, we own the golden egg."

The sound of Murphy's voice on speakerphone had a comforting, nurturing effect on him. He took a couple more deep breaths. "Before you called back, I saw Lambert walk into the park."

"Is that asshole pestering you? Is he? I hate that motherfucker so much! I'm just itching for an opportunity to make his life miserable. Say the word. I'll squash him like a bug. I'll slice off his balls and make a coin purse out of his sac. Swear to God! We'll get my old friend Stuart to incorporate it into one of the holiday windows at Barneys."

"Stop!" Wyatt couldn't suppress his delight in Murphy's eagerness to get even with Lambert for all of the pain he had caused. "I'm never going to be able to look at a holiday window at Barneys again without thinking about Lambert's ball sac." Both Wyatt and Murphy laughed hard.

"Listen, here's the deal. *Dress Up* is going to clean up at the box office," Murphy said. "No doubt about it. There's so much interest here in the press already, it would blow you away. I'll start sending you some links so you can get a feel for what we're sitting on."

Wyatt smiled at Murphy's enthusiasm. When wound up, he could sound just like a little kid on Christmas morning. It was part of his charm and an important tool when deep in negotiation. It was hard as hell to buck the Murphy train once it picked up steam.

"I couldn't do what you do, Murphy," Wyatt admitted with a sigh. "I don't know how you navigate around all the bullshit and still come up positive. You're incredible. Don't sweat the earlier call. More than anything, I'm very tired. I need to find a way to recharge my batteries before jumping into this Hollywood thing. I'm scared to death right now."

Wyatt wasn't able to disguise the weariness in his voice no matter how hard he tried. He was just starting to become aware of how spent he was. He had been going nonstop, jumping from one demanding project to the next with sometimes less than a week or two to collect his thoughts and gather up the necessary energy to make it happen all over again. What weighed heaviest on his mind was that hundreds of people now relied on him for their livelihood, and it would only get worse once this movie got going. It was a terrifying responsibility.

"Well, that's the other reason I called."

Murphy had some kind of plan up his sleeve. Wyatt crossed his arms and sat on the edge of his desk as he awaited the details.

"Remember the pictures you saw of the beach house I built in Maine? Remember you said how great it would be to have a place like that where you could get away from the busy city and not worry about anything other than sitting naked on the porch, soaking in the surrounding beauty? Here's what I'm thinking."

"Just for the record, I never said the part about being naked on the porch. I hated being naked until I lived with you," Wyatt pointed out.

"Whatever," Murphy continued unfazed. "Your calendar is relatively quiet this summer. The folks out here need some time to organize before they start preproduction and handing you stuff to review and approve. Why don't you pack up a bunch of your precious can't-do-withouts and spend the summer in Maine. I'm a tad biased here, I know, but the house is gorgeous. The cove is quiet and private. You don't have to put a stitch of clothing on from the time you get there until you leave. I know people who can keep you stocked in exotic cheeses and expensive bubbly like you're used to. Wy, all you need to do is relax and enjoy your time away. Replenish that fabulously creative mind of yours."

Before Wyatt had a chance to say anything, Murphy added, "Don't say yes or no right now. I sprang this on you and I know you need some time to noodle it. Call me in a few days. I'm going to be so busy out here negotiating there's no way I'm going to have the time to enjoy the place. It would make me feel good to know you were enjoying it, naked."

"I'll go!"

"Yeah, I have to go too," Murphy answered back. "Give me a call in a few days."

"No, butthead. I'll go to Maine," Wyatt barked into the air. "I've made up my mind. I'll take you up on the beach house. I need a break."

"Really? You're serious! You're not going to regret it, I promise. Give me a couple of days to put all the pieces together. How soon before you can leave?"

"I've got a couple things here I need to take care of...." Wyatt ran through a list of various obligations, the ones he could remember. "Hmm... let's shoot for next Monday. That gives me a week to clean things up here. Where do I fly into, Barn Swallowville?"

"Sport, I don't want you to spend a minute planning this. I'll have a driver pick you up Monday morning, say eleven? All you'll need to do is clear your calendar, and I'll do the rest."

"This feels like the right decision, Murph. Thanks for... well you know, all you're doing for me."

"Wyatt, don't forget the motto we trust and live by. When you're happy, I'm happy, the world's happy. It's the golden rule, my friend."

"Why is it you always seem happier than I am?" Wyatt asked in mock despair.

"I take time for sex. Lots of sex. It's that simple," Murphy answered without skipping a beat.

"Is it called sex when it only involves your hand and a computer?" Wyatt volleyed right back.

"Easy, easy my friend," Murphy cautioned, "I'm this close to going to bat for Lana and her dancing knockers."

Wyatt squealed into the phone before punching the End Call button. Only Murphy could pick him up and put him back together again so quickly. They had some of the best characteristics of lovers without any of the tension. He was lucky to have someone always covering his back, he thought, as he returned to his window above the park.

It was hard for Wyatt to believe—a good portion of the summer without any pressure, imagine that. He deserved this time away. No one could argue the fact. Would he get bored and want to come back, he wondered? It was a possibility. He wasn't known for his talent to slow down and relax. He vowed then and there he wouldn't allow himself to fall into the same traps that had plagued his ability to pause and enjoy life in the past. In the next day or two, he would make a list of books he had always wanted to read but never had the time. He would have his assistant track down all the movies he had missed over the years because of his intense work schedule. He would cook. There were a million things he could do with a summer on his own. Murphy had not only lifted the dark cloud of doom surrounding him, he had blasted it out of the universe.

Wyatt sat down at his computer and began making some notes. As he typed away, he fought off the nagging urge to remove his clothes. That could wait. He had a whole summer of nakedness ahead of him. He chuckled as he reached across the desk and hit speed dial.

"RYAN!"

Ryan peered up from his computer screen to see his boss, Murphy, explode into his office. He'd been typing up Murphy's atrocious handwriting onto a spreadsheet for a production meeting scheduled later that afternoon.

"I'm not done yet," Ryan said, returning to his work. "Your scribble sucks, and I'm trying to figure out what you've written without having to bother you."

"It's that take-charge attitude of yours that sets you apart from the herd."

Murphy plopped down on the small plastic chair across from Ryan and took a huge swig from the bottle of water he'd walked in with. "I like what you've done in here. It's impressive," he added, after giving the tiny corner office a once-over.

"So... you like it better now than when it was filled with mop buckets and cleaning supplies?" Ryan asked as he continued to type without looking up.

"It was?" Murphy asked, amazed. "I find that hard to believe. Wow, you have a knack. Is this new?"

In hopes of getting Murphy out of his hair, Ryan looked up from the tattered legal pad he'd been squinting at long enough to identify the object of Murphy's attention.

"You're asking me if my lunch bag is new!" *Give me a fucking break here! I've got less than two hours to hand this back and your pestering is the last thing I need right now.*

"Murphy, I'm not sure why you're here... in my office... right now. I've worked for you for almost eight months and this is, let's see... only the second time you've made the trip down the hall. The one other time, you were on a hunt for chocolate, and because you'd struck out with everyone else, you were forced to wander down here. Listen to me...." Ryan looked across his desk in desperation. "I couldn't be more serious when I tell you I'm going to be right down to the wire on this assignment. I beg you, please leave me alone."

"Don't sweat it. I cancelled my meeting for today. The notes can wait."

Although it was a relief to hear he was off the hook, Ryan refused to let down his guard until he knew for certain what this impromptu meeting was all about.

"Take a deep breath and relax," Murphy said as he demonstrated for Ryan how to breathe deeply, adding with a mischievous wink, "We never get quality time like this to shoot the breeze."

Murphy was up to something, Ryan was sure of it. However, with the pressure off, at least for the time being, he allowed himself to sit back and relax. Ryan enjoyed the rare opportunities when he could spend time with Murphy. Murphy was a terrific boss, and Ryan felt blessed to be part of his organization. Over the course of the last couple months, Ryan felt he'd won Murphy's respect by delivering quality work, on time, with little or no direction. He'd cautioned himself not to read more into it, but perhaps as a reward for his quest to be perfect, Murphy had begun taking more time with Ryan, supplying background information and providing him a welcomed glimpse of the big picture. Murphy made him feel like he was part of the team. The *Dress Up* Team. Most nights he went home from work convinced he was in the right place at the right time. And work was fun. A spirited banter had developed between them, and Murphy seemed delighted when Ryan shot back an unexpected zinger.

"It's strange the things that stick in my mind." Murphy offered, crossing his hands behind his head. "Didn't you tell me your parents sent you to a camp somewhere in Maine?"

"It *is* strange, the things that stick in your mind, but yes, I did tell you that. It was kind of a Ranger Rick camp designed to teach kids a respect for nature. I had to go several summers when I was in my teens. I detested it from the minute I got there until I boarded the plane back home. No television, no computers, just shitty food, and the camp counselors... fuck, what a bunch of hayseed geeks. Why?"

"I'm curious, if you hadn't had to go there for camp, do you think you would have liked it... being in Maine?"

Easy, this could be a trap. Murphy's office was filled with pictures of Maine, and Ryan was well aware he'd built some kind of dream home there as a retreat. This little visit was starting to make him feel uneasy.

"I thought it was... okay." Ryan answered, only to correct himself a second later. "No, I didn't think it was okay. At the time, I hated it."

It was better to be truthful until he had a better idea of what this was all about. "I was a rich city kid from Beverly Hills, who had a houseful of electronics to babysit me. Being yanked from home and shuffled off to Maine each summer... it felt like Siberia."

Murphy smiled back. Ryan couldn't tell if he was annoyed by his candor, or appreciative of it.

"I have a huge favor to ask. I need you to do a solid for me. I need you to spend the next several months in Maine."

"You've got to be fucking kidding me. Are you fucking kidding me?"

"I wouldn't fuck you."

"Really?"

"Well... maybe after a few really stiff cocktails. It'd have to be kind of a spontaneous thing."

The smile was still there, but any hope Murphy was yanking his chain was diminishing rapidly.

"You're serious? You want me to go to Maine?"

"It's a very important mission, my friend, and if you choose to accept it, I will be forever grateful. Wanna hear more?"

"Oh, do I," Ryan answered, barely able to disguise his disappointment.

"Wyatt Stark, who is sort of your other boss, in a strange, incestuous kind of way, is going to be spending the summer at my house there."

"Please don't ask me to stay there with him. Please don't ask that," Ryan pleaded, leaning across his desk for added emphasis.

"I'd never even dream of asking such a thing." Murphy appeared hurt Ryan had jumped to such a conclusion. "Honestly! Sit back! Relax! It's nothing like that."

"What's it like then?" Ryan asked with an overabundance of caution.

"Wyatt has been operating at breakneck speed the last couple of years. He's been under tremendous pressure, and he's tired. He's in no position to be taking on this movie right now. He's close to being worthless, and that's not a good thing... for any of us."

Ryan held his breath as he waited for Murphy to elaborate.

"Here's where you come in.... I've just got to ask, where on earth did you purchase that lunch bag ensemble?"

"Excuse me?" Ryan found himself completely caught off guard.

"The thermos... it's purple just like your lunch bag. A very tasteful approach to meal time on the go and snappy too! I bet people comment on it when you're strolling through the commons. They do, don't they. 'Fess up! I would, that's for sure."

"Please! Get to the point," Ryan begged, exasperated by Murphy's playful diversion. "I'm seconds away from tears. I'm happy... comfortable right here in my little world. I enjoy working here, right here. I love it... working right here, turning your crappy handwriting into beautiful, organized memos. Life is good!"

"I want you to be my safety net. I want you close to Wyatt in case something happens to him." Murphy was at once serious and businesslike.

"What do you mean, in case something happens?" Ryan sat motionless.

"For your ears only, Wyatt's had some panic attacks recently," Murphy offered in a hushed voice. "I hope by getting him out of the city and away from a few other nasty-nasties, he'll start to regain his strength, and these attacks will be history."

"I still don't understand. What are you asking me to do?"

Ryan was surprised at how direct his questioning had become. There was nothing even remotely appealing about the prospect of spending a couple months in godforsaken Maine with a famous Broadway director who was having mental issues.

"Be close. I want you to go out there a few days ahead of him and get the house ready. I want you to pick him up from the airport and make sure he gets to my house safe and sound. You'll shop for him when he needs things. For lack of a better way to put it, Wyatt is a very precious commodity whom I happen to care deeply about. I need someone I can trust to be there with him in case he finds himself in the weeds."

Ryan frantically worked to process what he was being told. This was by no means anything close to what he'd expected his day to be like.

"You don't know Wyatt," Murphy continued, "he's not going to need his hand held. He's not needy that way. He'd probably starve to death before he asked you for food. Ryan, you'd be doing this for me. To him, you'll probably be just some guy who is there to run errands. And honestly, that's all I need you to be. If all the planets are in the right orbit, hopefully, Wyatt will figure out a way to relax and get himself into shape for this film."

"Wow... this is heavy. I mean...."

"You're right! It's heavy because it requires our very best shot. You being out there ensures me I'm... we... are giving it our best shot. I can't be there myself, or, I would be."

Ryan wasn't sure how to respond. When put in those terms, only an asshole would have the bad sense to push back.

"I see something in you," Murphy added kindly, "a quality... it tells me if you're out there looking after him, somehow, we stand a good chance of making this plan work. So, what do you think? Will you do this for me?"

"Of course. I'll do it."

"Thank you. For one of the only times in my life, I don't have a plan B."

"I won't like it, but I'll do it."

Ryan was pleased to see Murphy was once again all smiles.

"There's nobody else I can send. A friend would only get on his nerves. It has to be someone who can stick in the background and be, like I said before, a safety net. You have no idea how much I appreciate this. I'll make it up to you, I promise! Any questions?"

Ryan knew there were a million questions he should ask, but to save his soul he couldn't manage to get any of them to surface.

"I'm in the process of making arrangements and putting together some notes for you. You'll have access to my cell phone. Never hesitate to call if you think you need to."

"When do I leave?" Ryan asked, reaching over to rearrange his lunch ensemble, a feeble attempt to show his boss he hadn't lost his sense of humor when, in fact, he had.

"Tonight!" Murphy announced as he bounded out of his chair.

"Tonight?" Ryan asked in disbelief as he jumped to his feet.

"You're flying out first class, and I'm making arrangements for you to stay at the Bridgeport Hotel—which, by the way, is by far the best digs my precious money can buy. You can bank all of your salary until you're safe and sound back here in Lalalalalaaa. I expect you to expense anything you need."

"And I'd thought about calling in sick today."

"Wyatt's a very nice guy and nothing like you'd think he'd be. He's a sweetheart, and he needs this time away more than he knows.

I'm going to be sick!

"Listen," Murphy said. "I realize I've dropped a bomb on you. Leave! Get out of here! Get as organized as you can. I'll have a car pick you up later this afternoon. Ryan, thank you!"

Ryan clutched his chest as Murphy left his office. He was certain this was the closest he'd ever been to experiencing his own panic attack.

Chapter 2

WYATT stared at the computer screen and frowned. Scrolling ahead on his calendar to the summer months, he spotted two events, one early in July, the other in mid-August that, in the excitement of having the entire summer off, had escaped his memory. He dreaded the thought of having to initiate contact with not one, but two wealthy and demanding theater mavens. The habitually boozy Bethany Orlock and the conniving fame whore, Bitsy June Plimpton. A sizable piece of his firm, curvaceous ass had been promised earlier to both of these pugnacious jackals. No way getting around it. To spend the summer at Murphy's uninterrupted, he would have to reverse his earlier promises by saying no to them both. Neither Bethany nor Bitsy had much experience with the word "no."

As he continued to roll back and forth, searching for a way out of this mess, a very frightening thing happened. Without warning, the fat, pampered images of both Bethany and Bitsy materialized on his screen. Their heavily powdered faces were scrunched together like caramel rolls. Each squabbled and yakked, vying for his attention, their stained teeth chomping at him like mad dogs.

Breathe deep. I'm seeing things. I'm a lunatic! I'm raving mad!

Closing his eyes and shaking his head from side to side, he sat motionless for several seconds before risking the opening of an eye. *Thank God!* Wyatt sighed with relief. The familiar template of his calendar had returned. It was time to end this madness. He planted both palms flat on the desk and took in a huge breath. He'd deal with Bethany first.

For the last several years, he had agreed to be guest director for Broadway 101. Bethany's pet project was set up to give kids under the age of eighteen a glimpse of what it was like to be part of a big Broadway musical. "To ignite the hungerrrrr...." she had slurred drunkenly out the side of her mouth one night when seated across from him at a benefit, no doubt an event that had something to do with Bitsy June. In a weak moment, he had agreed to donate his time and support.

What a fucking bad decision that was!

Wyatt looked up her private number on the contact list Murphy had set up for him. He understood his name on the program not only guaranteed all the spaces would be filled with adolescent Broadway wannabes, but it also insured ticket sales for the performances would be strong, if not a complete sellout. Bethany could be an absolute bitch if she didn't get her way. Wyatt inhaled twice and dialed her number.

"Hello," the cigarette-and-vodka stained voice slurred out of the speaker after several excruciating rings.

"Bethany, darling, it's Wyatt Stark." There was nothing darling about Bethany, he thought, as he waited for her to respond.

"Wyatt, my love, how wonderful it is to hear your voice." Clink. Clink. Clink.

Oh for God's sake! Wyatt rolled his eyes. The sound of ice cubes dropping into her glass was unmistakable.

Wyatt bit his lip and scurried to finalize a strategy. He had only two choices, he concluded, and neither was likely to release him of his obligation without a painful exchange with darling, Bethany. He could go the honest route. He could confess his need for a complete break from his schedule before the filming on *Dress Up* started. A lame choice, he knew, because Bethany wouldn't give a shit, and she'd tell him as much. Or he could lie and say preproduction on the movie was already so intense it was impossible for him to find the quality time now that her immensely important program deserved. This was total bullshit because it didn't take a director of his caliber to launch a production of *Hello Dolly* starring, for the most part, no-talent high school kids whose parents were rolling in cash.

"Bethany, I hope I'm not taking you out of anything important?" Wyatt asked, certain he heard the sound of liquor bottles clanging in the background.

"Nonsense, Love! How nice of you to call."

We'll see just how nice you think it is after I drop this bomb on you, you moneyed old bitch lush.

Wyatt forced himself to silence the inner narrative he had running. It was damned close to finding its voice. "Bethany, I'm literally sick to my stomach," the only part of his excuse that was truthful, he thought, before continuing, "because unfortunately, due to scheduling issues with the upcoming movie, I'm going to have to pull out of Broadway 101. Preproduction is already well underway and it's imperative," Wyatt lowered his voice for dramatic effect and continued, "I keep as close an eye on the decisions as possible."

"Slurp... slurp... slurp."

Wyatt listened on pins and needles as an entire cocktail was downed on the other end of the line.

"Oh Wyatt, you can't be at all serious," Bethany stated sadly after setting her glass down with a loud bonk. "I've simply got to have you aboard this year. The program is in a critical stage, and I'm counting... I'm relying on you... for its success."

Wyatt sat back in his chair and closed his eyes.

Breathe!

He hadn't counted on Bethany going right for the jugular. How unfair was it she was counting on his involvement for the entire success of her stupid program.

To hell with this! He scooted back up to the desk. *I'm going to tell her to take her program.... Wait! Wait a second!*

Wyatt sat straight up in his chair for the first time that morning. Why hadn't he thought of this before? Without a moment's hesitation, he leaned forward and, with just the right pitch of sincerity, offered, "Bethany, it's so, so flattering you think so highly of my abilities. I truly mean that. Now, you have to know I wouldn't simply call you to beg off my commitment without having not just a good solution, but a great solution for you to consider."

"And that would be...?"

Once again Wyatt heard the clinking of ice cubes and the rattle of liquor bottles.

"Jason Lambert! He'll replace me in a heartbeat!" Wyatt waited for this to sink in before he continued. "Only a few weeks ago, when I happened to mention to him my involvement with Broadway 101, he… this is what is so incredible, he confessed how envious he was he wasn't asked to be a part of Broadway 101. I know how particular you are, so I refrained from offering any hope. But if I had to pick someone to step in for me, if I had to pick anyone for my replacement, Bethany, my love," *my love, heaven help me,* "if I had to pick anyone who would achieve the results you're counting on, it would be my dear… dear friend and colleague, Mr. Jason Lambert. And I would be remiss, completely and totally remiss, if I didn't remind you of the delightful show he has running right now at the Oracle."

Wyatt placed a hand over his mouth as he fought off the urge to laugh. *Come on, my love, take the fucking bait, you fat-assed sturgeon.*

Lambert had been hired to direct *Tempting Tobias Tate*, which had turned out to be the surprise hit of the season. Lambert wouldn't have even come close to making the short list for director had he not paraded Wyatt's name and support up and down the line of investors. *How could I have been so blind?* Without a stitch of talent, Lambert found himself credited with a smash hit. He had been handed a foolproof script so finely crafted, it was virtually fail-safe.

Lambert and Bethany, a match made in heaven!

Lambert would be so impressed Bethany was interested in him, he would say yes to anything she requested. Wyatt's eyes twinkled with delight as he waited through numerous slurps before Bethany responded.

"I'm exsheemely disappointed you won't be with us this zoommer, Wyatt."

Oh crap, he almost said out loud. *She's shit-faced! Will she even remember I called?*

Slow, steady breaths!

"Have Lambfarts call me, darling. We'll shjuss half to live with shim."

"Thank you for understanding, Bethany. You have to know... I'm terribly disappointed, but you'll be in good hands. You'll be in good hands with Lambfar... with Jason. Bye and take care."

With a good deal of satisfaction, Wyatt pressed the end call button. He was done with Bethany.

Only one more bitch to go and you're free. No! Don't stop now. You're on a roll!

Wyatt searched for Bitsy June's number.

Each year Bitsy June hosted the Bitsy June Plimpton Foundation's Benefit for Actors of Age. Bitsy's event raised money primarily for New York actors who had reached the end of their careers and were unable to afford housing or medical insurance. Being awarded one of her "scholarships" meant you would be given care and housing for the rest of your life. It was a charity he cared about. He was proud to be a part of it. However, he didn't care enough about Bitsy's event to give up a precious second of his summer in Maine.

As he dialed the old fleabag up, he was reminded of the danger he faced, pulling out of this event. Opening yourself up to the devastating wrath of Bitsy was a risk no matter how you approached her. Critics, producers, and stars, no matter how successful, had long suffered the effects of falling out of favor with Bitsy, a woman so powerful in the New York theater scene she could, if allowed, sink even the most anticipated hit of the season if those involved with it didn't kiss her ass and kiss it good and hard. Bitsy's ass was plenty large, so no amount of kissing it ever seemed to be enough.

"Miss Plimpton's residence," a voice answered in a thick Hungarian accent.

Wyatt wasn't surprised his call was answered by Lenore, Bitsy's maid, who had been with her since Jesus was a child. He had always been suspect of Lenore's genealogy. The story, as it was so faithfully recounted by Bitsy, went like this: while on a tour of Europe with her first husband, Lars, Bitsy decided to visit an orphanage in Hungary.

God knows why. Wyatt couldn't get past this first part no matter how hard he tried to imagine it happening. The story went on to tell of a chance meeting between Bitsy and Lenore, who upon first sight won a place in Bitsy June's heart. Lenore was whisked out of her drab, pitiful surroundings and brought back to the States, where she would have a chance to pursue the American dream. This is the part that consistently cracked Wyatt and Murphy up. The American dream, as interpreted by Bitsy, meant drawing bathwater and scrubbing toilets. Could Lenore have gotten any luckier? The story was crap. Murphy joked that Lenore was probably some no-talent from central casting. Lenore, whoever she was, had been lucky, or unlucky, depending on how you looked at it, to cross paths with the fabulously wealthy Miss Plimpton.

There was another aspect of the Bitsy and Lenore story a few who knew them both subscribed to, which concerned Bitsy's sexual orientation and the fact that once Lenore had been firmly placed in the role of Bitsy's maid, Lars, minus a sizeable chunk of his vast fortune, had been given the old heave-ho. The two had been inseparable ever since. Wyatt had warmed to this portion of the saga more than any other.

"Hi Lenore. It's Wyatt Stark. Would it be possible to speak with Bitsy?"

"Hello, Mr. Stark." Lenore answered. "Miss Plimpton is in the sunroom having her morning tea. Please hold."

Wyatt tried to focus on what he was going to say to Bitsy but couldn't fight off the image of Lenore and Bitsy lying side by side on a large, violet velvet chaise lounge eating petite ham and cheese sandwiches and drinking mimosas.

"Wyatt?" Bitsy asked moments later, her voice dripping from decades of entitlement and world travel. It was the only thing about her Wyatt enjoyed.

"Thank you for taking my call, Bitsy." Wyatt couldn't lose track of the fact that, in Bitsy's mind, she was royalty and demanded to be treated as such.

"Nonsense, Wyatt, my dear boy. I wish you'd call more often. It's always a pleasure. How's that lovely friend of yours, Murphy Smith, doing? I never see him anymore now that he's spending all of his time on the West coast."

"He's doing very well." It was no secret to Wyatt Bitsy preferred Murphy over him. She always had. It was Murphy who had managed to charm Bitsy into providing the funding they required to go off on their own. Thanks to Bitsy, they were able to launch what would become their first major theatrical success. She was the only wealthy ear listening at the time. It wasn't important to her one little bit that she made a fortune off of them over the years, a fact that was of course never discussed. Years and miles of ass-kissing could all be wiped away with one slight misstep.

"Make sure to give him my best."

"It would be my pleasure." Wyatt took a breath before continuing. There wasn't room for any mistakes here.

"Bitsy, the reason I'm calling...." *Oh man, here I go.* "I'm looking at my calendar for the summer and running into a million problems. You must have heard by now we are going to bring *Dress Up* to the screen."

"Yes. What a brilliant idea. The Rosenburgs have been to see it four times. People won't be able to stay away."

"Well, the problem I'm finding," he continued, "is all the preparation needed to make this film happen is demanding much more of my time than I would have thought. I was wondering, would you consider having Murphy chair your benefit this year?"

He hated making Murphy the sacrificial lamb, but his choices for a replacement were limited. Wyatt knew, even though he'd be pissed as hell and would throw a huge fit when he found out, Murphy would do Bitsy's benefit in place of him. Murphy would do this, knowing it would allow Wyatt a summer free of responsibility. Murphy would attend the benefit in his place or they would no doubt suffer some form of retaliation down the road. Bitsy had muscle and she wasn't at all shy about using it. After all, an octogenarian chorus of thousands slept warm with bellies full of turkey dinner on her watch.

"Well...." Bitsy took her sweet ass time to answer. "Programs haven't gone to the printer yet, so that's good."

Oh for fuck sakes, Bitsy, you bitch. Yes or no! Will you let me off the hook or not?

"I had always wanted Murphy to chair the event, but I never thought he'd be able to find the time," Bitsy added, her voice as cold as a glacier.

Ouch! There it was. Bitsy, without saying it, had attempted to take a swipe at his ego. *And you know something, Bitsy Bitch? I couldn't fucking care less! Go fuck yourself!*

"Have Murphy give me a call so we can discuss the details. What?"

"Huh?" Wyatt wasn't sure what was going on. Was she talking to him or someone else? He thought it best to keep the ball in her court. Perhaps Lenore had passed stinky Hungarian gas. He'd find out in a minute.

"One second, Wyatt. What, Lenore?"

Wyatt waited, tapping his fingers on the desk in anticipation of ending this call.

"Wyatt, the mayor is waiting on the other line."

Of course he is Bitsy. The mayor of Bullshitsville! What a crock of poo poo! But hey, if it meant this conversation was ending, God bless the mayor's timing.

"I'll have Murphy give you a call, Bitsy. Thank you for being so understanding. Take care."

Breathe! You did it!

Wyatt sighed with relief. Unbelievable! His summer was free. The gods were smiling down on him. With the two deal-breaker commitments now history, he leaned back in his chair and closed his eyes. He remained motionless until his stomach rumbled, prompting him to think about Linda. Linda, Linda, Linda, what was he going to do with Linda while he was away?

Linda Hernandez, for all practical purposes, was the glue that held his life together. She ran his house with a no-bullshit approach he had grown to love and respect. After his first major success as a choreographer, he decided he needed a housekeeper to keep his hectic life organized. Linda was the only one who had responded to his detailed and intimidating classified ad. In his quest to hire the perfect domestic, he had listed no less than thirty-four requirements. If he was going to have someone in his house every day, he was going to get exactly what he paid for.

In hindsight, Linda had hired him. She made it very clear from the onset she could handle all of his requirements, but she worked on her terms. There would be no lists, no changing up the game plan to accommodate some bored and thoughtless prima donna's whim.

Before he knew it, Linda had become exactly what he had been looking for and so much more.

Wyatt knew he didn't want to take her with him. That wouldn't work. *What would be best for the both of us?* Although he wasn't going to be around, he wouldn't mind if his trusted housekeeper kept her regular schedule. It would be comforting, having someone in the place while he was away. Or she could take some time off, whatever she wanted. Wyatt would pay her regardless. They could both do with a break from each other.

"Linda!" Wyatt hollered from his office. Much earlier, he had heard the sound of pots and pans coming from the kitchen, so he knew he either had a very clumsy burglar who loved to cook, or more likely, Linda had arrived and started her daily routine.

"What?" the housekeeper hollered back from the kitchen. "You want lunch anytime today? I'm busy."

"Come here a minute," Wyatt hollered back, unfazed by her stubbornness. "We need to talk."

"You better have clothes on," the voice threatened.

"For Christ's sake, Linda, get your ass down here for a minute!" *Geez, what was it with everyone bringing up this no-clothes thing today?* It was starting to piss him off. Okay, it was true. He had accidentally crossed paths with Linda on several occasions when he was naked. He was gay, she was straight, no big deal, he had thought. He didn't shove it in her face on purpose, for cryin' out loud. He wasn't some kind of freak or anything like that. He enjoyed the freedom of not wearing clothes when he was at home. No big deal.

Wyatt listened as pots and pans clanged and banged from down the hall before he heard the defiant footsteps of his strong-willed housekeeper padding down to his office. Linda entered, bringing with her the aroma of freshly baked bread.

"What now?" the forty-something woman in lavender sweats asked without a hint of interest, all the while clutching her oven mitt to her chest with the seriousness of a relief pitcher stepping onto the mound late in the ninth. "I've got a million things to get done today," she added, as if there was a need to explain her disinterest. She held her ground, wiping a loose strand of wispy gray hair from her forehead with her mitt-free hand while waiting for Wyatt to speak.

"I'm going away for the summer. Murphy talked me into occupying his beach house in Maine while he oversees the preproduction of *Dress Up* in Los Angeles."

"So?"

There was no beating around the bush with this woman, he was reminded. He couldn't help but feel a little wounded by the fact she didn't require any further explanation.

"Ah… well… I just wanted to tell you that," he stammered back, unable to conceal his hurt. "And," he went on to explain "to let you know I will still need you here while I'm away. Or… you can take some time off, whatever you want." Her mere presence flustered him sometimes. Why was that, he wondered? "I will pay you regardless," he added, in hopes she would show some sign that he was human and had feelings or she even gave a shit about what he was telling her.

"You need to get away," she replied as she removed her chapped hand from her sacred mitt. "You're burned out. You have those scary spells now. You need to go sit by a tree for a while and relax. I will be fine here all by myself. Trust me."

Linda stared back at Wyatt with a determination that could only be compared to a mother shoving her reluctant son out of the house into the big world for the first time. Deep down, he knew she loved him like one of her own. *She would have killed me by now if she didn't.*

"Anything else?" Linda asked from across the room, her oven mitt dangling at her side as if she were sizing up the next batter.

"No. I'll make a list of what I want shipped to Maine and give it to you tomorrow. I'm leaving next Monday. What's for lunch?"

"Egg salad."

"Thanks for your time," Wyatt said as he turned back to his computer screen.

"Yeah, okay," the housekeeper hollered back, already halfway down the hallway.

RYAN wiped his mouth and replaced his tattered napkin with a fresh one from the tray. The bright spring sunshine bearing down on the weather-flecked red and white painted woodwork made the drive-in all the more surreal, he thought, as he bit into his cheeseburger. Looking around, he determined the color scheme was equally bizarre whether he visited the place at night or during the day. Until now, he'd only been here at night. What the owners of the Peppermint Twist neglected in upkeep, they sure made up in the quality of their food. *Damn! This burger is awesome!* He took another huge bite from the paper-wrapped sandwich. This was his third visit in less than a week. He had found himself waking up in the middle of the night desperate for one of their juicy burgers.

The last few days had been busy ones. He hadn't had a minute to spare, making sure all the preparations were complete for the arrival of Mr. Stark. Mr. Wyatt Stark. Several e-mails, with very precise instructions for him to follow, had been provided by Murphy. Murphy had made it very clear there were to be no screwups of any kind. And that was fine. He got it. What he hadn't voiced to Murphy, but what continued to play in the background of his thoughts, was what was this Wyatt Stark guy going to act like around someone in his position? For all practical purposes he had signed up to be this guy's on-call servant. Ryan suspected there was more than a better chance this guy could turn out to be a real shithead. Shitheads went with the territory in the entertainment business. *Bring it on!* Ryan had committed himself to this little adventure, and there was no way he was going to let some uppity jerk jeopardize his job or his relationship with Murphy Smith.

So far, the biggest challenge he'd faced had been filling Stark's grocery order. Ryan ended up having to drive halfway across the state to procure a cheese that was the guy's favorite. Wine, both red and white, varieties he had never heard of, were another challenge, but nothing like locating the cheese.

Looking over the stack of notes and e-mails he had placed neatly on the passenger seat, Ryan confirmed for about the zillionth time that Stark's plane was scheduled to land at one thirty, forty-three minutes from now. The airport was fifteen minutes from the drive-in. He had plenty of time to get there. On the off chance the plane was early, he finished the last few bites of his lunch and waved for the carhop to retrieve his tray so he could be on his way.

An attractive young woman—sixteen, seventeen years old he guessed—approached the car. She wore red shorts with a red and white striped T-shirt. A red name tag with white lettering introducing herself to the world as "Missy" was pinned directly over her more than ample right breast.

"You're finished already?" she asked while removing his tray.

"I am. Great burger! Thanks and have a good day," he said with a smile as he took his sunglasses down from the visor and put them on.

Missy had barely cleared the vacant parking spot next to him when a car came to a sliding stop on the rough gravel just inches from the sidewalk. Peering over to see who had come barreling into the lot so recklessly, he wasn't surprised to find the lime-green Volkswagen convertible packed solid with teenage girls.

"Hey, Hollywood," taunted a preppy blonde cheerleader type who was sitting in the car's front passenger seat. "Comin' or goin'?" she asked seductively in a voice much more mature than her young age could possibly have known from personal experience.

"Oh… I'm going," he answered with a warm smile.

"That's a frickin' pity," a voice barreled from the backseat, causing the entire carload to burst into giggles.

"Why's that?" he asked innocently. Ryan couldn't resist the opportunity to flirt.

"You're frickin' hot as shit," came the same voice from the backseat.

This time Ryan was able to identify the owner. The voice belonged to a fat-faced, pimple-adorned girl with short black hair. She was damned lucky to be blessed with an aggressive personality, he joked to himself. God knows, unless she went through an extreme makeover that included dumping half her body weight, she was going to need it.

"Thanks," he answered as he started his car and with a wave, backed out of the parking lot.

Pulling onto the narrow road leading into the tiny regional airport, he was relieved to see he had arrived before Stark's plane. The last thing he wanted was his assignment waiting around for him, or worse, Stark calling Murphy, wondering where the hell his ride was. Sprinting into the small building serving as the terminal, he glanced at the clock above the counter, which read 1:14 PM.

"Can I help you?" the guy behind the counter asked, glancing up from his computer screen after the bell over the door had chimed.

"There's a private plane coming in from New York and I'm here to pick up the passenger."

Ryan wasn't sure how much he should reveal. After all, Stark was a celebrity, at least to anyone familiar with theater and Broadway. He didn't want to cause any unnecessary excitement. The whole reason the guy was coming to Maine was to relax and get away from all of the attention.

"Right! I just heard them update over the radio. They're still a few minutes from landing. Care for some coffee?" The man gestured to a table near the window. Ryan looked over to find a small electric coffeemaker, containers of sugar and cream substitute, and a stack of white styrofoam cups.

"I'm good, but thanks," he said.

Sitting down on one of the beige vinyl chairs, the one not adorned with ragged duct tape on the arm, he reached over and grabbed a beat-up copy of *Aviation Today*, his only choice, and began paging through the magazine waiting for the plane to arrive.

"Here they come, if you want to watch," the man behind the counter said with a friendly voice.

Ryan stood and walked over to the window. The plane at this point appeared to be only a tiny light, barely visible in the bright blue sky. He watched as the plane cut the distance to the airport in just a few minutes. Seconds later it glided onto the runway and, after reversing its engines, turned and headed toward the terminal. The small, sleek white jet stopped several feet in front of the window where he was standing.

Okay Ryan, it's show time! Let's get Mr. Hyperventilation off the plane, into the car, and tucked neatly and safely into Murphy's. If he doesn't want to talk along the way, fine. It's a short drive and I couldn't care less.

Ryan had been distracted while watching the plane land. He was surprised to see the same man who had been behind the counter now outside. The man waved at the pilot and a door on the side of the plane opened, swinging down to create stairs to the pavement. Seconds later, Wyatt Stark stepped out of the commuter jet and into the bright sun. Carrying a small leather bag in his hand, he began descending the stairs. The man from behind the counter escorted him into the terminal.

THE air was cooler and smelled like pine needles, Wyatt noticed, as he stepped off the plane and walked across the aging concrete tarmac to the small, square, mint green stucco terminal. Stepping inside the door, he was stopped cold in his tracks.

Holy shit! Is that hottie here to pick me up? Stunned, Wyatt lost the grip on his carry-on, which landed with a dull thump at his feet.

"Mr. Stark! Hi there, I'm Ryan Taylor," the young man said as he stepped forward to shake Wyatt's hand. "I'll be taking you to the Smith residence."

Ryan, who appeared to be in his mid-twenties, was a total knockout. Every inch of this guy was a work of art. He could have been one of Wyatt's dancers. He was long, lean, and had the appropriate upper body development Wyatt sought out when casting. Although the summer was young, the stud had a good start on a tan and his short, sandy hair already showed signs of being sun-bleached. He was wearing dark glasses, so Wyatt was unable to see the color of his eyes. No doubt, like the rest of what he saw, the guy's eyes were stunners.

"My lucky," Wyatt chirped as he reached down for the shoulder strap of his carry-on and missed. After two more swipes and a grunt, he gave up on nabbing the strap. The flight, the champagne, and of course the handsome man who had stepped forward and was now offering to help with the bag, frazzled him. Determined to regain control of his situation, he bent over and scooped the bag up into his arms, holding it like a schoolgirl would a bundle of books.

"I have no idea where I'm going or where the heck I am," Wyatt confessed in a whisper as he forced himself to not giggle. He giggled often when he was nervous. Sneaking in a couple short breaths, he fought to maintain his composure as he looked around the terminal. He recognized for the first time since getting off the plane how buzzed he had managed to get during the flight. His face flushed as he realized he was not doing a very good job of hiding it. In an attempt to stay in the moment, he added, "Please call me Wyatt."

"Sure." Before Wyatt could protest, Ryan snatched the carry-on out of his hand. Wyatt stumbled along behind as he struggled to get his shit together. Out in the parking lot, he was directed to a shiny black SUV. Ryan opened the passenger door, and when he climbed in, Wyatt noticed the car still smelled brand new.

"Nice car," he said as Ryan shut his door for him. Thankfully, he was able to fasten his seat belt without asking for help. Ryan fired up the engine and they were on their way.

"We pass through town on the way to the Smith house," Ryan informed him as he turned onto the narrow highway. "Do you need to stop for anything? Wait, sorry," he paused, as a look of frustration fell over his face. "First, I should tell you I was able to find everything on the list Mr. Smith gave me."

"Mr. Smith gave you a list?" Wyatt could only imagine what Murphy had determined he'd need while in Maine.

"Yes, Mr. Smith provided a grocery list."

"Grocery list," Wyatt repeated. *Murphy, the gift that keeps on giving.*

"All of your clothes and stuff arrived yesterday," Ryan said, looking over. "Mr. Smith asked me to unpack for you. I hope you'll find everything is satisfactory."

"I'm sure you did just fine. That was very kind of you," Wyatt said.

He glanced over at his driver, who flashed him one of the sexiest smiles he had seen in a very long time. *God dang!* Wyatt had to force himself to look out his window.

Ryan slowed the car as they entered the small village. It sure didn't appear to offer much in the way of entertainment, or convenience, Wyatt noted. However, right off the bat he counted two bars and two churches—a fair balance, he chuckled to himself. There wasn't much else to speak of. A small grocery store named Taylor's Superette to the right, and a gas station a block further down the main drag. Taylor's Superette. Taylor's, why was the name familiar to him? *Hey wait a minute!* Wyatt looked back at the sign. *Didn't this guy say his last name was Taylor? I'm almost sure he did.*

"Ryan?" Wyatt asked, "By any chance… is the grocery store, the one we just passed, Taylor's, any relation to you?"

Wyatt waited for a response. Ryan didn't respond. *Maybe he didn't hear my question.*

"Wow! Yeah! I can't believe you picked up on that one," Ryan answered just as Wyatt was about to ask him once more. "It's my pop's store."

They drove for a few more blocks before Ryan added, "My mom cashiers and prepares some of the stuff for the little deli in the back of the store. In the summer, when I'm back from school, I do the delivering for them. We have a lot of summer residents who have groceries delivered to their boats and cabins along the coves. It's a living," he added along with another killer smile. "It gets my folks through the winter months, which can be pretty bleak in these parts."

Looking around, Wyatt couldn't agree more. It was beautiful now, but there sure didn't look to be much to keep a soul occupied during the long winter months. Well, the liquor stores, but that would grow old quickly or you'd be dead from liver disease. A musical in the church basement, he pondered. *The Full Monty,* perhaps? *Stop it!* This guy grew up here and it was his home. Besides, this place wasn't all that different from where he had grown up in the Midwest. As desolate as it appeared, it also had a comforting, welcoming quality Wyatt identified with.

"Where are you going to school?" Wyatt asked after they had driven a few minutes in silence.

Once again Ryan appeared not to hear. *Maybe there's something distracting him?*

Wyatt was just about to change the subject when Ryan looked over to Wyatt with a grin and said, "I'm at Boston University. I'm majoring in business."

Ryan had a hint of an accent, a hesitation to the way he spoke that Wyatt found irresistible.

"Well, I'm thankful you have your summers free to help your parents out. I don't know what I would have done if I had been dropped off on my own back there. I feel like I've already made my first friend here."

Okay, that was enough, Wyatt thought as soon as the word "friend" had vomited out of his mouth. He already felt guilty for entertaining "naughty thoughts," as Murphy would have called them. *Get a grip! I feel like I just made my first friend?* And what was that supposed to mean? It had to be a combination of the fresh air and champagne that was making him say and think in such a ridiculous and reckless manner. *I feel like I just made my first friend. Yeah right.* This guy was probably counting the miles and seconds until he could dump him off and be on his merry way.

"I left my card on the counter in the kitchen," Ryan said. "Please call me if you need anything. I would feel terrible if you didn't call. Oh, the other thing," Ryan added, "I don't know if Mr. Smith told you, but there's a Jeep for you to use if you feel like driving into town."

"Lovely!" The mental image of Murphy coming out of the house and jumping into a Jeep dressed from head to toe in pastel plaid, which he had picked up on clearance during one of his frequent trips to the L.L. Bean outlet store, caused his lower lip to tremble. Wyatt fought hard to keep his composure.

Okay, maybe he had made his first friend after all. His comment to Ryan didn't sound as bad as he had first thought. Ryan seemed sincere in his offer to be of assistance. Wyatt decided to trust his instincts.

Exiting the village, the road quickly narrowed. Huge trees canopied over them, creating a lush tunnel that went on for as far as the eye could see. Wyatt found the change in scenery fascinating. They appeared to be driving uphill for the longest time, but after a series of even steeper climbs, as well as a few breathtaking descents, the road leveled off, and Wyatt caught his first glimpse of the Atlantic since leaving New York. This sure didn't look like any coastline he'd ever seen before. Jagged rocks and tall pines covered the long, fingered peninsulas jutting out into the ocean. A sailboat here, a powerboat there, and thousands of colorful bobbers everywhere.

"What's the deal with all the bobbers?" Wyatt asked. The flightiness he had experienced earlier had dissipated. He was feeling almost normal and enjoying the drive to Murphy's. Being seated so close to such a handsome man wasn't all that bad either. Several times during the drive he had pretended to look over at something in Ryan's direction when, in fact, he was looking at Ryan. He couldn't help himself, and each time, he looked away, ashamed. He was reminded of the feeling he'd experienced masturbating as a teenager. It felt so great at the time, but the overwhelming shame that followed, made it almost not worth it. Almost.

"They're lobster trap buoys," Ryan said. "Beneath each marker is a lobster trap. Hard to believe there's so many, isn't it?" Ryan slowed the car down, allowing Wyatt to get a better look. "Most of the little bays and inlets are filled with them."

"I'm amazed." Wyatt, suddenly self-conscious, sat back in his seat. For the last several miles, he'd been sitting on the edge of it. His face reddened. *I probably look like some kind of geek to this guy.*

"I never get tired of looking at them," Ryan said. "Each buoy has its own distinct color combination. That's how the lobstermen tell them apart."

Interesting, Wyatt thought. *My buoy would be pink and lavender with dainty white lace. I wonder what color this stud's buoy would be?*

He quickly brought his hand up to his mouth, covering up the goofy grin he couldn't prevent from spreading across his face.

They turned away from the shoreline and drove for several more miles before Ryan slowed the car and turned onto a dirt road marked only by a shiny new mailbox.

"This is the only road leading to the house," Ryan offered as branches snapped and scraped the outside of the car. "If you come across someone in your driveway, they came to see you and nobody else, or they're lost."

Wyatt turned and nodded, a little freaked out by the remoteness. It looked like the perfect setting for an ax murder. He kept this to himself as Ryan maneuvered the SUV along the bumpy ruts on the verge of being overtaken by ferns and other wild plants. The road weaved a few more times before it crossed a wooden one-lane bridge carrying them over a stream.

A few hundred feet further, Ryan veered to the right, bringing them into a clearing and up to what looked like an old house. He stopped the car next to an even older-looking black Jeep. How uncharacteristically butch for Murphy, Wyatt thought as he peered out at the house. His nerves were on high alert because, if this was Murphy's place, there wasn't a chance in hell this was going to work.

Chapter 3

RYAN jumped out of the car and came around to open the door for him. An awkward moment passed while Wyatt sat, still tightly secured by his seat belt, with his mouth wide open. "Wow," was all he could manage to say. Ryan, after reaching into the backseat for his carry-on, waited while Wyatt unbuckled and staggered out of the car.

Breathe deep. Come on, Breathe, Wyatt! Don't have this happen now. Please God, not now. Wyatt felt his fingers growing numb. Another sign he was in trouble.

"So, you had no idea what to expect, I take it?" Ryan asked.

"Well, here's the deal," Wyatt said softly, not wanting to look at the house, "I saw some pictures a couple of years ago when Murphy was building this… this."

Breathe. You're going to embarrass yourself. Keep it together, at least until he's gone.

He carefully chose his words before continuing. "I certainly didn't remember it being this rustic." What Wyatt had thought he remembered were pictures of bright, spacious rooms. Certainly not the dark, cabin-like structure in front of him. The outside of the house was very rough and looked like it had seen better days. Few windows faced this direction, and the ones that did were dark and not offering up any clue as to what one could expect inside. The only hint the place wasn't a million years old was the grouting on the foundation. It was a shade too white and flawless. The wooden siding had been stained a dark green, causing the house to blend in with its surroundings.

"Oh, I know," Ryan agreed. "It looks kind of rough from out here."

Hang on. Slow steady breaths. You can make it through this one.

Wyatt closed his eyes and concentrated on his breathing, lest his fragile emotional state blossom into a full-fledged attack. He was in trouble. Big trouble.

"Mr. Stark? Are you okay?" Ryan asked, reaching out and taking hold of Wyatt's arm.

No! I'm not okay. I'm a fucking mess!

"I should be," Wyatt said in hopes he would be after taking a few more moments to try and calm himself.

"Maybe once we get inside, things will look more like you remember them." Ryan kept hold of him as they started toward the house.

Fat chance! Wyatt continued to fight off massive disappointment and anxiety as he followed Ryan up the steps to the door. He had signed up for a summer of relaxation, not a camping trip.

Taking the keys out of his pocket, Ryan searched until he found the one he was looking for. He opened the door and stood to the side, gesturing for Wyatt to enter.

The door opened into a narrow hallway painted some kind of neutral color, possibly a soft yellow. It housed a bench, a couple of floor mats, and various hooks for jackets and hats. They passed through the hallway, and what awaited him took his breath away. If the outside had been made to look rustic and unassuming, the inside was a complete about-face.

Wyatt found himself walking into a huge combination great room and kitchen. The appliances were state of the art and the stonework, which kept one's expectations low from the outside, became a work of art inside the house. "Incredible!" Wyatt mouthed as he felt the tightness in his chest loosen. As rapidly as the attack had come on, it began to retreat.

"Pretty impressive, don't you think?" Ryan asked while turning on the lights and removing his sunglasses for the first time.

Wyatt was overwhelmed by the cleverness and beauty. "It's like a practical joke. The difference between outside and in," Wyatt commented as he looked over to Ryan and chuckled with relief, the tension streaming out of his body. He had been right about those eyes all along. Ryan had gorgeous dark brown eyes with just the right hint of sleepiness. They were dreamy and sexy. A shiver of excitement ran through his body. At least he hoped that's what it was. "Now, this is what I remember. Except I don't think any of the pictures do the place justice."

"I was floored when I walked in here for the first time," Ryan admitted. "From the way it looks on the outside, you have no idea it's this cool inside. And this isn't even the best part. There's plenty more to feast your eyes on. Come on, I'll show you around and then I'll get the heck out of your hair. I'm sure you're tired from your trip and looking forward to getting situated."

There's no rush. Spend the summer. Show me the bedroom.

A million inappropriate responses flooded Wyatt's mind. Maybe, as the summer progressed, there would be more opportunities to get to know this handsome young man. And that was all he could hope for, he reasoned. His usually expert gaydar, foolproof in almost any setting, wasn't registering any encouraging vibes at the moment.

Ryan gave him a brief tour of the house, explaining where he had stored the items that had been shipped earlier, as well as certain important features like climate control and the sound system. It was obvious Ryan had spent time in the house prior to this tour; he had sure gotten familiar with it fast. *Who could blame him,* Wyatt thought. *It's not every day you find yourself in a fabulous house like Murphy's.*

Ryan pointed out a notebook stashed away in one of the kitchen drawers with Murphy's handwriting on the front, titled "House." Inside were the directions for everything, all neatly organized by room. Murphy couldn't have made this any easier for him. His excitement had returned full force and, at least for now, no signs of anxiety.

Ryan pointed out his card near the phone in the kitchen and made Wyatt promise to call for anything, anytime. Wyatt reached into his pocket for a tip, but was quickly shut down.

"I've been taken care of very well by Mr. Smith," Ryan assured him. "Please call if I can help you in any way."

Wyatt shook Ryan's hand and watched from the door as Ryan headed out to his car. He waved one more time as the young stud backed up and headed down the road, disappearing out of sight. Locking the door, to be on the safe side, he took a deep breath before he undressed. This, he thought, was the official beginning of his sabbatical.

Wyatt balled his travel clothes up in his arms and walked in the direction of the master bedroom, he hoped. Murphy had insisted the bedroom be his for the summer. Although Ryan had walked him through most of the house, he was still uncertain where he was headed. After making a couple of wrong turns, he eventually found his way. The master bedroom area faced the water on the opposite end of the house from a screened porch. Like the huge living room, it, too, was walled with windows facing the cove. If privacy was required, wooden blinds could be raised to any height desired from slats in the floor.

Moving past the sleeping area, Wyatt entered a spacious walk-in closet where he deposited his clothes in a heap. Ryan had left several of the drawers open to indicate he had unpacked the rest of Wyatt's clothes there. Past the huge closet, he entered the bathroom area, which was made up of several smaller rooms. The toilet, a shower room, and another larger room housing a spacious sunken bathtub framed with windows offering terrific views of the water. Each window could be opened to let in the breeze as well as the sound of waves, lapping onto the beach. It was a brilliant design.

He enjoyed a brief shower and after toweling off walked back into the bedroom. At the opposite end of the room, past a two-sided fireplace, he discovered a small, cozy office. Murphy had designed this area to be a private haven. The warm, comforting room was furnished with a desk, computer console, a small seating area with a leather couch, and a television mounted on the wall. The other two walls were filled with floor to ceiling bookshelves. The windows here were not at eye level but higher so, if needed, he could have privacy and still open them to catch the sound of the waves or, more dramatically, the passing of a summer thunderstorm.

Wyatt returned to the kitchen, where he made a fast track to the notebook. As Ryan explained, it held all the secrets to the inner workings of the house. Glancing around, he spotted something else he'd been looking for: alcohol. He removed a bottle of white wine from the beverage refrigerator. Pouring a glass, he sipped as he ruffled through the notebook, plotting his course. The kitchen still held many mysteries worth exploring.

Opening the large main refrigerator, he squealed when he saw it was a walk-in cooler stretching deep into the wall. On one side, rows of freezer cabinets were labeled: meat, vegetables, seafood, pasta, dessert, it was all there. The opposite side held racks with fresh items: dairy products, produce and everything else imaginable. Not wanting to chill himself, he grabbed a clipboard hanging on the inside of the door before scurrying out. Listed in very neat printing were the entire contents and the date when each item was purchased. Everything from the finest meats and seafood, to frozen pizzas had been stocked in preparation for his stay. Most items were his favorites. It was clear Murphy and Linda had spent some time on the phone planning all of this.

The next delightful discovery brought him back to the same hallway he had walked through when he had first entered the house. The wall opposite the benches and clothes hooks, at the mere touch of a fingertip, opened to magically reveal a complete laundry area. Shelves above the prerequisite washer and dryer units held every cleaning and laundry product one could ever need. Finished taking inventory, he once again pressed his finger to the small pad, closing up the wall and returning the area back to an unsuspecting hallway.

From the kitchen area, he walked to the end of the great room and ventured down the wide stairway to the lower level. Lights automatically lit his way as he descended the stairs to the entertainment room, anchored on one end by a huge stone fireplace and on the opposite end by a screening room, complete with its own little bar area. An assortment of games awaited him in the large room. Pool table, pinball machines, slot machines, and televisions hung everywhere. A large wooden bar had been inserted into one of the walls, which upon closer inspection, appeared to be the remnants of an old wooden ship deck. The rock jutting out at odd intervals here and there along the floor and walls was the actual rock foundation the house had been built on. Murphy had chosen to incorporate it into the architecture rather than remove or hide it.

Starting to chill from the natural coolness of the lower level, he headed back up the stairs. The entire expanse of the front of the house was an interesting mix of wood and glass, allowing the tranquil cove to be the star attraction. From the angle where he stood in the humongous living room area, he could see around the corner of the secluded beach to the ocean, which was dotted here and there by tiny, evergreen covered islands. Wyatt followed the flow of the room to the side, where double doors opened onto a spacious porch. He loved how warm it felt. Peering out one of the screened windows, he chuckled when he realized Murphy had designed the porch over a stream flowing from somewhere deep in the lush green forest out to the cove. The gentle sound of water cascading over rocks was intoxicating. Opening the screen door, he walked down the stone steps to the ground, which couldn't quite decide if it wanted to be all sand or grass. Eventually, the grass gave up its claim to a curved, silky sand beach, framed on the right by massive old pines and on the left by a series of large rocks jutting out to the water.

The late afternoon sun was still high enough in the sky to warm his skin. Soon, the shadows of the house would stretch themselves out to the shimmering blue water. Wyatt spent several minutes glancing up and down the cove. He couldn't remember seeing a more beautiful, tranquil setting. Looking back to the house, he realized Murphy had created the ultimate north woods paradise. If he felt like it later, he would go for a swim before dinner. Now it was time for another glass of wine.

Back in the kitchen, he filled his glass and paged further into the notebook, which pointed him to another hallway, located just to the left of the fireplace in the great room. With glass in hand, he started down to the far end and into an area of the house designed to accommodate Murphy's guests. As he walked, he discovered a series of spacious yet cozy guest bedrooms, each with its own bathroom. Further down the hallway, he came upon a workout area that included a large whirlpool and a cedar plank sauna. Murphy had thought of everything. Every square inch of living area benefited from his wonderful knack for design and exquisite eye for detail. It all made sense. Everything inside the house was state of the art, from the appliances in the kitchen to the futuristic sound system, entertainment center, and climate control. He smiled as he journeyed back to the kitchen, which at least for now, he nicknamed "ground zero."

Looking over the clipboard with the grocery list, he planned dinner. He would have a steak, baked potato, and small salad. Already hungry—he hadn't had any food since breakfast—Wyatt sliced cheese onto a plate and carried it, along with the remainder of his bottle of wine, out to the porch, where he relaxed on one of the cushioned recliners. A flock of gulls circling over the cove lulled him into a deep, warm sleep.

When he woke up several hours later, the light was nearly gone and the air had chilled considerably. Going through his clothing choices, he picked a pair of soft, flannel pajama bottoms and a T-shirt. He was just about to start grilling his steak when the phone console on the wall began beeping, startling the daylights out of him.

"Hello," Wyatt answered tentatively, recovering from his scare.

"Stay the hell out of my underwear drawer, you perv," the familiar voice barked on the other end. "I see you haven't managed to burn down the house yet."

"Hey, Murphy," Wyatt laughed as he leaned into the counter. "I gotta tell ya, this place is incredible. I am so impressed."

"Thanks! I hoped you'd find it acceptable."

"You're a genius. But then you already know that. Seriously, I think I'm going to love it here."

"How was the flight? Did my guy pick you up on time? Everything go smoothly?" Wyatt thought for minute. *Should I make a big deal about Ryan or just let it go?*

Wyatt decided to play it safe and not go into too much detail. He wasn't sure if he'd be seeing much of Ryan. This summer was about relaxing and taking a break. It would be a big mistake to fixate on his attraction to Ryan more than he already had. The guy was hot and Wyatt had reacted the way any healthy gay male in his position would have: he'd drooled, embarrassed himself, and envisioned nonstop hot sex with the young stud.

"Your guy was there right on time. The flight, everything, went great. Thanks for making it all go so smoothly." The way Murphy watched out and took such care embarrassed him if he thought about it long enough. *How could I have gotten so lucky, to have such a wonderful person in my life?*

"I'm not going to be bugging you much, Wy," Murphy said. "More importantly, I don't want you bugging me much. I'm crazy busy right now and there's nothing you can help me with. But I want you to work very hard too, at doing nothing but relaxing. Is that understood?"

"Yes, Mr. Smith," Wyatt answered respectfully.

"I'm not shittin' you on this one. I know you're going to get antsy, and bored, and probably nuts with ideas for the movie with all this free time you're going to have, but that's just too bad. Live with it. I want you to make every effort to make this a summer away from work."

"Yes, Mr. Smith," Wyatt answered again, less respectful than before. Okay, he was tired of being lectured. He understood Murphy's point, but now, right now, he didn't care. He was hungry.

"I'm going to be so disappointed in you, and Daddy's going to spank you if you give up on this opportunity...."

"Okay," Wyatt interrupted, hollering into the phone. "I fucking get the message. Give me a fucking break!"

"I know how you are," Murphy responded, completely unfazed.

Wyatt, with the phone nestled between his chin and his neck, walked over to his wineglass and downed it. No matter how frustrated he got, he had to marvel at Murphy's technique. It made him smile. Had Murphy outlined any sort of structure or rules prior to Wyatt making the trip, Wyatt—and Murphy knew this better than anyone— would have balked and closed the door on the idea. Now that Murphy had him relocated, and the plan was already rolling, Wyatt was captive and Murphy took full advantage of Wyatt's disadvantage. Masterful!

"Murphy, I'll do my best. I understand how important this is and I think I'm going to love it here. It's not going to be a problem, so don't make it one. Now, we can talk for hours in the morning if you want, but I'm starving and unless you want me to hang up on you, say good-bye now.

"Good-bye now!"

"Good-bye now too. I love you," Wyatt said with a smile in his voice.

"I love you too, Wyatt. Call me if you need anything. Wait, check that. Call Ryan if you need anything."

"Good-bye now, too, again." Wyatt waited for Murphy to drop off the call first before putting the phone back into its cradle. A huge yawn sprang from out of nowhere. He wouldn't swim tonight, he decided. There would be plenty of time for that. He really needed to eat something substantial. Mastering the appliance controls would be a challenge, but the notebook had all the information he needed.

Tired as hell, he decided to eat in the little office right off his bedroom. Food had never tasted this good, he thought, as he watched a documentary on the Great Wall of China. Leaving his dinner dishes to deal with in the morning, he climbed into one of the most comfortable beds on the planet and was soon asleep.

THE next morning he awoke to bright rays of sunshine pouring in from the large windows facing the water. From the looks of it, it was going to be a glorious day. Just what the doctor ordered. Being a creature of habit, he woke up at about the same time every morning, early, often before sunrise. Mornings were his favorite time of day, but because of the nature of his work, the countless late nights, he didn't always have a schedule that permitted him to enjoy them.

This morning he woke up with a raging hard-on the likes of which he hadn't experienced in a very long time. Unsure why he was in such a state, he ignored it, or tried to. Strolling naked into the kitchen with a penis insisting on leading the way, he rummaged around until he had tea brewing and a bagel ready to toast.

"Shit," he said as he waited for the tea to steep. He hadn't given it a thought until now, but he had forgotten to make arrangements for delivery of the morning paper. Oh well, he would just have to live without, or if he was really starved for news, fire up his laptop and take advantage of Murphy's extensive wireless network, which no matter how it was promoted, would never be the same as hunkering over the paper. He could arrange through Ryan to have it delivered if he really missed it. For now, he'd find some other distraction. After all, at least for the summer, it might be a good idea to wean himself off of the news. Back home he was a regular junkie.

Stepping out on the porch with a mug of piping hot tea, he gazed out over the cove to the vast ocean beyond. The bright morning light beaming down on the water reminded him of a plush resort he and Murphy had stayed at a long time ago. He inhaled the warm, moist air. The cove was calm and lovely. He decided after he finished his tea, he would test the water. Murphy had warned him it would still be cold, but he was game to give it a try. The sooner he became used to it, the sooner he could begin swimming in earnest. Another daily routine from home he couldn't live without.

Wyatt padded down the wooden steps leading from the outside deck onto the beach. The sand was warm beneath his toes. The early summer sun was surprisingly intense and warmed his skin. The idea of a cool swim seemed even more inviting. Running at full clip from the beach into the water so he had no risk of chickening out, he gasped when his body made contact, but there was no stopping him now. Using the momentum he had going, he dove under the surface, the cold water sending shock waves throughout his body. Eventually, the shock wore off and he managed to swim a couple short laps before noticing his fingers were starting to turn blue. Still, it felt incredible. He enjoyed the sensation of being naked, gliding through the water.

HOT water pelted Ryan's face as he stood directly under the nozzle. It's one of the things he enjoyed about being in a hotel, the unlimited amount of hot water at his beck and call. Turning around, he positioned himself so the showerhead pointed at his shoulders and neck, where he still felt tension from his morning workout. Leaning forward, the intense spray moved down past his broad shoulders to the small of his back. Spreading his legs, he palmed the wall and savored the sensation created by the water rushing between his muscled ass cheeks. Hanging his head, he stared past his dick to watch the water cascade down his legs. This was the way he preferred to end every shower.

Pushing himself off the tiled wall, Ryan twisted around and shut off the water. Sliding the glass door open, he stepped out and grabbed a thick, luxurious towel. This was another hotel perk he looked forward to—plush, freshly laundered towels.

The cool air collided with his warm skin, sending plumes of steam into the air. He took his time toweling off, making sure to reach every nook and cranny of his strong, well-toned body. Tossing the used towel back into the shower, he moved to the main part of the bathroom, which contained a large vanity, heated mirror, a toilet, and a Jacuzzi tub.

Murphy had lived up to his promise. The hotel was posh. Now that he had settled in and gotten used to its amenities, his life away from home was turning out to be much more pleasurable than he'd expected.

Finished shaving, he walked into his two-room suite and stepped into his black boxer briefs, which he had set out in advance, alongside the rest of the clothes he had picked out: shorts and a faded Los Angeles Lakers T-shirt he'd wear everyday if he thought he could get away with it.

Grabbing his backpack off a table near the door, he pocketed the keys to his rental car and stepped out into the hall.

I'm forgetting something....

Sometime between the end of the porno he'd ordered up last night and waking this morning, he'd formulated a plan for today. There was something connected to the plan he hadn't remembered to do.

That's it! Check my cell for messages. Something might've come up.

So far, Wyatt had yet to contact him. Murphy had mentioned this would probably be the case. Despite his weakened condition, it had been planted in his head that Wyatt wasn't likely to become needy or require his services very often. This was part of the reason he'd planned today's outing. Not knowing how his prized charge was doing was starting to cause concern, though. He needed confirmation for himself that things were going well.

Flipping open his phone, Ryan wasn't surprised to find there were no calls. He and Murphy had spoken several times in the last week, since he'd arrived, and to his knowledge, everything was going as planned. There wasn't any real need for him to be doing this, and yet he was eager to check things out. On one level, he wanted to squelch any anxiety from not knowing Wyatt's status firsthand. On another, deeper level, he felt compelled to make some type of contact with Wyatt.

Stepping out of the door into the hallway, he remembered one last thing he'd forgotten to put into his pack. Ryan walked over to a dresser opposite the bed and pulled out a pair of bright-red swimming trunks. If the day turned out to be as warm as expected, he thought it would be fun to pick up lunch and stop at one of the beaches between here and Murphy's house to spend the afternoon. Ryan was looking forward to checking out more of the little villages that surrounded the area. As long as he carried his phone, there was no reason to limit himself to the hotel pool, where he had spent much of the last few days, surfing the Net on his laptop and reading.

Pulling onto the highway, he was surprised at how anxious he was to get to Murphy's. He fought the urge to call Wyatt and ask if he needed anything. That wasn't the way it was supposed to work. Wyatt would call him. He needed to stick to the plan. Murphy had been clear: "To him, you'll probably be just some guy who is there to run errands. And honestly, that's all I need you to be." *Fine by me. Well....*

Wyatt had turned out to be anything but what Ryan had expected. He was very charming and he seemed appreciative of Ryan's services. There was no question about it, Wyatt appeared exhausted and vulnerable, and for some inexplicable reason this made him very attractive to Ryan. There was a charismatic element going on with Wyatt too. Ryan had read somewhere that talented people, successful people, had a quality about them you could feel when you were in their presence. In the past, he'd assumed this quality was the product of arrogance. In Wyatt, it wasn't arrogance at all. It was something more. He was magnetic. This vibe made Ryan feel like being with Wyatt was special in some way. As if he was privy to a secret. An exciting secret.

Whatever it was he felt, he was becoming aware of a need to feel it again. Coming around the corner, he spotted the shiny new mailbox marking the road leading into Murphy's. Ryan pulled his SUV over to the side and put it in park. He spent several minutes contemplating what he was about to do.

What if there's no sign of him? How close should I get before I call it quits? Play it by ear and don't do anything foolish you'll regret later. Remember that plan you left the hotel with? Stick to it. Take a little peek and then leave.

If he couldn't spot a glimpse of Wyatt today, he could always try it again. And besides, maybe he'd hear from Wyatt in the next day or two. Putting the car in gear, he turned off the highway.

Slowly, he crept down the bumpy road leading to the house, careful not to gun the engine and give himself away. Inching forward, he continued to fight a fierce inner battle pitting what he knew to be right against what he knew to be wrong. What he knew to be wrong was precisely what he was attempting to do now: spy on Wyatt Stark.

"To him, you'll probably be just some guy who is there to run errands. And honestly, that's all I need you to be," Ryan repeated as he approached his destination.

Why am I doing this? I'm doing this because I can't control myself, that's why!

Maybe if he was a stronger individual, he'd be able to keep better control of himself. The fact he had gotten himself this far, he reasoned, was proof positive he lacked the necessary self-control expected of him.

Ryan pulled over and turned off the engine. He'd come far enough. Even if Wyatt decided to take a walk, this would be a considerable distance for him to travel.

This is safe.

Stepping out of the car, he reached in and grabbed his pack, slinging it over his shoulder as he carefully shut the door. A trail, located several hundred feet further down the dirt road, would bring him to a spot he had explored during a break in preparing the house for Wyatt's arrival. Never expecting it to be of importance, today it was the perfect solution for what he was attempting.

Leaving the road, twigs snapped under his feet and branches whipped his body as he headed down the trail through the dense forest.

After walking for several minutes, he heard the faint sound of waves crashing against rock. Ryan stopped. Something else had been needling him and he needed to take a minute and address it.

What about the lies you told? When are you going to deal with those?

Ryan knew he could rationalize the lies. It was all part of his attempt to stay in the background. That's what he'd say if they ever came up.

That's all you have *to say. Besides, wasn't it Wyatt who made the assumption I was a local in the first place? Relax!*

Farther down the path, he descended a small embankment and continued through a valley of ferns. A few more feet and he spotted a clearing. Up another easy hill and he was out of the forest and standing on huge, dark rocks, lining the shore. To the left was the open ocean and to his right, he could see the gentle curve of the cove and the beach that stood directly in front of Murphy's house. With a considerable amount of caution, he worked his way further out onto the rocks until he was able to glance across the cove at the house. The spot was exactly as he had remembered, and a perfect perch for him to be an undetected observer.

Ryan soon noticed how warm it had gotten. The sun beating down heated the rock, causing him to sweat. If nothing else, he would work on his tan and perhaps explore the rock for a place to splash around in the water where he would be protected from the powerful waves. Retreating back to solid ground, he opened his pack and pulled out his swimsuit. Shedding his clothes, he stood naked on the rock and again questioned his motives. Nothing about this breach of common sense came close to anything outlined in the job he'd been hired to do.

None of that mattered. His heart was racing a mile a minute. He needed to be here. Ryan felt a familiar sensation as he pulled up his swimming suit. The real motivation for what he was doing was no longer a mystery to him.

Wyatt Stark makes my dick hard.

Chapter 4

WYATT stayed in the water as long as he could stand it. When he realized no amount of exertion was going to warm him, he swam to shore. Dripping wet, he glanced up the beach to the rock point. A figure in red swimming trunks caught his eye. Almost as soon as it registered he'd seen someone, the person scurried over the rocks and vanished. Wyatt kept his eye on that side of the cove as he walked back to the house. The figure never reappeared. There was enough distance between them that being naked didn't bother him, although it did cross his mind.

That must be where Murphy's property ends, he thought as he entered the house, not giving it another thought.

Wyatt spent the remainder of the morning and much of the afternoon with a book, trying without much success, to unwind. Although he started out with the best intentions, the ability to relax was a constant struggle he lost more often than won.

For the first few days, he was fine. The newness of his environment was enough to keep him occupied. By the end of the week, he was, despite the paradise Murphy had provided for him, close to losing his mind.

To pass the time, Wyatt placed calls. He placed many calls. Friends and acquaintances he hadn't spoken to in years received calls. Many received more than one. The telephone had become Wyatt's lifeline. The calls became his bridge back to civilization. Eventually he ran out of names. Wyatt felt trapped.

In total agony, he knew he had to do something or he'd go crazy. *What the hell have I done? What could I have possibly been thinking when I agreed to spend a summer in complete isolation? I hate this!*

I'm lonely. Give me some fucking noise that isn't from a gull or a loon, or some other stupid-ass creature of the wild. The sound of a piercing, screaming, emergency vehicle would be music to my ears.

Faced with nothing else to do, Wyatt found himself thumbing through a cookbook specializing in soups, its large, colorful pictures a temporary distraction. A recipe for lobster bisque caught his eye. *Yummy!* Wyatt yanked the phone off the wall.

Pick up. Come on, pick up. I know you're there. You were there just an hour ago.

"Stark Residence."

"Hey Linda," Wyatt chirped, "It's me again!" Wyatt waited for his housekeeper to speak. Seconds passed without a response. All he could hear on the other end was labored breathing. "You there?" he asked, desperate for any type of conversation even if it was strained, like he knew it was now with Linda. He didn't care.

"What now? I was on the ladder cleaning the blinds in your office," Linda answered testily.

"Wow! I bet they look great!" Wyatt waited for Linda to acknowledge his appreciation of her efforts. It never came. Instead, he was treated to silence on the other end of the line.

"Say… the reason I'm calling," he charged on, "is to find out if you've ever made lobster bisque. I'm looking at a recipe right now and I gotta tell ya, Linda… it sounds tasty and it looks easy to make. And hey, I'm here, right here in the middle of the land of lobsters." Wyatt forced himself to chuckle. "I was wondering if you had any good lobster bisque tips."

"No tip, just make it."

Wyatt couldn't ignore her unwillingness to move the conversation forward. He scrambled to think of something else to talk about that might be more engaging. *Please Linda, I'm dying here. Like a captive koala deprived of eucalyptus, I'm dying.*

Wyatt's heart sank. There was nothing left for him to say. He couldn't argue that it would be in his best interest to end the call.

"Well… okay. I guess I'd better let you go." Struggling to protect his dignity, he announced, "I got stuff to do around here too." *Like slit my wrist and guzzle drain cleaner.*

Click!

"Huh? Did she.…" *She just hung up on me! Can you believe that? My housekeeper just blew me off!*

Wyatt stormed around the house like a caged animal. There was nothing about this arrangement that was working. *I don't give a shit if I'm living at the Taj Mahal, I want out. I want out now!*

It was time to throw in the towel. He dialed Murphy's cell, and with nostrils he knew were flaring, stood poised to do battle. It wasn't Murphy's fault. Nope! It wasn't his fault at all. Spending the summer here had been an idea that, on paper, seemed like a good idea, but in reality, a monumentally stupid mistake. Wyatt paced in circles, willing Murphy to pick up the phone.

PICK UP THE PHONE! So help me God if you don't pick up your phone.…

"What now, Wyatt?" Murphy answered flatly.

"Excuse me? What do you mean, what now?" Wyatt could feel the veins in his neck bulge.

"What I mean is this is your third call today. What could we possibly have to talk about that we haven't already covered in your previous calls?"

Wyatt closed his eyes and took several deep breaths. He could feel his fingers going numb. Mr. Anxiety Attack was knocking at the door.

Breathe! Keep it together. You're talking to Murphy.

"Here's a new topic," he answered in a measured voice laden with smugness. "I've fucking had it with this fucking north woods nature bullshit. I want to go home NOW!" Wyatt leaned over the counter for support. His anger and frustration had begun to trigger a full body shutdown. Perhaps an attack of monstrous proportions.

Several fat, bloated seconds passed before Murphy responded. "You're doing that loud, breathing through your nose thing again. It's so not attractive."

Wyatt knew on some level what he'd just heard from Murphy was funny. He just couldn't go there, and to prove his point, remained silent. He'd had it.

"Listen to me, Wyatt. I knew going into this that changing your daily routine was going to be a huge challenge. You're such a creature of habit. Frankly, I'm surprised it's taken this long for you to make this call."

"Please, Murphy...."

"Listen to me," Murphy said patiently. "I never ask you for anything. I never demand squat from you and you know that. I'm going to ask you to do something for me now and it's very important. It's very important to me. Why is it very important to me? I'm going to tell you why. It's very important to me because if you get out here in a couple of months and you're distracted and tired, and not in the right frame of mind to take on the challenges of making this movie, we're going to be screwed. Our careers are going to be over. In everyone's eyes, we'll be losers. Fucking losers! I'm not threatening you, I'm not telling you this to make you scared. I'm telling you what I know to be true."

Wyatt leaned farther over the counter as he listened to Murphy. What he'd just heard, it all made sense. It made Murphy sense, which meant that on some level what he'd heard wasn't arguable or negotiable. Murphy sense. Wyatt had a love-hate relationship with Murphy sense.

"Now, you have to believe me when I say I know what you're going through," Murphy continued. "And because I know you know I know, I'll make a deal with you."

Wyatt perked up when he heard the words, "make a deal with you." Perhaps he'd get his way after all. There would be a minimal price to pay, a Murphy tax, but no matter what it was, he'd be able to afford it.

"What's the deal?" Wyatt asked as he started to pace again.

"Give our fucking north woods bullshit plan one more week. Seven short days, and if you still feel the same way about staying as you do now, then I'll have you home the next day. Do we have a deal?"

Not seven days. Oh please not seven more days, I can't do it. I can't do it! Wyatt paced faster as if trying to catch up to the thoughts racing around in his mind. *It's a fair deal. I hate it, but it's a fair deal.* What was worse than it being a good deal, it made Murphy sense.

"God damn you, Murphy. Okay, I'll stay here seven more days." Wyatt spun around looking for the nearest clock. "It's 2:45 my time. One week from now, at 2:45 my time, I'm going to call you, and you'd better answer your phone, if you know what's good for you, and I'm going to ask you very politely to send the plane for me and, Murphy, are you listening?" Wyatt stopped pacing as he waited for Murphy to answer.

"I'm listening, Wy."

"You'll very politely tell me, without any further argument, the plane to take me home is on its way. Is that understood?"

"Sounds like a plan to me. I understand."

"Okay then." Wyatt resumed pacing. He was charged. He'd cut a deal. He had nothing more to say.

"Wyatt?" Murphy asked.

"What?"

"There are a couple more points to this deal and we can shake."

"What?" Wyatt bit his lip. He hadn't anticipated there'd be more provisions to Murphy's deal.

"One," Murphy stated in a friendly, but authoritative voice, "Barring an emergency, this is the last call you'll make to me until two forty-five, your time, one week from today."

"Fine!"

"Two," Murphy continued, "you'll stop calling Linda every thirty minutes. You're driving her bat-shit crazy and she's already complained to me several times. This is her break too. Respect it."

Murphy's last condition hit Wyatt like a ton of bricks. He was instantly overwhelmed with shame. He hated being caught like this.

"Agree to the second condition, please."

"Murphy?" Wyatt asked, devastated by the acknowledgment of his own selfishness. "Would you please call Linda and tell her I'm very sorry for being such a self-centered asshole?"

"Hon, you're neither of those things. You're so far out of your element right now, you don't know what to do with yourself. I'll let her know."

"Thank you."

"Are you still my special pumpkin?" Murphy ventured playfully.

He's on your side, Wyatt!

"Yes, because you'd be hard-pressed to find anyone else this stupid to fall for your tricks," Wyatt answered, forcing himself to start the process of putting himself back together.

Murphy laughed hard.

Wyatt said good-bye and walked out of the kitchen into the huge living room. The view of the cove was breathtaking. The reflection of the light off the water danced everywhere he looked.

What the hell is wrong with me? Why is it so hard to appreciate this?

WYATT woke up feeling ashamed for not trying to make this whole sabbatical thing work out. The call with Murphy had troubled him, and he had spent much of the night replaying their conversation in his head. He felt embarrassed to have been lectured.

Looking out over the cove, he was overwhelmed by its beauty and tranquility. This was a special place. Starting today, he'd make every effort to make the most of his time here. If he still felt the need to go back to the city, so be it. But he wasn't going to allow that to happen without putting up a fight. Who the hell knew when he'd ever have an opportunity to do something like this again?

Wyatt decided he would start by going for a swim. After that, he'd put on some clothing and go for a hike. And after that, he'd read, or watch a movie. He would start cooking. Wyatt had forgotten how much he had been looking forward to trying new recipes. Maybe even a little baking. He would work on doing all the things he'd planned to do here.

Enough of this bullshit! This is my fucking time, goddamn it. Setting his mug down on the table, he ran down the stairs to the water.

Wading near the shoreline, warming his body in the sun, Wyatt looked down to the point and spotted what he thought was the same guy in bright red swimming trunks. Being so far away from him, details of the figure were hard to distinguish, but he was confident it was the same person he'd spotted several days before. He watched as the figure sat down, and from where Wyatt was standing, the guy appeared to be staring in his direction. *Is he watching me? How strange.*

Reminded that he was naked, he dove into the water and began swimming his laps. When he had finished swimming, he treaded water until he was able to confirm the unwelcomed visitor was no longer in sight. He was gone.

Murphy had made it clear the beach in front of the house, as far as you could see in both directions, was his private property. Twice now, this same individual had violated property lines and was trespassing. One thing Wyatt knew for certain, he wasn't about to play this cat and mouse game any longer. Maybe a sign fell down and the guy didn't know he was trespassing. If he was there tomorrow, Wyatt would throw on some shorts and go have a chat. He hated confrontation, but he loved having his privacy more.

As he reached the steps to the porch, he heard someone call out, "Wyatt! Hey, Wyatt!"

He looked over to see the man in the red trunks waving his hands up and down. Straining his eyes to make out more detail, Wyatt finally put two and two together and figured out it was Ryan. *What the hell?*

To his horror, Wyatt watched as the young man climbed down the rocks and began running on the beach toward him. He weighed his options. He could hustle up the stairs and grab some clothes, or he could hold his ground and hope Ryan liked what he saw. Before he had a chance to choose an option, Ryan's long, muscled legs had cut the distance between them in half. A rush for clothes was no longer an option. Ryan was close enough now for Wyatt to hear huffing and puffing.

"Wyatt!" Ryan panted as he ran up next to him. "I'm sorry to bother you. I realized when you didn't acknowledge me the other day you might not see all that good without contacts or glasses. When you headed back to the house, I was sure you didn't recognize me."

Wyatt was too embarrassed to do anything but smile back, causing visible uneasiness in the young man, who was struggling to find a comfortable way to ignore Wyatt's nakedness.

"Wow! You're in really great shape," Ryan said, flashing his killer smile.

There's not a single thing I can do right now that's going to change the fact that I'm standing here naked in front of one of the most handsome men I have ever met in my life. Okay, Wyatt, here's the deal. Pretend you're fully clothed. You know… the Emperor's New Clothes. "Well… thank you." *Oh yeah… brilliant!* Wyatt valiantly fought the urge to cover his bits with his hands.

"Ah shoot," Ryan said. "I should have called to let you know I was coming by for a swim. I wasn't using my head. Sorry, man."

"Naw, it's cool," Wyatt reassured him. *Cool you're here, not so cool I'm butt-naked.*

"Dad used to send me up here to check on the property for Mr. Smith," Ryan continued. "I discovered a trail from the road to the cove. There's a great place at the end of the point where you can get in and out of the water without banging yourself up. I didn't mean to sneak up on you like this. I'm really sorry."

"No apology needed."

"I didn't want you to freak out, thinking it was someone you didn't know hanging around, so I thought I'd better make sure you knew it was me."

"Don't worry about it, Ryan. Really, I don't mind at all." Wyatt felt himself beginning to relax. "Listen, if you have the time, let me throw on some shorts, and we can sit out on the porch and visit. I've got a couple of cold ones in the refrigerator."

"That isn't necessary."

"I insist."

Wyatt felt bad Ryan was so worked up about intruding on his privacy. Until now, he hadn't realized how starved he was for conversation. A handsome face didn't hurt either, and Ryan certainly had that and more. With his legs and chest exposed, Wyatt could tell this guy had devoted a few hours of his time to the gym. He had one hell of a hot body. A manly patch of chest hair contrasted nicely with his boyish face. Ryan's sandy-haired legs and arms sent a shudder through Wyatt, reminding him he had better make a beeline for those shorts. His dick had a mind of its own these days. It, too, was eager to become better acquainted with Ryan.

"Please stay. Make yourself comfortable and I'll be right back," Wyatt said over his shoulder as he hustled up the stairs while it was still just the tip of his nose leading the way.

Moments later, dressed in baggy cargo shorts, Wyatt came back to the porch carrying a couple of cold beers. He handed one to Ryan, who was sitting on the sofa looking out at the water. Wyatt took a seat across from him.

"You'll have to show me the path you mentioned."

"Oh sure, any time," Ryan said, taking a sip. "This really hits the spot."

An uncomfortable moment passed, which they both filled by sipping on their beers. Wyatt felt tense, but not in a bad way. He was anxious, eager to feel comfortable with Ryan. Wyatt wondered if Ryan had any idea how attractive he was.

"You spend your summers away from college helping your mom and dad out, right?" Wyatt knew if he threw a couple more exploratory questions out there, one of them would take, and they'd be on their way.

"There're a couple of us who make deliveries during the summer. It gets busy. Besides all the vacation homes and the summer rentals, there's a large boat community who shop at the store. We have flyers around town listing our products. People call in their orders, Dad and Mom fill them, and we deliver for a small charge. I'm thinking in the next couple seasons we'll be able to move the whole process online. Dad's a hard sell on that idea." Ryan chuckled, inviting Wyatt to see the humor in his dad's reluctance to accept change.

"Well, there is the old adage, if it ain't broke, don't fix it." *Perfect! You just told him he was stupid.*

"Do you enjoy working on Broadway?"

Wyatt was thankful Ryan wasn't intimidated by his last comment. He had kept the ball in the air. "I can't imagine doing anything else. I'm lucky that way, I guess," Wyatt said. "I've always known what I've wanted to do with my life. I had a goal from very early on."

"My life isn't that mapped out," Ryan shared with a laugh. "I'm still searching for something I can lock onto and run with. I'm going to have to start making some decisions soon, or I'll end up running the store when Dad and Mom are no longer able to manage it."

"There are worse ways to go through life," Wyatt assured Ryan with a smile.

"Oh I know. I'm lucky, I guess, to have the store to fall back on if something else doesn't work out." Ryan reached for his beer. "I want to get out and experience the world while I'm still independent and not saddled down with a ton of responsibility."

And we're off! Wyatt typically held court over a herd of ass-kissers, eagerly hoping for some tiny sign of approval. He didn't get any of that now. Ryan was delightful.

Wyatt fought off distraction as they talked. Silly thoughts were rolling around in his head, popping up left and right without warning. He found himself speculating, or wishing—no, hoping like hell—Ryan was gay. *Stop it right now!*

Ryan was the real deal. Although he was several years younger and possessed a handsome, boyish face, there was very little else about Ryan that was boyish. He was one of those rare human beings you meet who haven't a clue how attractive they are, or in this case, how *very* attractive they are.

It took considerable effort, but Wyatt made a promise to himself to enjoy the friendship Ryan offered for just that, a friendship, and to keep his lustful thoughts to himself, where they belonged.

Only the truly disappointing news Ryan's dad was expecting him to make a few evening deliveries prevented Wyatt from inviting the young man to stay for dinner.

"Is there anything I can pick up for you?" Ryan asked as they walked from the porch to the kitchen, carrying their empty beer bottles.

"Let me see...." Wyatt opened the refrigerator door and stepped inside for a look. "You could bring some lettuce. Romaine, if you have it."

"We can do romaine. Anything else?" Ryan asked.

Ryan was standing very close, looking over Wyatt's shoulder. It felt good to have Ryan standing so close. Comforting and exciting at the same time. *Do you want to touch me, Ryan? I want to touch you.*

"What about some fruit?" Ryan asked.

"Fruit?" Wyatt laughed. "Sure, I'll take some fruit. Surprise me." Closing the door to the walk-in, Wyatt noted the inquisitive look on Ryan's face. The reference to fruit hadn't registered in the same way it had for him.

Ryan promised to return with the groceries the next day. Resisting a temptation to hug him, he thanked Ryan and patted him on the shoulder. Wyatt walked him out to his car.

THE next morning, Wyatt discovered a cooler by the back door filled with the groceries he had requested. A piece of yellow notebook paper had been taped to the cover, which read:

> *"Wyatt—Thanks for the brews! It was GREAT getting to know you. Give me a call if you need anything else. Busy couple days ahead.*
>
> *See you soon, I hope, Ryan."*

What a sweetheart, Wyatt thought as he hauled the cooler into the house. Whoever wins the key to this guy's heart, he lamented, they're going to be one very lucky… person. The jury was still out on that one. Wyatt wasn't about to give up hope.

He spent the morning, as he had done almost every morning since arriving, out on the porch reading and enjoying his tea before swimming. Relaxing, the concept of kicking back, was starting to take, but he still felt the urge to be productive. As he swam back and forth across the cove, his thoughts turned to his baby, *Dress Up. I miss dancing.* It was time to take a break from all this grueling rest and relaxation and do some actual work.

When *Dress Up* was first starting to come together, he had envisioned a soft, yet powerful number in the show where Casey, one of the hunky male runway models, in a solo dance contrasting with all the glitz and energy of the rest of the show, contemplates his future in the harsh world of fashion. The lyrics would be simple, allowing the actor to communicate primarily through dance.

Wyatt understood his audience. Women and gay men would leave a wet spot on their seats as the actor portraying Casey danced his heart out in nothing more than a pair of sexy briefs. Ah yes, these calculated moments couldn't be taken for granted. The sequence was eliminated during previews in Minneapolis. No matter how Wyatt staged the dance, it just didn't play the way he had intended it to.

The film version, however, gave him a second chance. He knew in his heart he could finally realize this scene's full potential. He looked forward to the challenge and felt certain he could make the dance not only successful, but a much more potent statement than even he had originally thought possible.

Lying on the sofa, remote in hand, he listened over and over to the music created for *Casey's Dance.* The music gushed out of Murphy's billion-dollar sound system, enveloping him in a blanket of sound. With his eyes closed, Wyatt felt the familiar rush that signaled to him he was about to create. When he was first starting to choreograph, he had permitted himself to analyze what was happening during this creative trance, which brought the process to a screeching halt. Over time, he had taught himself to keep his mind free of any distractions until he had what he needed.

Wyatt listened several more times to the music, and then it happened. In his mind, he leapt off the sofa and onto a bare black stage. This was how his process of choreographing a piece started out. Visualizing a barren stage was easy. Filling the stage with quality work, wasn't. It was his habit to replay the music over and over, each time building on his creation by adding more layers of movement. As he choreographed the sequence in his mind, it was he who always danced the male or female lead. It didn't matter.

By late afternoon, he had moved the whole process, including sound from the speakers located in the porch, out onto the sand in front of the house, where he began to actually dance the choreography he had been creating in his head. He danced the new work over and over, each time adding more and more character and flair until he, and the piece, became one. Soon he would get to a point where he could begin to sell the piece. He would dance the role, holding nothing back. Holding back now, as he reminded his dancers, meant less to work with later down the road. Now was the time to be big and bold. He could take out or scale down their improvements later.

His concentration was so intense when he was in this creative state, he lost track of everything around him. Hours passed, and before he knew it, the light had begun to fade. The afternoon had been a personal victory. He sipped from his water bottle, staring out at the water and beyond. A part of him had been frightened off by this solo moment of Casey's. He'd considered the failed attempts at making the sequence work in the stage version of *Dress Up* his failure to communicate.

Do I have limitations? Am I losing my touch? He had always approached his work fearlessly. Somehow, he'd always been able to find a way to make whatever he was working on succeed.

The tops of the pines on the small islands protecting the cove were still lit by the early summer sun, but deep, elongated shadows had begun to creep across the beach. The natural lighting during this part of the day was extraordinary. Wyatt relished the gloaming. *Very theatrical!* He made a note to try and remember the dynamics of the light so he could attempt to recreate it in the future.

Taking a gulp of water, he made a deal with himself. *Just one more time through the routine and I'll call it a day.* Setting the bottle down next to his towel, he picked up the remote and pressed Replay. As the music drifted out onto the sand, Wyatt danced. He had discovered Casey's voice. This time around, the moves felt more honest, more gritty and real. He felt liberated as he danced. The piece was becoming comfortable. Wyatt knew his work today had been solid. Something he could definitely build on. When the music finally ended, he held his pose, savoring the satisfaction he felt in knowing his efforts had produced something special.

The sound of clapping startled Wyatt. To his surprise, Ryan was seated on the steps leading down from the porch.

"That was totally, totally… incredible," Ryan gushed as he continued to applaud. "It's one of the most beautiful things I've ever seen. I'm serious."

"Ryan," Wyatt panted, struggling to catch his breath. "How long have you been sitting there?"

"Only a few minutes. When you didn't answer the door, I figured you were out swimming… or lounging…."

Wyatt watched as Ryan's smile faded. His face turned deep red.

"… lounging on the beach," Ryan finished with less confidence, unable to look anywhere but at his feet.

Does he really think I'm pissed off at him for stopping by? God, if he only knew.

"I sure hope I'm not disturbing you," Ryan said, hanging his head and adding, "I should have turned around and left when you didn't answer."

"Heavens, no! Not to worry," Wyatt assured him. "I'm glad you stopped by. Yesterday's visit was way too short." *Oh great! Ryan stops by and once again, here I am, naked. What a freak he must think I am. It's time to say something.*

"I like being naked. I don't know what else to say."

"Oh hey, don't worry about it. You have no idea how your nakedness…well… how powerful… your body is so… it made your… ah hell, it was just incredible." Flustered, Ryan gestured behind him. "On the way over I picked up some live lobsters from Frosty and

Lil's." Ryan reached into a plastic bag and pulled out a large, fresh lobster with strands of seaweed dangling off it.

"Lil Hinnenkamp is a friend of my folks," Ryan said, placing the wiggling crustacean back in its plastic kennel. "She picked out a couple of winners. I wasn't sure if you liked lobster or not, but if you do, these are some of the freshest. Oh, and I also brought along some champagne my dad had sitting around. One of his regulars gave it to him and he hates the stuff. I was going to offer to make you dinner if you haven't already eaten, but it looks like I might have caught you at a bad time. Wow, I can't stop talking. Sorry, Wyatt. The last thing I want to do is intrude on your time."

"Relax. I'm cool. I'm really glad to see you," Wyatt assured the young man with a smile as he strolled over to the steps. "I've been at this all day long and I need to call it a day. I'd just go on and on and on forever if somebody didn't stop me."

"You're sure?" Ryan asked. "I tried calling, but I bet you were out here and couldn't hear the phone."

Wyatt could tell Ryan wasn't convinced he had made the right decision to show up unannounced. "Ryan, my friend, I can't think of a better way to spend an evening than with fresh lobster, a bottle of bubbly, and last but not least, enjoying it with a handsome lad like yourself." *Careful, the "handsome lad" comment may have crossed the line, especially given the fact I'm standing here naked.*

Wyatt gestured to the box and asked, "So what flavor of bubbly did you bring anyway? I love this stuff."

"Oh... you know...." Ryan rummaged through the box and pulled a bottle out and handed it over to Wyatt. "Some brand I've never heard of before. I haven't heard of too many brands to begin with."

"Sweet!" Wyatt squealed as he accepted the bottle, unable to contain his joy. *What were the odds? He's got a bottle of Krug, 1990.* "Oh man, this is incredible! I'm not kidding you. This is my absolute favorite. My very favorite in the whole wide world."

Wyatt was amazed, enough so that when his astonishment at the fact it was a bottle of Krug had ebbed, he stepped back in horror after realizing his naked body was now close to rubbing up to Ryan.

"We need to get this baby on ice and I need to get some clothes on." He handed the bottle back and bolted up the stairs. "I'll meet you in the kitchen. This is going to be great! Wow, you're cooking dinner for me. Sweet!" he hollered over his shoulder. "I still don't know my way around Murphy's kitchen, but I would venture to guess anything and everything we need is there somewhere."

By the time he had freshened up with a quick douse under the shower, put on a pair of shorts and a T-shirt, and strolled into the kitchen, Ryan was already well on his way to preparing their dinner. A large pot of water was on the stovetop and he was in the process of washing off a few baby red potatoes. Two champagne flutes stood empty at the other end of the kitchen counter.

"Wow, you don't waste any time, do you?" Wyatt asked with a hearty laugh as he stepped into the room. "What kind of music do you enjoy? Murph's got a little bit of everything here."

"I love all types of music. Seriously, put on anything."

Wyatt went into the living room and selected Catalogue on the flat screen mounted on the wall near the bar. Icons appeared, displaying CDs Murphy had on the system. It didn't take long for him to make his choice. In seconds, music could be heard throughout the house. *I have to get one of these.*

He hurried back to Ryan, who in the short time he had been away, had moved from potatoes to rinsing off ears of corn.

"Let me guess, Miles Davis?" Ryan asked, looking over at Wyatt with a twinkle in his eye.

"Something tells me that wasn't really a guess. Are you a Miles fan?" Wyatt asked as he wandered back around the counter to inspect the dinner preparations. He allowed himself a quick once-over of his handsome young guest. Ryan must have left his flaps at the door, for he stood, like him, barefoot. *God, even his feet are beautiful.* Wyatt forced himself to bring his eyes back up to street level.

"Yeah, I love Miles. My dad is really into Miles. We listened to him all the time while I was growing up."

He liked that Ryan referred to his father in a positive way. He liked how they shared in their love of Miles. The comment produced a quick snapshot for him of Ryan as a kid, at home, happy and loved. Love always seemed to breed confidence in a person. A childhood that lacked love was almost a prerequisite for showbiz folk. It seemed to fuel their creativity. They darted from here to there in various states of perpetual insecurity. On the rare occasion when this wasn't the case, those who brought secure, confident personalities to the table stood out. *Like this one. Ryan is a standout on every level.*

"Can I help with anything? Holy crap! Look at the size of these things," Wyatt said in amazement as he picked up one of the wiggling lobsters and held it up for inspection.

"You can start on the salad if you like," Ryan offered, chuckling at Wyatt's reaction to the lobster.

"How old is this guy, a hundred years or better?" Wyatt put the lobster back in the sink and went over to the bag of salad fixings Ryan had brought along. He pulled out lush green lettuce, a tomato, red pepper and a small sealed container. Some kind of salad dressing, Wyatt guessed.

"What's this?" Wyatt asked, holding up the container.

"Oh that's my killer salad dressing," Ryan answered. "I hope you like it. It's vinegar-based with all sorts of herbs in it. I just happened on it one time when I was putzing around in the kitchen. Everyone I make it for loves it. Oh, and to answer your earlier question, it takes a lobster about seven years to get to be a pound. My guess, these dudes are roughly twenty years old. Tragic to have their young lives end in such a violent way, dontcha think?" Ryan flashed an evil grin at Wyatt while gesturing to the pot of boiling water on the stove, cracking them both up.

Wyatt took a knife out of a nearby drawer and began slicing up the tomato and the pepper. The knife slid with little effort as he sliced and diced. *Like how little effort it takes to be with you,* Wyatt thought. How comfortable he felt being with Ryan.

"Hey, just because the champagne isn't chilled yet doesn't mean we have to go without something to drink. I have a bottle of Sauvignon Blanc already chilled—can I talk you into a glass?"

"That would be great. I'm almost done here," Ryan said. "The lobsters only need a few minutes. I can drop them in anytime. We can coast for a while if you want."

"I like the coasting idea very much," Wyatt answered as he chopped and diced. "I'd like to coast my way back out onto the porch when I'm done with the salad." He reached under the counter, opened up the wine refrigerator, and pulled out a bottle. Removing two wineglasses from above, he went about opening the bottle.

"What's your drink of pleasure when you're out on the town?" Wyatt asked as he peeled away the wrapper, exposing the cork.

"Hmm... I'd have to think about that." Ryan paused to contemplate Wyatt's question. "I'm not much of a drinker, but when I'm out with friends, I'll usually order a beer, or maybe a margarita. I like wine, but don't know much about it."

"Well, check this out. It's a nice, gentle sipper." Wyatt walked over and handed Ryan a glass. "Let me know if you don't like it. There're plenty of others to choose from. Here's to your health, your wealth, and... a light jail sentence for the murder of Crusty and his friend."

They both sipped in unison. Taking a step back, he waited for Ryan to render a verdict.

"Mmm, I can see why this would be a favorite," Ryan said, smacking his lips before taking another sip. "It's very refreshing. Not too sweet either. My mom drinks this pink crap I can't stand. It's so damn sweet."

"I'm glad you enjoy it. I'm not into sweet either. At least not in wine." Wyatt walked back over to where he had been chopping. "Okay, the tomato. When I'm done with the tomato, let's move this party out onto the porch." He finished his salad preparation and after tossing everything into a large bowl with Ryan's homemade dressing, he stashed the bowl in the refrigerator behind him. Ryan adjusted a lid over the boiling pot so it was vented and, with wine in hand, they made their way through the house and out onto the porch.

The hour or so before sunset was a magical time on the cove. The birds chirped and flew from tree to tree in a frenzy to get everything completed before darkness set in. The evening light off the water danced and shimmied onto the sand and trees surrounding the house. Content with the show in front of them, minutes passed before either man spoke.

"This is quite a place Murphy has here, I'll sure say that. Did you enjoy growing up in this area?" Wyatt asked.

"Huh? Oh… sorry." Although he appeared to be listening, it was clear Ryan had drifted. "I was a million miles away just now," he confirmed. "What did you ask me?"

"Well, how about a penny for your thoughts?" Wyatt smiled and sipped.

"Oh boy", Ryan said, after taking a hefty sip of wine.

Is it my imagination or is he beginning to blush again?

"I was just thinking about the summer and how much I had hoped to meet someone like you," Ryan answered.

"Like me?" Wyatt asked playfully. "Your goal was to meet an old dancer who can't seem to keep any clothes on to save his soul?"

Ryan laughed. "Exactly! You can imagine how amazed I am to have met my goal this early in the season. It's like a miracle."

"Touché," Wyatt yipped.

"I really like you, Wyatt and.…"

"And I really like you too," Wyatt interjected, sensing Ryan needed to hear something affirming about now.

"… and I hope I don't make you uncomfortable by saying this, but for the record… I mean not that you haven't already figured it out by now.…" Ryan gulped down another slug of wine before looking down and staring at his feet.

Wyatt had to stifle a giggle. *If I had feet that pretty, I'd look at them every chance I got too. Oh how the mind of a crazy person works.* Leaning toward Ryan, Wyatt prodded, "Yes?"

Setting his glass down on the table, Ryan looked up and blurted out, "I'm gay."

Chapter 5

RYAN'S disclosure caught Wyatt by surprise. It's not that he hadn't thought about it. It was the timing. Wyatt was surprised he hadn't seen this one coming. Usually you can tell what a person's leading up to. You have some sense at least of the direction they're headed.

"That's it?" Wyatt asked, praying his voice came off even and steady, lest he give away his absolute elation over what he'd just heard. Although he had speculated about Ryan's sexuality—well, hoped to dear God he was gay was more like it—he was beside himself with joy that Ryan's "Friends of Dorothy" membership had been confirmed.

Ryan nodded back, managing a sheepish smile. His face had turned as red as a strawberry.

"Me too," Wyatt offered up for the sake of brotherhood. "And what better way to celebrate our collective homosexuality," he continued without skipping a beat, "than by enjoying a lovely bottle of Krug together. Be right back!" He patted Ryan on the knee before darting out of his chair and through the door.

YES! he screamed silently as he hurried to the kitchen, his feet barely touching the ground. He paused with his hands on the counter, forcing himself to take a couple of deep breaths as he processed this extraordinary development. *This means nothing, nothing at all. Ryan didn't ask me to bed. He simply shared something personal with me. Okay, okay, Ryan's gay. I'm gay. South Beach is completely gay. It's no big deal.*

Satisfied he'd allowed himself enough time to regain control, Wyatt collected champagne glasses and the chilled bottle from the cooler and headed back to the porch. When he returned, Ryan had moved from his chair to the deck railing outside of the porch. He stood motionless looking out over the cove.

"You know, Ryan, I'm very happy we met," Wyatt said, setting the glasses on the railing. "I had no idea what to expect this summer, but I can tell you one thing, there's no way I could spend an entire summer here by myself. I enjoy being around other people too much. Sometimes I don't realize it, but I get lonely when I'm not around tons of people. Even though we haven't known each other for all that long, I feel a natural comfortableness being with you. That's what I wanted to tell you tonight. So you see, we both had things we wanted to share."

He patted Ryan on the shoulder and smiled, satisfied with his response. Aiming the bottle in the direction of the water, he sent the cork flying through the air with a loud pop! Quickly, expertly, he defused the explosion of foaming liquid by tapping the top of the bottle with the palm of his hand. He filled their glasses and handed one to Ryan before he offered a toast:"Here's to being comfortable with who we are. May we both live for a million gay years!"

"To a million gay years!"

Both men stared out at the water. The light was retreating at a fast pace. Rich tones of gold highlighted only the very top of the trees. The birds had quieted and the water lapped up onto the sand.

"Christ, this view sucks," Wyatt said with mock disdain, causing Ryan to spit champagne over the side of the rail, which in turn caused Wyatt to laugh so hard he had to sit back down on his chair in the porch so he could catch his breath. The earlier tension had vanished. Ryan, his eyes moist from laughing so hard, plopped down in the chair next to Wyatt, who refilled their glasses. They both seemed to realize at the same instant that Miles Davis was well into his second, or perhaps even third, encore. They had lost track.

"Mind if I pick something this time?" Ryan asked.

"Of course not. Be my guest. If you can't figure out the technology in there, just give me a shout. I know how to select a CD and play it, but that's about it." Wyatt caught himself licking his lips as Ryan passed in front of him. He tried not to go there, but he was beginning to lose the battle. There was potential here. He was sure of it. At the same time, he countered his optimism with reality. He was older than Ryan. That was the reality. Age almost always screwed things up. A sobering thought—a deal-breaker, as Murph would say. Just as he sat up to shake away those pesky demons, the familiar strains of the music he had spent the entire afternoon choreographing flooded out onto the porch.

Ryan came bounding back, grinning from ear to ear.

"Okay… the provocative smile, the *Dress Up* music, what's this all about, little mister?" Wyatt sat back and gave Ryan the best Sunday-school-teacher face he could manage.

"Well…." Ryan blushed as he continued. "I have a favor to ask."

"A favor? Okay, give it a shot." Wyatt sat breathless as he waited to hear what Ryan had in mind.

"I was wondering… would you please dance to this music again? It was so incredible, watching you dance. I can't get it out of my mind."

Even though a healthy sweat had broken out on his hands as he hoped for something perhaps a bit more intimate, Wyatt was charmed by the request. After all, he could have asked to use Murphy's Jeep. Ryan was so sincere, how could he refuse? Besides, he was a show-off at heart. Everyone who knew him well knew that about him.

"You really want to see it again? Technically, it's still a work in progress, you have to understand." *Shut up and dance.*

"Yes, please," Ryan answered with an enthusiastic nod.

"Well… then of course. I'd be honored to dance for you." Setting his wineglass on the table, he stood and walked down the steps to the sand, where he listened for a minute to find his place in the music, and then after taking a deep breath, began to dance.

"Wait, wait, there's more." Not only was Ryan grinning now from ear to ear, his eyes were twinkling like traffic lights.

"More you say," Wyatt teased, "More?"

"Would you dance for me… naked?" Ryan stood at the top of the steps with his hands crossed over his chest. There was the slightest hint of a challenge in his body language, Wyatt observed, which gave him an idea.

"I will dance naked for you," Wyatt agreed, sauntering back up the stairs. "However...." He stole a quick sip from his glass before he looked back over at his new friend. "I will dance naked for you on one condition only."

"Name it."

Ryan is jousting with me. This is fun.

"When I dance naked, I prefer my audience naked as well." Setting his wineglass down, Wyatt mirrored Ryan and stood facing the young man with his arms crossed.

The challenge is on.

Ryan seemed surprised, but after he had a moment to register Wyatt's counter-request, he threw his head back and doubled up with laughter. Regaining his composure, but not losing the smile or the twinkle in his eye, he reached for his glass and took a long, slow sip. Setting the glass back onto the table, and without taking his eyes off Wyatt, Ryan moved a few steps backward and peeled off his shirt, laying it across the back of a chair. He flashed his megawatt smile while he unfastened his belt and, ever so slowly, pulled it out of his shorts and draped it over his shirt.

Wyatt, beside himself in anticipation, sat back in the chair and emptied his glass in one gulp. With those beautiful, dark brown eyes still locked on him, Ryan, with a wink, unfastened the button on his shorts. Pausing for a brief moment, he stretched his arms high above his head, accentuating his leanness and flashing his fuzzy armpits at Wyatt. Wyatt brushed his hand across his mouth to check for dribble. *Oh... my... God!*

Turning his muscled back to Wyatt, Ryan unzipped his cargos, letting them fall to his feet before stepping out of them. Picking the shorts up with his toes, Ryan met his hand halfway and placed them on the chair next to his shirt, leaving nothing but his black boxer briefs to remove.

Those feet again!

Wyatt squirmed in his chair. A parched mouth wasn't the only effect Ryan's striptease was having on him. He helped himself to another slug of champagne, this time directly from the bottle. Ryan, with his back still to Wyatt, hooked his thumbs in the waistband, and in one slow, steady move, brought his underwear all the way down to his ankles and off. Moving slightly to place his shorts on top of the rest of his clothes, he finally turned and faced Wyatt, feet slightly apart and his arms folded in front of him, smiling like a Cheshire cat.

Ryan had certainly met the challenge.

"Oh my," Wyatt whispered as his eyes feasted on the exquisite, naked body standing just a few feet away. The man's physique was perfection. As Wyatt was scurrying to come up with something a little more substantial to say, Ryan sauntered over to the table and filled his glass to the top, emptying half of it and smacking his lips together in satisfaction. "Let me know when you're ready," he said nonchalantly, picking up the remote in his hand.

"Well then," Wyatt said as he clasped his hands together in an attempt to regain his composure. Standing, he moved past Ryan and walked down the steps and onto the sand. He peeled off his shirt and dropped it behind him. Next came his shorts, and in what certainly wasn't a surprise by this point, when the shorts hit the sand he, too, stood naked.

Before the music started, Wyatt turned his back to Ryan. This was as important an audience as any he'd danced for before. When he was creating the musical, he had often wished he was still young enough to cast himself as Casey. Wyatt identified with the character on so many levels. Tonight was his chance, at least in part, to give the role a test drive. He had never wanted to dance for anyone as much as he wanted to dance for this man. With the waves rolling up onto the sand, he turned to face Ryan, who had moved down and was seated like before, on the steps, with his champagne flute in his hand.

"I'm dancing the role of Casey," Wyatt explained to his naked admirer. "Casey is a young hopeful, a runway model who is struggling to keep true to his ambition, to have a successful career in modeling. He's just had an unfortunate encounter with a casting agent who told him it would be in his best interest to find another career. Heartbroken, this number exposes his drive and, hopefully, shows the audience he does have what it takes, no matter what the jaded agent thinks of him. Okay… I'm ready. Start the music."

RYAN sat his glass down on the step beside him and watched as Wyatt began to dance. The lighting from the porch and deck illuminated Wyatt in a way that was both flattering and dramatic, although Ryan knew special lighting wasn't necessary. The warm glow accented Wyatt's natural beauty. Ryan caught himself sitting with his mouth open as he watched in breathless wonder.

You are one very hot man, Mr. Stark. Yes indeed, you can hold your own with the best of them. There's no doubt about that.

Ryan had been uncomfortable when he'd watched Wyatt dance earlier. He was torn between staying in the sidelines unnoticed, or interrupting Wyatt by making himself known. In the end, Wyatt's dancing had been so powerful, Ryan had forgotten this conflict. The rest of the world had stopped during the performance.

Watching Wyatt this time around, Ryan was once again at odds. He struggled to keep at bay the dark, foreboding clouds working their way to the front of his thoughts. As Wyatt's athletic body soared into the air and whirled around in the sand with the grace of a swan, the clouds in Ryan's mind twirled around with increasing speed.

What are you going to do about the lies? The lies matter now. What if he doesn't understand? You're not a good person. Wyatt is going to hate you and that's what you deserve.

No! Ryan screamed from deep inside. *Stop it!* Obeying his command, the destructive forces that threatened reluctantly retreated. They were no match against Wyatt's formidable talents. Like before, Ryan was overwhelmed by Wyatt's skill. Because Wyatt had introduced the piece, providing the story line for him, Ryan could see how effective Wyatt's moves were at communicating Casey's story.

As the music built to a thunderous crescendo, Ryan's heart swooned. With each passing phrase, with each turn and twist of Wyatt's body, Ryan's body surged, as if he, too, were dancing.

Feeling a drip land on his ankle, Ryan looked down between his legs and watched a long, clear, slow moving strand of pre-cum make its way to his foot. From deep within, he was aroused. He knew at that very minute he was at Wyatt's mercy. He longed to caress Wyatt. To run his hands up and down Wyatt's long, lean body. As the music moved toward its climax, Ryan's body rocked back and forth. No longer was there a doubt in his mind. *I'm falling in love with you, Wyatt Stark!*

TOWARD the end of the piece, the music builds as Casey makes the decision to forge ahead with his modeling. Wyatt soared into the air, calling on muscles he hadn't had to use for years. Wyatt felt liberated. His body responded to his commands. He finished the piece within a few feet of where Ryan was seated. With his chest heaving from his efforts, smiling and exhilarated, Wyatt bowed.

When he came back up, he glanced at Ryan, who sat motionless. The look on Ryan's face was hard to read. Wyatt thought something was wrong. Perhaps he had missed the mark. The extra he had put into his performance might have been a mistake. Maybe, he thought as he tried to bring his breathing under control, maybe he had ruined the dance by submersing himself so deeply into the character of Casey. He had fooled himself. Wyatt frowned as he tried to catch his breath. Perhaps the intensity he'd just added in his performance had confused Ryan. The setting, the beach and the cove, had all worked against the piece. Ryan had yet to say anything. Wyatt, prepared for the worst, took a few steps forward. Ryan's face had been in the shadows, but now that he was closer, Wyatt could see the tears welled up in Ryan's eyes.

"I'm sorry," Ryan said, standing. "I get emotional when I see something... you...." He paused to reach down and pick up Wyatt's shirt lying on the sand in front of him. Ryan wiped his face. "Oh shit! This is your shirt. Damn it, I'm sorry."

"Hey, it's okay. Just don't blow your nose on it." This cracked them both up. Wyatt was bursting inside, just bursting. *Thank you! Thank you! He really liked it!*

Wyatt stepped forward and took Ryan into his arms. They stood for several minutes, holding each other. It was Ryan who finally broke the embrace. Not to move away, but to slowly bring his lips to Wyatt's.

The music had ended and with the moon beginning its climb over the bay, they shared their first long, lingering kiss.

Your mouth... your lips... you taste so sweet!

Wyatt felt Ryan's body tremble. Unsure of how to proceed, he pushed himself away. This created an awkward moment, and they laughed out of nervousness. The reaction of both their bodies to the kiss couldn't be ignored. Wyatt made a mad dash for his shorts.

"Wow," Wyatt said, his voice cracking and unsteady. He buttoned up his shorts. The effects of the kiss were still very obvious. "Wow," he repeated with a timid smile as he stood before Ryan, the fly of his cargos tented. "The kiss...."

"I know what you mean," Ryan admitted, looking down at himself. "Wow works for me too."

Ryan climbed up the stairs. Wyatt watched him carefully tuck himself into his briefs.

"I don't know what to make of it yet. This wasn't in the plan," Wyatt said as he followed Ryan up the stairs. "I don't feel at all bad about what just happened."

"I don't feel bad about it either," Ryan said as he buttoned his shorts. "But it sure as hell made me hungry."

"Me too," Wyatt agreed with a laugh. "Let's have dinner and let everything settle down before we try and analyze this too thoroughly. Wait." Wyatt reached for Ryan's hand before continuing. "I'm very attracted to you. I felt something... an interest, shortly after meeting you at the airport. I don't want to rush or make you feel uncomfortable. Your friendship means too much to me."

Ryan paused for a couple of seconds before he spoke. Pulling his shirt over his head, he kissed Wyatt. "I'll do my best, but I'm not great about going slow with anything."

"Oh shit, this is going to be like the blind leading the blind," Wyatt joked as he pointed Ryan toward the kitchen.

"How long does it take to boil Crusty and his friend here?" Wyatt asked as he walked over to the sink to spy on the lobsters.

"Not long at all," Ryan answered. "A couple of minutes once the water is boiling." Ryan had already turned the burner on underneath the large pot. "Why don't you grab a bottle of wine and sit at the counter while I put dinner together? We can talk."

"Sounds like a plan." Wyatt went over to the wine refrigerator and pulled out a bottle. Grabbing a couple of fresh glasses, he moved everything over to the counter across from Ryan and opened the bottle.

"Here, take a sip of this," Wyatt said, handing Ryan a glass. "It's an Orvieto. I like this one because it's so clean-tasting. Refreshing, like you."

"I feel wonderful." Ryan flashed Wyatt a huge smile as he placed potatoes into the microwave.

"I'm so glad you're here," Wyatt confessed without filtering for carefulness or control.

Ryan turned back to the counter. "Cheers!" he said as he sipped.

Wyatt soaked in Ryan as he watched him sip. His smile, those dreamy bedroom eyes, he couldn't remember a time when his willpower had been tested to such a degree. It took everything he had to keep from leaping over the counter and throwing himself at the young stud.

"This is the best wine I've ever had," Ryan said after savoring another sip. "I'm serious. It's not too sweet, it's not bitter, it's amazingly clean, and like you said, refreshing. It's refreshing, just like you, Wyatt." They both cracked up at how Ryan shamelessly returned Wyatt's compliment.

What if I invited Ryan to spend the night? Would the night be steamy and satisfying? Would Ryan prove an experienced lover who shared his expertise? Was he simply a hot stud who cared more about pleasing himself than anyone else? Not a chance! Ryan is much too kind a soul to be any different in the bedroom.

"Pour me some more, please," Ryan said as he moved over to the sink and grabbed the lobsters, holding them high in the air. "What did you call this guy, Smelly?"

"Crusty. I didn't name his friend. I like Smelly." Wyatt turned around and in his best announcer voice said, "Ladies and gentleman, meet Crusty and Smelly, known collectively as… dinner."

"Okay, here we go." Ryan eased the lobsters into the boiling pot of water. Once they were both in, he grabbed his glass of wine. "I hate this part," he squealed as he raced around the counter and hid behind Wyatt for protection.

"What do you mean, you hate this part?" Wyatt asked, laughing. "This was your idea."

"I know. I love lobster, but I hate cooking them."

Wyatt turned around on his stool so he faced Ryan. He pulled the handsome face down and kissed him on the nose. "What am I going to do with you?"

"Hopefully not throw me out because I'm a wimp when it comes to executing lobsters," Ryan said, leaning back down and returning a kiss to Wyatt's nose. "It's a common problem, just ask Woody Allen. You probably know him."

"Nope, I don't. We've been to a few of the same parties, but I've never been introduced to him." Wyatt fought off the urge to wrap his legs around Ryan's strong body. He needed to slow this down. He needed to slow himself down.

What's happening right now? Please let it be exactly what I want it to be. Please let this be what I've been waiting so long for.

"Get back over there and deal with those lobsters," Wyatt ordered, playfully pushing Ryan away.

Wyatt congratulated himself on an absolutely uncharacteristic display of good sense. A virtual tour de force if ever there was one. He had called upon every last ounce of self-control he possessed to put the brakes on luring Ryan into the bedroom.

"I'm good," Ryan said with a chuckle. "It's the putting them in water part I really don't like." Ryan moved over to the other side of the counter and inspected the boiling pot. "Grab some plates, Wyatt. We're comin' down the home stretch."

Wyatt hustled around the kitchen, setting up a couple of places on the counter, and then returned to his seat. Ryan plucked out a steaming lobster, added a piece of corn and a potato, and placed the feast in front of him. A shell cracker in one hand and their salads in the other, Ryan sat down beside him.

"Here's to our first dinner together," Wyatt toasted when Ryan was seated. "Here's to many more, I hope," he added.

"To many more!"

Wyatt felt so comfortable and relaxed. Crusty and Smelly were cooked to perfection. He made a mental note to ask Ryan to cook for him again sometime. There had to be other culinary surprises up this guy's sleeve.

As the night progressed and the wine flowed, the two men talked nonstop, sharing more intimate details about themselves. They covered favorite foods, movies, music they enjoyed, and even past boyfriends were discussed. Wyatt held back on divulging much about his past relationships, sharing only a few escapades. Hand-picked, self-deprecating experiences he hoped would come off as endearing and funny. Out of his deep respect for Murphy, who was so much more to him than a past boyfriend, he chose to not go there. He would never have dreamed of including Murphy in such a lineup. Murphy was family. And other than Murphy, he didn't have all that much to talk about.

"I'll remember this night forever," Ryan said as he took Wyatt's face into his hands and kissed him. "Fuck, it's almost two in the morning. I have to be into the store to help my dad early."

Does he really have to go? Yeah... it's probably for the best. Whose best?

Before Wyatt had a chance to say anything, Ryan asked out of the blue, "Hey, I know this is kind of out there, but our county fair is coming up. Would you like to go? It's trippy, in a fun way. We'd have a blast. I'd love it if you'd go with me."

"Sure," Wyatt said without hesitation. "I love trippy."

"Awesome!"

Before leaving, Ryan insisted on helping him clean up. Not much was said as they busied themselves around the kitchen.

"Thanks for the terrific dinner," Wyatt said when they had finished loading the dishwasher. "I had a blast tonight."

"Me too," Ryan said, unleashing another smile.

Wyatt stepped forward and took Ryan into his arms. They swayed back and forth in a tight embrace until Ryan broke the spell by planting a wet, sloppy kiss on Wyatt's eye.

"Gross!" Wyatt chuckled as he wiped his face dry on his T-shirt. *Does this make us blood brothers?*

"Call me soon," Ryan said with a grin as he eased out the door.

Wyatt's body trembled. Reluctantly, he allowed Ryan to escape into the night.

Chapter 6

WYATT waltzed around the house in a heightened state of giddiness following his marvelous evening with Ryan. Life in the wild now had a purpose. He woke up each morning looking forward to what the day held in store. He actively went about getting in touch with his lush surroundings, adjusting his pace so he could relax and appreciate the splendor. But no matter how he chose to occupy his time, Ryan was never very far from his thoughts.

Wyatt wanted to see Ryan again but resisted the temptation to call. He knew he needed some distance from Ryan to evaluate the new developments. *Do yourself a favor and take time with this one.* He wasn't sure how to read Ryan. His affection, was it an act? Did he leave wanting more? By abstaining, did Wyatt jeopardize his opportunity to become intimate with Ryan? These questions rolled around in his noggin like rocks in a polisher. Wyatt was confident their attraction had been mutual, but as dictated by his core being, he cultivated unfounded insecurities.

Seconds after plopping down on the sofa with his tea, he heard the phone ringing. Calls were so infrequent he never thought to bring the phone out to the porch. Anyone who knew him well understood his cell phone was not something he used very often, or in all probability had within reach, let alone charged.

Please let it be Ryan!

Setting his mug down on the table, he bolted back through the house to the kitchen, where he managed to squeak out a hello while struggling to catch his breath.

"Wy, how's it going? You sound out of breath. Did I interrupt a serious session of monkey spanking? I can call back in what... say... a minute and a half?"

"Oh it's just you, Murphy. I ran in from the porch." Wyatt wished he hadn't inserted the "just" in his greeting. Of course he was eager to talk to Ryan, but he missed Murphy too, and was glad his partner had called.

"Whaddaya mean, just you?" Murphy asked with a hint of hurt. "Are we entertaining gentleman callers these days? You dog, I knew you wouldn't be able to resist those burly, smelly lobstermen," Murphy teased, laughing at his dig.

"You guessed it," Wyatt shot right back, falling into a familiar rhythm characteristic of their conversations. "The bigger, the smellier, the better! My tongue is raw, raw from licking rubber boots."

"Well, good for you," Murphy said encouragingly. "I was worried you were lonely. I should have known you'd solve that problem on your own."

"Okay, I'm hoping there's a reason for this call, because if there isn't, you're keeping me from some serious porch time before I swim."

"You're swimming in the cove? For real? Isn't the water on the chilly side?" Murphy asked.

"I like it chilly. It energizes my body. I feel great all day."

"I'll just bet it does. Not to change the subject, Sybil, but 2:45 passed. Then 2:46 passed, even 3:05 passed by yesterday, and I didn't hear from you. I got worried. You doin' okay?"

Wyatt was tempted to tell Murphy all about Ryan, but held back. It was too early and, in all honesty, he wasn't sure himself what to make of the whole thing. He had spent the last several days trying to put Ryan into perspective. No matter how he looked at it, he couldn't hide from his heart. He was falling in love.

"I'm finally relaxing. You win. You were right. So bring me up to date," Wyatt said, changing the subject. He was curious about what Murphy had been up to and welcomed the opportunity to be brought up to speed on any new developments concerning *Dress Up*.

"Hey, before I get to the *Dress Up* update, I want you to check this out. I couldn't show this to you earlier because you were calling me every ten minutes. This will be fun. The flat screen on the opposite wall of the fireplace, go ahead and turn it on."

"You want me to go into the office off the bedroom and turn on the television?"

"God damn, you can be dense sometimes, Wy. From where you're standing right now, look toward the great room. See the shiny flat thing on yonder wall? Turn the shiny flat thing on. Geez, you mean to tell me you haven't used this television yet?" Murphy asked, dumbfounded. "I have it on all the time when I'm there."

"No. I never think to watch television in here. How do I turn it on?" Wyatt asked, after he'd walked over in search of the On button.

"Honestly! In the drawer, the one where I keep the book of house stuff, you'll find a remote," Murphy instructed. "Point it at the screen and press the green button on the top left."

If Murphy had a flaw, Wyatt thought, it was his lack of patience with those who were nontechnical. He couldn't quite grasp the fact that there were people who, despite the abundant technology available to them, just didn't give a shit. The only defense anyone had against Murphy in situations where you were humbled and made to feel the fool was to capitalize on the rare occurrence when something technical wasn't working as Murphy had anticipated. This choice was neither productive nor rewarding, because Murphy would be hurtled into such a frenzy as he searched for the solution, whatever time you had hoped to spend with him would be lost.

Wyatt opened the drawer and, sure enough, over to the side was the remote. Pointing it at the shiny flat thing on yonder wall, he pressed the green button. Watching from across the room, the television buzzed, flashed, and went dark except to display the words "Channel One."

"There's no picture. On the television I see the words 'Channel One', that's it. The screen's dark except for that. Sorry!" Wyatt reported, immediately furious with himself for pointing out a potential technical nightmare.

"Good," Murphy said, unfazed. "Now go over to the phone console on the wall and press the button marked TeleConference. Then let me know what happens."

Wyatt walked over to the phone console on the wall and did as instructed. There was a louder buzzing over on the television and then, after a few seconds, Murphy's image appeared on the screen. He was seated behind a desk with a wall of glass behind him, showcasing a palm tree over his left shoulder.

"Wow!" Wyatt was impressed. Seeing Murphy live reminded him at once of how much he missed his partner.

"Hey, moon pie," Murphy greeted him with a chuckle.

"Hey, stinky! Is that a pimple above your upper lip?"

"It's a worry wart. And guess who caused it? Hey, see the little black dot up on the wall to the left of the entry leading into the living room?" Murphy inquired before Wyatt could blast one off. "Smile, you're on candid camera."

"No kidding, you can see me too? This is so cool. Seriously, you look good, Murph!"

"Whoa, Trigger! Now that's what I call a pair of low-hangers. Wy, I think you can special order a skid plate with a nifty little elastic band that goes—"

"Oh fuck!" Wyatt had forgotten he wasn't wearing clothes. In a panic, he darted over to take cover behind one of the barstools along the counter.

Murphy laughed hard. "My shy kitty!"

"Shut up now," Wyatt said, feeling his face turn red. "Tell me what's going on."

"Well, it has been a hard-fought battle," Murphy began, sounding like a Weekend Update anchor, "but I've finally gotten the producers to think about casting somebody in the lead other than Lana. Christ, do they love them some Lana out here. She's like Hollywood's golden girl. Anyway, I've presented the names you and I discussed, and if all goes as planned, we should be flying them out over the next couple of weeks for screen tests. I'll keep you posted."

This news pleased Wyatt. Not casting Lana Melville in the lead had been his number-one concern. If the part wasn't brilliantly danced, the film would tank.

"You want me to go into the details?" Murphy asked.

"Not yet. I trust you're doing what you need to do," Wyatt assured his partner's crotch. Murphy had zoomed his camera in for a close-up of his dress-pants-clad nether region, taunting Wyatt, who stoically refused to acknowledge Murphy's silliness.

"As long as things are moving in the direction we want them to, I'm fine for now." Wyatt meant what he said. For the first time in as long as he could remember, he was comfortable sitting back and trusting the negotiations to play out in his favor.

"Hey, have you ever had lobsters from Frosty and Lil's?" Wyatt asked, changing the subject.

"Hmmm... I don't think so. Frosty and Lil's... where the hell is that?"

He was surprised Murphy hadn't heard of the place. "It's a local joint. I had a lobster from there and it was incredible. The best I think I've ever had."

"God, you're that desperate? How'd you manage to keep the claws away from your lil' thingy," Murphy joked, leaning into the camera. "Come on, move away from that bar stool so I can see little dinky. Don't worry, I can zoom in on a speck of dust. I bought the same camera they have on the Hubble. Come on, Wy, make dinky do the happy dance!"

"Hardy-ha-hoo," Wyatt countered sarcastically.

"You're just a ton-o-fun today," Murphy said with a yawn. "I know there's a bunch of little lobster shacks around. Frosty or whatever it was you said, I'm sad to say I haven't been to."

Wyatt was boring Murphy because he wasn't acting playful enough.

"I'll have to check it out in five years, when I can arrange for some time to take a vacation," Murphy whined, this time with his camera pointed to the inside of his ear. You should take some notes for me while you're there."

"Pledge."

"Huh?" Murphy asked, his face returning to the screen.

"I was thinking wax buildup."

"Really?" Murphy used his middle finger to dig into his ear while at the same time crossing his eyes.

"God, you're like fucking Red Skelton. Just a box full of silly. Better plan on six years. You can vacation after *Dress Up Part Three* opens in a theater near you. Anything else on your mind?"

Wyatt was surprised at how impatient he sounded. Part of it, he reasoned, was because he, too, was bored with being stuck standing in the same spot behind the bar stool. And, he was anxious. He had more pressing things to contemplate.

"Well… yeah, a couple of things… can you can spare a minute?"

Shit! I wounded him. Wyatt could see it in Murphy's face.

"I'm sorry, Pooky! Tell me what else is going on."

Wyatt blew Murphy a kiss. He watched for Murphy's reaction. A split-second later, Murphy ducked, as if Wyatt had lobbed a cow pie at him.

Enthusiasm reappeared in Murphy's voice as he described some of the production concepts being tossed around. The production aspect of whatever they were working on was always of greater interest to Murphy than talent negotiations. He loved getting involved with the technical elements. Murphy had a great eye for theatrical design. Wyatt relied on his opinion on everything from lighting, set design, even costumes. This beach house was as much a testament to Murphy's creative talents as anything. The man had impeccable taste. Together, they were a force to be reckoned with.

"We got really fucking lucky!"

The degree of excitement in Murphy's voice caused Wyatt to perk up and pay closer attention. He adored the childlike way Murphy got when he was charged up about something. He sounded like a poor orphan kid gushing over his new bike.

"I have to take care of a few contractual details yet, but it's almost a certainty *Dress Up* will be filmed by...."

Wyatt bit his lip as he waited out the pregnant pause that was another characteristic of Murphy's excitement.

"Pablo Von Stilton. Can you believe that?" Murphy slapped the surface of his desk with delight.

Wyatt did a split-second search through the archives in hopes of pulling up a winner. No such luck.

"He's the same cinematographer who shot the Ford blockbuster last summer," Murphy added.

Wyatt didn't have a clue, and he knew Murphy could read it on his face.

"He's a genius. And the best part, he's genuinely eager to work with you even though this is your first film. He loves working with first-time directors. Who knew? He assures me he'll watch your back every step of the way. It's a match made in heaven. It really is. His style plays into everything we have going already. Stilton is a prime example of how the tinsel-town buzz is starting to work in our favor."

"Von Shilton? Really? That's the best news yet."

"Stilton, like the cheese. Nice try. I know you don't know who he is." Murphy couldn't mask his disappointment as he waited for Wyatt to confirm his ignorance.

"Sorry, I don't." Wyatt shook his head sadly for Murphy to see. "But he sounds tasty. I do love that he's interested in working with us. We need everyone in our court, that's for sure."

"That's okay. You'll thank me later. I'm also having lunch on Wednesday with Tucker Lewis. He approached me, can you believe.... Wyatt, please tell me you know who Tucker Lewis is. He's a huge fan of *Dress Up* and practically begged me for a piece of the action."

"You're shittin' me! Of course I know who Tucker Lewis is." Wyatt moved out from behind the chair and began walking in circles.

"Tucker Lewis, wow, I can't believe it. I never told you this… but Tucker Lewis has always been my number-one choice for art director."

"Well, Mr. Dangly Downs," Murphy answered pointing his finger at Wyatt's exposed junk, "you have very good taste. He was my number-one pick too."

"I never dreamed he'd be interested," Wyatt said, hustling back to his spot behind the chair. "I always thought *Dress Up* fed so naturally into his style."

"That's exactly how he put it in his pitch to me," Murphy confirmed.

"Listen, we can cut corners in other places. Please don't be stingy negotiating with him," Wyatt implored. "He's the real thing. He's a perfect choice. Wow, imagine Von Shilton filming his sets."

"Stilton. S.T. I. L. T. O. N. Stilton."

"Sorry. Von Stilton, I got it. Wow! We are going to set the town on its ear," Wyatt squealed, unable to contain his excitement.

"You don't have to worry, I'm all over it." Murphy assured him, once again showing Wyatt the inside of his ear, the left this time. "It will all play out. Leave it to me to work my magic and write the check. Now go back to enjoying the summer. You're going to need to hit the ground running once this thing ramps up. I'll give you a call next week with another update. Until then, behave yourself and don't go lusting after any of those local boys. They're much better at boxing than they are at dancing. If you got in a tussle with one of them, your only hope would be to pinch like crazy and then run your ass off."

"Fuck you!" Wyatt couldn't help laughing at the visual Murphy had just provided, and worse yet, what he had said wasn't too far from the truth. Although he had considerable upper body strength, the thought of being in any type of physical altercation with another person scared him to death. A speedy retreat would be his best defense.

After saying their good-byes, Wyatt headed back to the porch. Sitting in the morning sun, he sipped cold tea and ate his bagel before heading onto the beach for his swim. Wyatt ran toward the cove and dove into the water at a full clip. Either he was getting used to the chill, or the water was warmer this morning.

I feel so alive.

His strong arms and legs propelled his naked body from one end of the cove to the other with very little effort. Wyatt lingered much longer than usual after completing his laps, diving deep down and swimming for as long as he could underwater. Exhilarated and refreshed, he stepped back onto the sand.

The day was going to be hot. The warmest since he'd arrived. Standing spread-eagle, Wyatt raised his head to the sun. The droplets of water rapidly evaporated off his skin.

Can I really afford to start a romance right now?

Turning around to dry his back, Wyatt wrestled with the thought of romancing Ryan while attempting to direct a major motion picture for the first time. It would be a miracle if he could pull them both off. Wyatt knew what he could be like when he was focused on a project. His concentration could be ruthless. Could Ryan make it through filming without feeling neglected? Wyatt considered adjusting his work process in order to share his time between the movie and his new love as he headed into the house. If things were to develop further with Ryan, was it really fair to subject this wonderful man to the craziness he called his life?

I have to figure out a way to make this work. If I take it slow, and talk out the challenges, I can do this. I want to do this.

Wyatt spent the rest of the morning, and a good portion of the afternoon, rambling aimlessly from house to beach. There were so many things to take into consideration. A relationship, a solid relationship, affected every aspect of your life.

Grabbing his laptop from the bedroom, he headed back to the porch. Stretching his feet out over the table in front of him, he typed "Ryan." Wyatt stared at the name while contemplating what to type next. Handsome, hunk, hot, huge cock. *This isn't working.*

Forcing himself to stop thinking in a physical sense, Wyatt typed Ryan's name again and waited. Handsome, hunk, hot, huge cock. *Fuck the pros and cons analysis.* Wyatt slammed the laptop shut and placed it back onto the table.

Frustrated and unable to relax, he walked several hundred feet down the shore and sat on the warm sand. Other than that asshole Lambert, it had been a long time since he had allowed himself to fall for anyone. The only person he had really fallen for had been Murphy. Occasionally, he would meet someone and, for a few weeks, they would enjoy each other's company, pretending they were a couple. Then his hectic schedule would heat up and his attention would be forced back to his work. This was his pattern. His shitty love pattern. Sure, he felt lonely sometimes, but those feelings never seemed to last long enough for him to make the necessary change to allow a long-term relationship to develop. His work always rescued him.

Ryan was making him analyze his life. *So this is why Murphy wanted me to spend the summer here? So I could torment myself by analyzing my fucked-up love life?*

Wyatt sat for a long time, staring out across the cove. The sun was softening, signaling evening's approach. Hungry, he began walking in the gentle surf back toward the house. *I barely know this Ryan. Maybe I can make some changes. You can't ignore feelings like these.* The feelings he felt when he was with Ryan were intense and unrelenting. Wyatt was stricken with a terrible thought. *How selfish I've been. How self-centered I was, to think Ryan was mine for the taking.*

Maybe Ryan was just hungry for sex. Maybe he wanted a summer fling and nothing more. Ryan might have a more primal, a more temporary vision about what was developing between them. Wyatt was surprised to feel fear.

Ryan had been aroused. Wyatt had felt the man's eagerness as it pressed up against the side of his thigh when they kissed. It was possible Ryan wanted and needed him only in a sexual way. *That's not good enough. It's not want I want. I need to be loved. I want someone to love the shit out of me.* Ryan had ignited his hunger for love.

WYATT woke the next day impatient and in need of some kind of diversion. He'd tossed and turned all night, consumed by what ifs and insecurity. Standing in the kitchen, sipping his tea, he found himself staring at the keys to Murphy's Jeep. *That's it! I'm goin' to town. I'll check out some of the local shops, maybe buy some magazines, and have a nice lunch.*

Fortified with a couple of bottles of water and an energy bar, Wyatt took a few minutes in the Jeep familiarizing himself with the controls before turning on the engine. Confident he could handle the Jeep after a brief inspection, he inserted the key. Seconds later, the unmistakable voice of Barry Manilow warbling about a weekend in New England blared out from the speakers.

Holy Christ!

In a panic he fumbled with the dashboard dials before silencing the singer's cheesy lament. *A little Barry goes a long way.*

Wyatt bounced and bucked as he fought to keep the Jeep on the bumpy dirt road leading from the house to the main road. Once he had reached blacktop, he was able to relax the death grip he had on the steering wheel. He hoped he was headed toward town. It didn't really matter. This was an adventure.

Fuck!

Wyatt pulled over onto the side of the road. How would he remember where the turnoff was onto the dirt road leading back to the house? Closing his eyes, he tried to visualize what he had just passed. The mailbox marking Murphy's road. *What else?* It looked shiny, brand-new. Right after turning onto the highway he had gone over a short bridge with a creek running underneath. With any luck, those two references would be enough. Wyatt hadn't thought to bring along his cell phone, or even Ryan's number if he found himself in trouble. *You idiot!*

The dense forest lining either side of the road was interrupted periodically by meadows filled with wildflowers. Wyatt must have been too excited to notice the beauty weeks ago on his ride from the airport. Ryan had distracted him.

As he got closer to town, a few homes and other buildings began to appear. Smallish homes, all painted white. What kind of people lived inside? Strong, hard-working families with modest taste. Nothing like city people. More like the people back home in the Midwest.

He slowed the Jeep down to a crawl as he entered town. The first building on the right was an old church, dazzling in the morning sun with its fresh coat of white paint. The steeple reached upward to an amazing, deep-blue sky. Alongside the church, a small cemetery stretched back until it was halted by a grove of pines. On the opposite side of the street, a series of old two-storied brick office buildings ran all the way to the end of the block. On one of the large storefront windows, printed in gold and black lettering, he read *"The Sentinel." I bet that's the local newspaper.* A bank, Abrahamson's Savings and Loan, was wedged between the newspaper and a small café at the end of the block. The rusted sign over its door read "Enga's" and displayed a large, piping-hot cup of coffee and a slice of pie in red neon. The houses lining the avenues that intersected with the main drag looked almost identical. Wooden, boxlike structures with big porches in front sat in the middle of large, well-kept lawns.

Further down Main Street he came upon another outcropping of brick buildings. In this group he spotted a liquor store, a hardware store, and the post office. On the opposite side of the street, another café, which looked closed, and a parking lot adjacent to a grocery store. Taylor's Superette, the store owned by Ryan's parents.

Wyatt eased the Jeep into the lot and parked alongside a banged-up old pickup truck. Ryan's SUV wasn't among the half dozen or so cars parked in the lot. Chasing away a pang of disappointment, Wyatt decided to go in anyway and have a look around.

A bell tingled over the door as he entered. Directly in front of him sat two checkout lanes, both without cashiers. An elderly woman maneuvered a small, elfin-like grocery cart around the corner before turning and heading down the center aisle. Wyatt walked the first aisle to the end. A small deli stretched across the back of the store. Standing behind the deli counter stood an older man sporting a white paper hat. *I bet that's Ryan's dad.* They shared similar facial features. On impulse, Wyatt decided to strike up a conversation and perhaps introduce himself as Ryan's friend.

"Hi there," Wyatt said, standing in front of the counter.

"Hello! What can I get you?" the man asked with a smile.

"Are all the salads homemade?" Wyatt asked, fighting back an attack of unexpected nerves.

"They are indeed," the man answered. "Care to try any? The chicken salad is our specialty. The wife makes it. People come from all parts to buy it."

"Sure! I'd love a taste."

The man had been cutting up a large hunk of red meat into smaller chunks. Wiping his hands off on a towel, he walked over to the counter where Wyatt was standing and scooped up a generous spoonful of salad and handed it to him with a napkin. "Thanks," Wyatt said before he emptied the spoon into his mouth. *Wow! Yummy!* "That was delicious," Wyatt wiped his mouth with the napkin.

"I can take care of that for you."

Wyatt handed back his spoon and napkin. "I'll take a container of the chicken salad. The small container, please. I'm on my own."

The man reached for a plastic container and began filling it up with salad.

"I'm a friend of Ryan's. I bet you're his father. I'm Wyatt."

The man slid the container full of salad over to him. "Not sure who this Ryan is you mentioned. I don't know anyone by that name. I could ask the wife. You lookin' for some steaks or burger?"

"Oh, I'm sorry. I thought you were Mr. Taylor."

Fuck that's weird. Really weird. I'm positive Ryan....

"You got that part right. I'm Bud Taylor, chief meat chopper and bottle washer. You on vacation, or visiting one of the locals?"

Wyatt didn't know how to proceed from here. Something wasn't right. This was Bud Taylor. Bud Taylor was Ryan's father. It was his family who owned the store. Wyatt was sure he had understood Ryan to say that.

Breathe!

"I'm spending the summer at Murphy Smith's." Wyatt's mind was racing a mile a minute. He couldn't wait to meet up with Ryan and get to the bottom of this mix-up.

"Sure, I know Murphy. Nice guy. Don't see him around here all that much, though." Bud Taylor walked back over to the wooden counter opposite the salad case. "Look around and let me know if I can help you find anything else. I better keep after this," the man gestured over to the hunk of meat, "or I'm not going to have my steaks ready for delivery this afternoon."

Wyatt grabbed his salad and headed for the cashier. The more he thought about it, the more uncomfortable he felt. The urge to get to the bottom of this misunderstanding drove Wyatt to turn and step back up to the counter.

"Hey, Bud," he called out, getting the man's attention. "I met this guy from around here and his name is Ryan. I thought he told me his father owns this store. Are you sure you don't know a Ryan? I'm sure that's what he told me."

"I'm the owner of the store and like I told you before, young man, I'm not familiar with any Ryan here or anywhere."

Breathe!

"Okay, thanks." Shell-shocked, Wyatt turned and walked to the front of the store where he paid an older woman—probably Bud's wife—for the salad and headed out the door.

Wyatt spent several minutes wondering what the hell had just happened before he turned the key and put the Jeep in drive. In a daze, he got back onto the road and continued out of town in the opposite direction of the house.

He had no idea where he was headed and he didn't care. He needed to be doing something. His thoughts bounced back and forth as he processed his encounter with Bud Taylor.

This is craziness. I'm not wrong on this one. Is Ryan lying to me? Why would he lie? Why would Bud Taylor lie? Deep, steady breaths.

The road made a gentle curve, bringing him down into a lush ravine. Crossing a narrow one-lane bridge, he steered the Jeep up a hill. A sign pointing to the right read "Hinnenkamp Fisheries - Freshest Lobsters in Maine" and below it, printed in smaller letters, "Arnie's Cove, Maine USA."

Something about the name was familiar. Wyatt brought the Jeep over to the side of the road and stared at the sign. Of course! Ryan had mentioned the lobsters he'd brought over the other night had come from Hinnenkamp's. *Hinnenkamp! It's not a name you hear every day.*

Turning onto the dirt road, he headed toward Arnie's cove. He drove for several miles before he spotted water through the trees. A couple hundred feet further, he came to a series of dark red buildings.

Wyatt parked the jeep and followed the signs pointing him to the sales area. Stepping through the screen door, the stench nearly brought him to his knees. *Wow! This place sells fish all right.* Squinting, he tried to get his bearings.

"What can I do you for?" a voice crackled out of nowhere, causing him to nearly jump out of his skin.

Wyatt searched around the dimly lit room in desperation until he spotted movement in the far right corner. The sound of running water seemed to be coming from all directions. A rotund woman in denim overalls she had accented with a tattered blue gingham scarf stood and waved at Wyatt. Sticking out her lower lip, she attempted to blow long strands of dull silver hair out of her face before giving up and using a thick, black rubber-gloved hand to clear her vision. She waddled out from behind a large sink. Wyatt was reminded of a picture he had seen from a book he had as a kid about a sea hag and a whale. The likeness was frighteningly similar.

"You looking to buy yourself some lobsters, fella?" she croaked.

"I was wondering… I was wondering if you knew how I could get in touch with a friend of mine. His name is Ryan Taylor. I thought his dad owned the grocery store in town."

As if to jog her memory in some way, the woman put her hands on her hips and blew a stream of air upwards, causing the strands of loose hair dangling in her face to flutter before settling back down and sticking to her sweaty forehead.

"I can't say I know any Ryans from these parts. Ryan, is that a boy name or a girl's?" she squawked, blowing another upward puff of air that failed to lift any hair off her face.

"Boy, er… man," Wyatt corrected himself. "He's a young man."

He tried to mask his disappointment. It was obvious she didn't have a clue who he was talking about. To make sure, he added, "He bought some lobsters here last week. I wondered if you remembered him. He's a good-looking guy, slightly taller than I am. And younger, Ryan's younger." Wyatt felt it necessary to add the last part, even though he was sure it wasn't going to do him a lick of good.

"Well he can't be any more good-looking than yourself," the woman said with another juicy cackle.

The fact she spit while she talked wasn't lost on Wyatt, who, in defense, moved back several steps for fear another cackle might launch a volley of phlegm his direction.

"Okay," he answered, wishing he had never stopped here in the first place. "Sorry to trouble you. I was just checking."

He turned to leave, but before he could get out the door, the woman hollered out, "Listen sonny boy, I'm just a relative here from Borden helping my sister out while her husband's in the hospital. He got himself some kinda infection they're treatin'. Lil, the owner, my sis, she's out hauling in lobster traps with her sons Jake and Gill. Maybe they know him. I can ask fer ya if you like?"

"No, that's okay," he answered as he bolted for the door. "Thanks anyway." Wyatt made a beeline for the Jeep.

Barely cognizant of what was passing by, he struggled to come to grips with today's developments. Never for a second did he dream the day would have ended up being such a disaster. Who was this Ryan? Why didn't his story check out? Why hadn't he thought to consult Murphy before allowing his feelings to take over? He reentered town and as he passed by the grocery store, his mood lightened momentarily when he thought he spotted Ryan's car in the parking lot. Saddened when he realized it wasn't, he drove himself home. He couldn't wait to get his hands on a drink.

RYAN leaned back in his chair, rubbing his eyes in an attempt to ease the strain he'd subjected them to. Glancing at his watch, he confirmed what he'd expected. He'd been at it without interruption for over four tedious hours. Without interruption, except to take a piss and grab another Diet Coke. Closing out the spreadsheet, he opened an e-mail and attached his edit with a short message to Murphy, pointing out some particulars he thought his boss should take a look at, and then hit send. *Back at ya! Hugs!*

Except for a few calls, Ryan hadn't had much contact with Murphy. He knew his boss was crazy-busy right now, and it worked better if they communicated via e-mail or an occasional text message. In addition to watching over Wyatt, his duties had switched from transcribing Murphy's handwriting to proofing. Someone else in the office now had the unfortunate task of trying to decipher what mysteries were embedded in Murphy's chicken scratch. He enjoyed proofing. The deal was this: Ryan would redline whatever changes he felt necessary, and Murphy would then review them. Ryan hoped there would come a time in the near future when Murphy would agree to have the document sent back edited without the redlining step. They weren't to that point yet.

Ryan was thankful for the distraction the work from Murphy provided. The last couple days had been an interesting mix of elation and dread. He was elated by the new developments with Wyatt. Their evening together had been one of the greatest nights of his life. Ryan could blame the feeling of dread he was experiencing on the lies he had told. *How deep is the shit I'm standing in?* There had to be a way out of this. A gentle way to make what he'd done endearing or funny to Wyatt. If he was patient and waited, there would come a moment when the time to own up to his lies would feel right. The timing on this was very important.

Ryan had been tempted to confess his situation to Murphy a couple days ago when they'd finished up a work call. He was glad he'd held back. After all, it wasn't anyone's problem but his, and God knows, Murphy had enough to think about right now without the additional worry that Wyatt might freak out when he found out. Besides, what would Murphy think of his involvement with Wyatt to begin with?

Ryan stood over the sink and splashed cold water on his face. The refreshing shock helped to soothe the ache he still felt deep beneath his eyes. Looking up into the mirror, the dripping-wet image staring back at him made him smile. *You crazy shithead! What were you thinking?* As worried as he was about the lying, nothing could dull or mask the joy he felt from being with Wyatt. Nothing about the connection he experienced while in Wyatt's embrace or the wonderful kisses they had shared felt false. The hardness Ryan noticed against his leg when Wyatt took him into his arms after he'd danced was unmistakable. You can say many things about a man and his dick, but one thing Ryan was certain of, a guy's cock rarely lied.

Spending a few days away from Wyatt had been a good idea. It had given him a chance to try and sort out his feelings. It also confirmed for him how strong his desire was to be with him. Wiping his face dry, he walked out of the bathroom and threw on a clean shirt.

Wyatt, here I come!

WYATT lost track of how long he had been staring at the water when he was brought out of his daze by a loud knocking. Jumping up from his chair, he rushed through the house and opened the door. Standing on the steps, with his signature grin, was Ryan.

Chapter 7

"HEY, Prince Charming," Ryan chirped.

"Come on in," Wyatt said, stepping away from the door.

One look at Wyatt and Ryan could tell something was wrong. The warm, inviting man he'd enjoyed so much a few evenings back had vanished. It was Wyatt's body, but the characteristic energy was gone, and the bright smile was nowhere to be seen. Maybe if he asked a few questions, he'd discover why Wyatt was acting so strange.

"I'm not keeping you from anything, am I? It's no big deal, you know. I'm the dummy who keeps showing up unannounced."

The last thing Ryan was expecting was to feel awkward. Being welcomed into Wyatt's strong arms was more along the lines of what he'd had in mind. What's more, he was getting the feeling fast that Wyatt didn't want him around. When Wyatt didn't answer him, he asked, "You feeling alright, Wyatt?"

"We need to talk. Let's sit out on the porch."

This isn't good.

"It's nice to see you," Ryan said as he followed Wyatt through the house. "Are you sure I'm not interrupting anything? I was just passing by and… well, that's a lie…. I missed you, Wyatt." *You've got to be kidding me, did I just say lie?*

Ryan hoped telling Wyatt he missed him would bring about a warmer response. Several seconds passed, and it became clear he wasn't going to get one.

Is he pissed off because I stayed away a few days? Is it something about the movie, or Murphy? Oh Christ! Is it the lies?

"I took the Jeep into town today."

It was painful for Ryan to watch Wyatt. He looked a mess. The contrast between now and the other night was scary. *He looks so sad.*

"You did? Ah hell, I was delivering for Dad all day. I wished I'd known, I could have gotten one of the other guys to take over for me. I could have shown you around town."

One thing Ryan knew for certain, this was not the time to come clean. Whatever this was about, he needed more details before he formulated a plan. He sensed he was on shaky ground, but wasn't sure why.

"Well...." Wyatt paused.

Ryan noticed for the first time how nervous Wyatt was. His hands were trembling. He was forcing himself to take deep breaths. Was this the beginning of one of his attacks? Ryan slowly moved his hand down and felt his pants pocket to confirm he had his cell phone with him in case something bad happened.

"When I was in town today," Wyatt's voice cracked, "I thought it might be fun to stop in and take a look at your... your parent's grocery store. You weren't around, so I went in and I met the owner, Bud Taylor." Wyatt stood up and wiped his palms on his shorts.

It's all over. There wasn't a thing he could do. Ryan sat and waited for the shoe to drop.

"I met the guy who owned the store," Wyatt paced back and forth, averting his eyes, "and when I told him I was a friend of yours, he...." Wyatt's voice cracked again. Ryan winced. "He didn't know who the hell you were," Wyatt turned to face Ryan. "I asked twice to make sure he wasn't confused. Twice! What the fuck is this all about?"

Ryan needed to come up with a way out of this. He was losing Wyatt. *Please, please don't let that happen.* His mind raced a mile a minute. His head began to ache. He was frantic, desperate to come up with anything. *Wait! Go back. Yes, yes....*

He had something. It wasn't much, but it was something. This thought, he'd visited this one before. It would help him now if only he could call it up. Seconds seemed like minutes as he strained to concentrate. Just as he was about to give up, he had it. Like holding onto someone dangling over a cliff by a single finger, Ryan forced himself to stay calm as he slowly pulled his thought up and over the ledge to safety. Relief motivated Ryan to laugh in a way he hoped fooled Wyatt into thinking this was all a silly misunderstanding. He also hoped Wyatt wouldn't notice he, too, was trembling.

Run with it. Yes, it's another lie, but you need to buy yourself some time. For fuck sakes, will another lie really matter at this point?

"Wyatt... my dad's name is Wilbur, but everyone knows him as Bud. Wow, that's funny. I mean..."

"What's so fucking funny?" Wyatt barked back, exasperated. "Bud... Wilbur.... I'm missing the funny part. Whatever the fuck his name is, he didn't know who you were."

The anger in Wyatt's voice caused Ryan to sit up in his chair. He was angry enough to cut him off. "Wyatt... I'm sorry you're upset. Please don't be mad. I have some explaining to do. Wilbur was just protecting his son. That's all it was."

Okay, come on, Ryan. You tried this one out before, remember? This is the lie you planned to use if the other lie about your parents' store was ever discovered. Oh, you're a good little liar. You rehearsed.

Ryan didn't want to consider the alternative. Not now, not with Wyatt already so agitated. He'd tell this one last lie, this last one, and then, at the earliest opportunity, he'd confess to Wyatt. He'd confess when he had a foolproof plan worked out. He'd come clean when he was in control of the moment.

Unbelievable! Murphy sends me here to look after Wyatt, and who fucks with him worse than anyone could imagine? What a piece of work you are. You should be ashamed of yourself. Look what you've done to this man. Are you insane?

Ryan stood and walked over to Wyatt. Taking him by the hand, he led Wyatt back over to the couch. "Here, sit down, and I'll tell you why Dad was being so freaky."

One shot is all you're going to get.

Wyatt eased himself onto the couch. Ryan joined him.

"Look at you," Ryan said as he moved closer to Wyatt. "I would never do anything to hurt you." Ryan reached up and stroked Wyatt's face. "I feel horrible," he continued. "I shouldn't have laughed when you were so upset. I'm very sorry. This can all be explained."

Thinking Wyatt might want to say something, Ryan paused. It was clear after a few dead seconds that Wyatt had nothing to say.

"Early last summer," Ryan began his lie, "when I was walking down the beach after work one evening, I passed this guy who was walking alone. Once I'd gotten twenty, maybe thirty feet past him, I turned around to take another look and saw he had stopped too. I wasn't really looking for any action, if you know what I mean, but I wasn't opposed to the idea either. It was a beautiful evening and I was horny."

Ryan sat back on the couch and faced forward with his eyes shut. He needed to concentrate. Keeping his eyes open or a glance toward Wyatt right now would only distract. It was a risk he couldn't take. He hoped Wyatt would interpret this shift in body language as him being ashamed for hooking up with someone he had passed on the beach. An acknowledgment of how careless and reckless this type of encounter could be.

"There are benches a little further up from the water," Ryan went on, "and I decided I was interested enough to sit down and wait and if this guy was at all willing to play, he'd join me, which is exactly what happened."

So far, so good. This is a good lie. It has meat!

"We sat and talked while watching the sun set. It was nice. The guy seemed regular enough and he wasn't bad-looking. Nothing like you," he confirmed. To emphasize this, Ryan took a risk and opened his eyes. He looked over to Wyatt and, with a wink, added, "I really mean that."

"Let's move on," Wyatt said with more than a hint of impatience.

"Sorry." *Stick to the story, fool. This is the fucking last lie. The last one! I swear, Wyatt, if you let me off the hook, I'll never ever lie to you again.*

Ryan resumed his position on the couch with his eyes closed. It was clear by Wyatt's heightened level of irritability that Ryan was far from out of the woods. This lie was a familiar one. He'd gone over it several times in his head. Broken down, the lie was a combination of a fantasy he visited from time to time and more recently, a lie he had devised to counter against getting caught in a lie about Taylor's. Converting the entire scenario over to a lie wasn't as hard as he had thought. If anything, it tripped off the tongue too easily, and that was beginning to frighten Ryan more than anything.

"Well… we hit it off, is I guess the best way to put it." Ryan threw in a pause here, to show Wyatt recalling this memory wasn't easy. *Yes, that's it. Show some struggle.*

"I started spending all my time with him when I wasn't working. Oh… his name was Mark. He said he was a writer and he was spending the summer here working on a book. He was staying at one of the resorts up near Wellington."

Ryan risked another look over at Wyatt. He was rewarded with a single nod.

"I don't really want to tell you this, but I think I have to for you to understand what happened." *Oh that was good. Keep it going.*

"I really fell for this guy. This was the first time in my life I'd let down my guard and allowed myself to become involved. I just never wanted to before. To this day I'm not sure why I did it for him. I guess I could have been lonely. Mark was funny. I love to laugh."

Ryan paused again, this time to organize his thoughts. He had gotten so wrapped up in his performance, he had lost his bearing in the lie. *You're becoming reckless.*

"Anyway, I'm getting kinda off track here. I started screwing around with my schedule at work. Mark would beg me to take the day off, and I would. A day here, a day there, no big deal. Before I knew it, I was avoiding the store, my parents, my friends. It was out of control. I lost control of myself."

"You're not the first person that's happened to," Wyatt offered.

Thank you! He's buying it.

"Dad started to get pissed off. He had his hands full, managing the other morons he brought on for the season, and the last thing he needed was to have to worry about his own son. God, it pisses me off so bad now to think how stupid I was."

"You weren't stupid. You thought you were in love."

No, I was stupid. Holy fuck, was I stupid.

"Dad, in his typical fashion, started to call me on it," Ryan plowed ahead. "He was frustrated and he wanted me to know I was being a jerk. Mark got wind that Dad was starting to give me a hard time, and before I knew what was happening, he sort of declared war on Dad. It got back to my father that Mark was bad-mouthing him around town and calling him names."

"You've got to be kidding me." Wyatt seemed amazed. "How could someone be such an asshole?"

Careful, that last one might have been too much. Tone it down. You're almost there.

"I know, this guy was a complete asshole, but I was too into him by now to realize it. The final straw... oh, this really hurts to think about. The final straw... Mark called my dad the 'village idiot' to his face when we crossed paths at the liquor store. To hear somebody trash your own father... it was a huge slap in the face."

Wyatt leaned over and squeezed Ryan's arm.

I hate myself. If you weren't such a spineless prick, you'd end this now. You'd take your licks and be on your way, Ryan scolded himself. There was very little relief in knowing that, so far, he was succeeding in his attempt to explain away the confusion Wyatt had encountered at Taylors. Not a single ounce of satisfaction. Ryan could feel the familiar, distant pounding in his temples signaling a headache of epic proportion, and his stomach had begun to ache. He deserved worse and he knew it.

"It's okay," Ryan said. "I'm glad this still hurts. I'll never allow something like that to happen again. After apologizing to my dad, I met Mark one last time to tell him it was over. He didn't take it well. For about a week he came into the store asking where I was, and my dad, man, I love him, he'd lie for me."

A world of lies, that's what we have here.

"A couple of times I was standing in the back room when Mark came in, but Dad would tell him I was out delivering. Soon after that, Mark stopped coming in. I took the long way around explaining this. Sorry."

"No... it's fine. I get it. Your dad was being protective when I inquired about you. I totally get it," Wyatt said with relief in his voice. "I'm surprised you even looked twice at me after all that," Wyatt joked.

"I haven't told a soul about you," Ryan said emphatically. "I didn't want anyone to think I was losing control of myself like I did last summer. I want so badly to tell them. My parents are going to love you when they finally meet you. I want to do this right. That is, if we decide there is something...." Ryan looked away. He couldn't stand himself.

"I feel something very special happening here, I can't lie," Wyatt said, turning Ryan's face back to his.

The words "I can't lie" cut through Ryan like a knife. His lip quivered as he fought to stay in control of his emotions. He needed to leave, right now. He repulsed himself. His stomach was churning and he felt dizzy. The lie had worked like a charm. Better than he could have ever dreamed possible. What he hadn't counted on was the awful guilt he felt and the revolting self-image he had created of himself from lying to this kind, beautiful man. He hated himself for it.

Ryan held it together long enough to excuse himself. Words, he said words and Wyatt said words back as they both walked through the house toward the entryway. His vision was blurred as he stepped from the house and walked to his car. This lie, this whopper he'd just told, had allowed him to see a side of himself he never wanted to see again. It was an evil side that demonstrated first-hand how he could control someone's very being by being deceitful. How powerful dishonesty could be. How ugly. It made him sick.

He fought back tears. Wiping them away, he tried to keep up with their flow so he could guide his key into the ignition. It took several attempts before he succeeded. He was crying now. The car was moving, and he sobbed. Several hundred feet away from the house, Ryan put the car in park. Without a moment to spare, he opened his door and emptied his stomach. Wave after violent wave erupted from deep within. Through all of this, he continued to cry.

Ryan sat, motionless, staring out the window at nothing. The SUV's powerful engine revved, reminding him the car was still running. Grabbing a few napkins from a compartment under the ashtray, he wiped his face and mouth. The smell of vomit caused his stomach to heave once more, but he knew there was nothing left. Rolling down his window, he took several slow, careful breaths of fresh air and put the car in gear.

Back at the hotel, he stripped naked and turned on the shower. Feeling weak from the strain his body had just gone through, he sat on the shower floor. There would never be a lower point in his life, he told himself. It was impossible. When the warm, cascading water from the shower offered no relief, he threw on a robe, turned off all the lights in his room and crawled into bed. His last thought before falling asleep was one of defeat. Ryan doubted he'd ever have the courage to tell Wyatt the truth. It was this overwhelming realization he held onto as he escaped into a deep sleep.

"HEY, it's Boss man," Murphy said when Ryan had managed to dig his cell out from the pocket of his shorts.

"Hey, Murphy, what's going on?" Ryan looked at the time display on his phone. It was after ten, seven a.m. on the West Coast.

Did Wyatt say something to Murphy about yesterday?

Ryan sat on the edge of the bed, his phone shaking in his hand as he waited for Murphy to speak.

"Nice work on the spreadsheet you sent yesterday, Ryan. I have one more for you to work on and I'll e-mail it to you later this morning. Have it back to me in a couple days. I'll be too busy in meetings to do anything with it until then. You sound strange. Everything going okay out there? Everything going well with Wyatt?"

Well, Murphy... here's what's going on. I'm telling these terrible lies to Wyatt because I'm a mean, hurtful person. When he finds out

I'm lying to him, he's going to freak out and have a panic attack, and this whole vacation is going to go right down the shitter.

"I didn't sleep well for some reason. I'm fine." Ryan stared at the carpet, hoping the call was finished.

"I hate when that happens. I've been so tired at the end of the day with everything going on, I sleep standing up these days. Anyway, I have to run. I'll send you the doc and if there's any problem with it or you have questions, give me a call. Later!"

Ryan waited for Murphy to drop off before snapping his phone closed. What day was it anyway, he wondered as he laid back on the bed.

Oh shit! I'm supposed to pick Wyatt up tonight to go to the fair.

He'd completely forgotten. Ryan weighed his options. He could cancel, but honestly, he didn't want to. He was looking forward to spending the time with Wyatt. Now that he was back in good standing. Unless something changed between now and then, Wyatt would be back to his old self. The question he had to ask himself was, *can you be back to your old self?*

Okay, so you hate yourself. Who cares.

Ryan hated whiners and he refused to become one. He'd lied. He would no doubt have the rug ripped out from under him for it. But until that time came, until he was confronted by Wyatt or Murphy or both about what he'd done, he was going to enjoy himself.

Screw it! I'm falling in love with Wyatt and I know he's serious about me too. Who knows, maybe by some miracle, when the shit does hit the fan, I'll escape with my prize. Stranger things have happened.

Right now the important thing was to keep Wyatt happy, and if he ended up feeling happy too, better yet. Heading into the shower, Ryan was determined to show Wyatt the time of his life. Enough is enough.

Chapter 8

GLANCING at the clock, Wyatt hustled to get ready for his first official date with Ryan Taylor: the Baker County Fair. He'd forgotten all about it until Ryan called to remind him. Primping and posing before the mirror, modeling his third choice of shirt in so many minutes, Wyatt settled on a basic black T-shirt to wear with faded jeans.

"Wyatt, where are you? You ready?" A voice called out from the other end of the house.

Wyatt rushed from the bathroom to the kitchen, where he was stopped in his tracks by his twin. Ryan had on, with very little variation, the same jeans and T-shirt combo Wyatt had on.

"Hey, boyfriend," Ryan said.

"Hi, sweetie!" *Fuck, we're wearing the exact same thing.* "I should change, we're twins."

"Why, Wy?" Ryan laughed at his own funny.

"You sure?" Wyatt wasn't sure. *Won't it look kind of funny for us to be hanging out together wearing the same clothes?*

"I'm positive. You look hot as hell and I don't want you changing a thing. Besides, half the guys in the county will have on what we have on, so it won't matter. Get over here."

When Wyatt was close enough, Ryan grabbed him by the hand and pulled him up close, smacking a wet sloppy on his lips.

Wyatt wrapped his arms around Ryan's waist and returned a less reckless kiss.

"Mmm... you taste good," Wyatt said when they eventually parted.

"You can snack on me all you want... later. I'm taking you to the fair." Ryan hustled Wyatt out the door.

A mile outside the city limits, Ryan slowed to a crawl as they joined the other cars inching past flag-waving Cub Scouts in charge of making sure everyone entered the huge field serving as the parking lot for the fair in an orderly fashion.

I'm so excited to be with you. I feel... young at heart? That's it.

Parked in their Scout-approved spot, they headed through the gates and into the fairgrounds. Ryan waved across the crowd at several people, who smiled and waved back. Wyatt wondered if they were friends or relatives but was too overwhelmed at the moment to ask.

Rows of booths gave way to a midway that appeared to go on forever. The aroma of mini donuts, cotton candy, and horse manure felt at once familiar and comforting. Wyatt refused the urge to reach over and lock arms with Ryan. They walked side by side through the flag-draped archway marking the fair's official entrance.

One of the first booths they came upon belonged to the local Rotary club. Wyatt struggled to remember what a Rotary club was all about. He remembered there was one in his town growing up, but couldn't recall if his father had belonged or not.

"Hey, Jerry," Ryan said, extending his hand to the guy behind the booth.

"Hi, Russell," the silver-haired man answered in a booming voice much too big for the small frame it originated from. He took Ryan's hand and pumped it enthusiastically.

"I'm Ryan," he corrected the old geezer.

Wyatt stood in the background waiting to see if he would be introduced.

"That's right. You're Ryan. I get so confused in my old age."

A couple seconds later Jerry perked up and added with a hint of what Wyatt perceived to be, for lack of a better word, nervousness,

"You just missed your folks. They're probably still around if you take a good look."

"Okay. It's no big deal. I see them plenty, I guess."

Ryan looks awkward. Was this guy off his rocker or in some way embarrassing to Ryan? Before Wyatt could further analyze the exchange between Jerry and his companion, Ryan introduced them.

"Jerry, I'd like you to meet my friend, Wyatt."

"Hello, Jerry! It's nice meeting you." Wyatt extended his hand and was rewarded with the same vigorous handshake Jerry had given Ryan.

"Wyatt, it's good to meet you too! You boys enjoy the fair now. Say...." Jerry lowered his voice into a "this is a secret" mode and perked up his furry eyebrows. "I hear tell there's a pretty little filly working the ring toss in the midway this year. I wouldn't waste any time before heading that direction myself if I wasn't trapped inside this booth for the rest of the night. Check her out for me and come back with a full report. Better yet, come back with her on your arm." Jerry clapped his hands together and roared.

"Thanks for the tip," Ryan chuckled, minus the uneasiness he had displayed earlier. Once they were a few feet away he stopped and asked with a sarcastic smirk, "So... are you a tits or an ass man?"

"On you," Wyatt answered with a devilish grin, "both!"

Ryan blushed.

The sun sank below the trees and the fair took on a whimsical, magical quality that brought back fond memories for Wyatt. For a split second, with all the colored lights surrounding him, he was reminded of walking down Broadway on a warm summer night. He was unable to control his delight, periodically stifling a giggle.

Ryan led him deeper into the fair. He couldn't believe how little he'd thought about New York since he'd been staying at Murphy's. As much as he loved the big city, he didn't miss it at all. It felt good to be released from the pressure and it felt really good to be here with Ryan.

Wyatt again fought the urge to take Ryan's hand. *How incredible it would feel to walk hand and hand through the fair together as a couple.* He frowned. *How unfair the world is. How is my love any different from anyone else's?* The scores of young lovers walking hand in hand around him only seemed to accentuate this injustice.

Passing a foot-long hot dog stand, he was brought out of his temporary funk when Ryan flipped a camera out of his pocket and insisted on taking a picture of Wyatt in front of the booth. Wyatt laughed, catching onto the joke. "Let me take a picture of you instead," he protested. "I don't want to be accused of false advertising."

"From what I've seen," Ryan said with a wink, "you're a far cry from leading anyone on. Now smile pretty for the camera Mr. Kielbasa Man!" Ryan snapped the shot and the two men laughed hard.

It had been fifteen years or longer, Wyatt thought, since he'd been to a fair. This county fair seemed larger than the one he remembered from his childhood. A few hundred feet into the midway and they were engulfed in its frantic world of music, scents, screams of both terror and delight, and flashing lights in every direction.

"Do you like rides?" Ryan asked with the innocent enthusiasm of a ten-year-old with a twenty-dollar bill burning a hole in his pocket.

Christ, I hate rides! "I don't think I've had much experience with rides," he answered bravely, not wanting to bring Ryan down.

"I'm a maniac. The faster, scarier, the better. I'll tell you what," Ryan looked around before continuing. "How about we compromise and try something on the mellow side for starters and see how you do?" Before Wyatt could respond, Ryan pointed down the row of tents and rides to the end of the midway, where a large, brightly lit circle of seats rotated slowly. "There! Will you ride the Ferris wheel with me?"

"Sure," Wyatt answered before he could think of a graceful way to say no. As they approached the ride, he began to feel weak. *Fuck, what did I just say I'd do? Look how high the top chair goes. I'll have to make this work. I can do this!*

Wyatt climbed into the chair and Ryan saddled up next to him. Once they were both seated, a burly man grabbed a belt from the side of the seat and buckled them in tight.

Wyatt attempted a smile, even though he was dying inside. Before he had time to launch into a full-fledged anxiety attack, to his horror, they began their ascent, backward. *You've fucking gotta be shittin' me!* He snatched Ryan's hand and held it in a death grip.

The ride stopped and started several times, causing their chair to rock back and forth as the wheel loaded up new passengers. Wyatt spent an agonizing few minutes with his eyes closed at the very top, praying for the operator to lower him safely back to the ground.

"You doin' okay?" Ryan asked.

Wyatt hadn't let go of Ryan's hand since getting on the ride. In fact, he scarcely allowed himself to breathe for fear it would add to his mounting terror. It was obvious that Ryan found his sissy ride-terror amusing.

"Yeah," Wyatt managed to eke out. "I'm doing okay." He attempted another smile but aborted the effort as too risky. Talking seemed to help, so he continued. "This is a new experience... this twirling around high above the earth with a guy... a guy... five front teeth short of a mouthful, in charge of my life. Yes, indeed... this is a very new experience for me."

Wyatt's heartfelt confession fueled Ryan on until he was laughing so hard tears welled up in his eyes.

"I'll say one more thing, more than likely the last thing I'll ever say before my death. I can't believe the view from up here." Aware of how funny he was being, he forged ahead. "Hey look! There's Manhattan."

In the distance, a glowing light appeared above the treetops, indicating a city that certainly was not Manhattan. In the opposite direction, you could still make out the end of the tree line and the edge of the vast Atlantic. The sky was tinted orange in the west as the last rays of sun faded deep into the horizon.

Wyatt was jerked back into terror as the giant wheel increased speed and began to make full revolutions, putting an end to his impromptu comedy routine. There was no disguising his distress. He was flat-out miserable and couldn't care less if he did squeeze all of the blood out of Ryan's hand

Get me the fuck off this piece of shit, right now!

After what seemed like an eternity, the same burly guy with the thirty-five-dollar smile undid their belt and released them back into the crowd of noisy fair-goers. Stumbling to regain his balance, Wyatt followed Ryan, who herded them back into the flashing chaos.

Half an hour later, once his stomach had calmed, Wyatt realized he was hungry. They shared a bag of mini donuts as they walked down the other side of the midway. Ryan paused before a large tent housing several games. They watched as baseballs were hurled at lead milk bottles. Over to their right, a group of overweight women seated on stools sprayed water at a target in hopes of advancing their pig over the finish line. How funny, he thought as he called Ryan's attention to the absurdity of it all.

"Want me to win ya a teddy bear, sugar?" Ryan asked out of the blue in a voice fit for the mayor of Hicksville.

"Well, I'd rather you presented me with one of those tantalizing foot-long wieners we passed on earlier, Jethro Earl."

"Oh they'll be plenty of wiener for you when we get home to the trailer, Joe Bob Dean. Don't fret yourself none."

I love that you're funny! It was Wyatt's turn to laugh until tears rolled down his cheeks.

I've got it so bad for you. If you're willing, tonight would be the night. I've waited long enough to experience the full meal deal.

Past the game tent they found themselves standing before the Lover's Tunnel. Wyatt didn't have a second to protest before Ryan grasped his hand and marched the two of them up to the ticket-taker. "Two, please," he said as he thrust a handful of money at the middle-aged woman sitting inside the ornately lit red and gold booth. Behind her and down a short walkway, little bucket-shaped gondolas waited motionless. Presumably, they carried the lovers through the tunnel before exiting on the opposite end, rejoining them with the other empty buckets.

"You plan on taking him into the tunnel of love, young man?" the rail-thin woman asked Ryan before accepting his money.

Wyatt felt the hairs on the back of his head stand on end. Everything was going so well. The time and place didn't seem right to test the woman's level of acceptance. This wasn't the big city after all. *Nothing good was going to come of this.* Wyatt started to back away.

Ryan wasn't budging an inch. Before Wyatt could get too far away, Ryan reached over and grabbed him by the shoulder, returning him to his side.

"I sure enough do, darlin'," Ryan answered, as relaxed as could be. "You're supposed to take the one ya love in there, ain't ya?" he asked in a voice full of pride and confidence.

"Well, young feller," the woman responded dryly, "I'm not sure what the hell kind of an accent that is, but I'll tell ya'll one thing I know for certain. I'm not taking your money."

Ryan pumped out his chest in anticipation of an all-out confrontation. Wyatt stared down at Ryan's flap-clad feet. They were prettier than his.

Before the moment could escalate, the woman leaned in toward the two stunned men and added with a smile, "I've a son living down in Fayetteville who's struggling with the same challenges you boys face. I'll be goddamned—" She paused only long enough for the smile to disappear. "—if I'm going to bow down to those red-necked ass-heads preventing him, or you, or anyone else on God's green earth from enjoying themselves and living their life in whatever the hell way they want to live it. It just ain't right."

The woman banged her fist on the counter, causing Wyatt to yelp. "This ride's on me and God bless ya both!"

It was as if the world had for one brief moment, come to a complete stop. Seconds, perhaps minutes passed before anyone moved. When Wyatt finally found the courage to look up, he was surprised to discover a softer, kinder face on the woman than he'd expected.

"Oh, one last thing...." The woman gestured for them to come closer to the booth.

When they were inches from the glass window, she looked at them both and said, "If either of you ever use an insulting hick accent around me again, I'll climb out of this booth and kick your ass so hard you'll see stars. Understood?"

The woman smiled and ripped a couple tickets off the large roll in front of her and slid them over to Ryan. Wyatt was so stunned, he was incapable of coming up with anything to say back. Ryan fared a little better, thanking the woman and wishing her son well before grabbing the tickets and leading them down to a disheveled and bored younger woman who accepted their tickets with a grunt.

"Outside or inside?" Ryan asked as they headed up the ramp to their "love" bucket.

"Outside," Wyatt said as he waited for Ryan to hop in.

They watched as the woman walked over to a gray fuse box. She pushed a large metal lever down and, with a violent jolt, their bucket launched into motion.

"Woo-hoo," Ryan hollered out as they rolled down the track to the opening of the tunnel, a plywood archway painted army green covered with faded plastic pastel orchids. Seconds past the tunnel's opening, they found themselves immersed in darkness.

"Keep your hands to yourself," Ryan cautioned, while at the same time doing his best to mess up Wyatt's hair.

"Quit that," Wyatt giggled, taking a jab at Ryan's armpit.

"You better watch yourself. You're messing with the master here," Ryan said.

Wyatt felt Ryan's wet, sloppy palm rub over his entire face before he had a chance to reply. He was equally disgusted and delighted, a combustible combination of feelings he hadn't experienced since being with Murphy.

"Oh, gross! That's so fucking gross," Wyatt squealed, slapping Ryan back over to his side of the bucket.

They rattled down the track in cool, damp darkness. Wyatt felt Ryan move closer. Bracing himself for another silly ambush, he was taken by surprise when Ryan's powerful arms wrapped around his waist. A wave rocked his body as Ryan's warm lips began kissing his neck and up past his chin to his lips, where they paused, then brushed and teased and nipped.

"Mmm," Wyatt moaned, shifting his body so he was facing Ryan. He wrapped his arms around Ryan's neck and drew him in close for a kiss. Bright, flashing lights startled them.

"What the hell," Wyatt said as their bucket inched its way along an old, worn-out diorama of Paris. On their right, the Eiffel tower loomed over the cityscape. Several feet further down the track on the left, they rolled past the Moulin Rouge, complete with a mechanical line of cancan dancers.

"I've always wanted to visit Paris," Ryan confessed as he snuggled up against Wyatt.

"It's the city of lovers, you know," Wyatt said as he reached for Ryan's chin, pulling him up for another kiss. Ryan's hand slid back Wyatt's T-shirt, brushing up against his nipples. They abruptly left Paris, and after a sharp curve found themselves smack-dab in the middle of Venice.

"Sei la mia rosa," Wyatt purred as his tongue twisted around Ryan's.

"Say it isn't so," Ryan purred back, sliding his other hand under both of Wyatt's legs. "What's that mean, tiger?"

"I think it means you are my rose. It's from a movie."

"I'll be your rose. I'll be anything you want me to be." Ryan's lips again found Wyatt's. This time they locked together for a long, sensual kiss.

Wyatt reached over and cupped the back of Ryan's head. Their tongues took turns probing and exploring. Ryan's hand continued to pester and play with Wyatt's nipples as they inched their way past Venice and back into darkness.

He was becoming aroused. His entire body tingled and shivered in response to Ryan's touch. Closing his eyes, Wyatt let his head hang backwards. He welcomed and savored the sensations. The bucket made another quick turn, and at the same time, Ryan hoisted Wyatt off his seat and into his lap, facing him. In one quick movement, Ryan lifted Wyatt's T-shirt up and off him. Before he knew what had happened, or could protest, Ryan had his left nipple clenched gently between his teeth.

"Oh my gawd," Wyatt gasped, surrendering himself to Ryan's assault, only vaguely aware their gondola had passed out of darkness and into a blizzard of dirty white and powder blue.

"I think we're in the Alps," Wyatt moaned.

"What's the Alps got to do with love?" Ryan asked, pausing briefly from working over Wyatt's nipple to reposition him on his lap.

Wyatt was beside himself with passion. He could feel Ryan's eagerness underneath him and he wanted it all, *right now*.

"Maybe it has something to do with breasts," Wyatt offered along with his nipple.

Ryan took it eagerly. In response, Wyatt rubbed his butt across Ryan's lap, inciting a groan of pleasure. "Oh man, I want you so bad," Ryan urged between bites.

"Don't stop. Please don't stop," Wyatt shouted above the yodeling coming from a distant speaker. Tossing and turning his head, weathering the incredible sensations he felt, Wyatt pushed his chest out to meet Ryan's mouth. Ryan bit back hard and Wyatt's entire body shook in response.

"That's it... oh yeah... oh yes." Wyatt's eyes glazed with pleasure as they lurched out of the darkness. "Oh yeah... bite those tits. Harder! Bite 'em harder," he begged as he reached under himself and groped Ryan's crotch.

Wyatt's eyes sprang open in response to a sudden jolt. Their bucket had returned itself to the beginning of the ride. Frozen in horror, he sat, straddling Ryan, naked from the waist up in front of a small crowd of astonished fair-goers.

"Had enough of the fair?" Ryan asked dryly.

"What do we do now?" Wyatt whispered, horrified.

"We could go again," Ryan suggested, sneaking a quick lick of Wyatt's nipple.

"Ryan, STOP! There's people watching!" Wyatt sat on Ryan's lap, frozen in fear.

"Okay, okay. We're fine, Wyatt. I think its off-season for shooting gay guys. But come to think of it, that could start next week. You don't see any guns, do you? Here, put on your shirt." Ryan picked Wyatt's T-shirt off the floor of the bucket and handed it to him. Wyatt fumbled as he tried to put it on in a hurry.

"There's nothing to be embarrassed about," Ryan said as he helped Wyatt off his lap. "Walk out of here like you own the place. Unless you spot a rifle, then fucking bolt!"

Wyatt avoided eye contact with the small group of onlookers who had assembled to watch. A piercing whistle forced him to look up. Ten feet away stood Lil Hinnenkamp's sister, waving and smiling.

Laughing hysterically, Ryan grabbed Wyatt by the arm, and together they made a mad dash to the safety of their car.

"Oh man, that was the best," Ryan said, clenching his stomach when he was finally able to talk.

"No one back home is going to believe that one," Wyatt added, wiping the tears from his eyes. "I don't think we're ever going to be able to top that. I can't laugh anymore this year."

"I'm starving," Ryan confessed as he navigated the car out of the field and past the brigade of Scouts. "I can't believe I was just at the fair and only ate a handful of donuts. I'm usually a total piglet at these things."

"I'm hungry too," Wyatt admitted, squeezing Ryan's knee.

"I've got an idea. I'm going to bring you to one of my favorites. It's nothing fancy, but it's on the way home."

In truth, Wyatt wasn't sure what he was. He wasn't in control of himself. He was so in love, he was vibrating. He'd fallen hard. There was no turning back. He rested his head on his new love's shoulder.

A few miles down the road, Ryan turned off onto a dirt parking lot in front of a little shack called The Peppermint Twist. It was clear, the closer they got to the building, it had seen better days. The red-and-white paint job—the peppermint twist part of the motif—was peeling in more places than not and at least half of the light bulbs outlining the overhang were either burned out or missing. The Peppermint Twist was the quintessential old drive-in, like out of a movie, Wyatt thought.

Ryan eased the car into one of the parking spots under the canopy and shut off the engine.

Wyatt was just about to open his door and get out when a young girl with short, spiked hair the color of a fire engine came flying out the screen door toward them. She was wearing a short tennis-style red skirt, a white cotton blouse with a red sweater wrapped around her neck, and blinding white sneakers. The only thing she was missing was a mouth full of bubble gum, but a mouth full of braces finished off the look nicely, Wyatt noticed. Removing a red pen from behind her ear, she leaned down and peered into the car window.

"Hey, guys! Welcome to the Peppermint Twist. You dudes know what you'd like or should I give you a couple of minutes?"

"May I order for you?" Ryan asked, looking over for approval. The girl's face, framed by the car window, was threateningly close to Ryan's.

"Please do," Wyatt said. His senses were on overload and had it been left up to him to decide on something to eat, they would still be around to consider breakfast.

"Why don't you give us two deluxe cheeseburgers, one order of fries—they're really large—and two...." Ryan turned to Wyatt, "chocolate, vanilla, or strawberry?"

"Chocolate," Wyatt answered without risking another look in Ryan's direction. The image of the girl in the window was more than he was able to deal with right now. He bit his lip as he valiantly attempted to stifle one of his legendary giggle fits. This could be the perfect storm of giggle fits if he were to relax his concentration.

"And two small chocolate shakes, please. That should do it," Ryan added with a flourish.

"Okay," the little firecracker fired off with an unprecedented display of efficiency, "that's two deluxe peppermint cheese, one fry, and two chocolate shakes. Be back in a flash, fellas."

They watched as the girl in the amazingly white tennis shoes disappeared around the corner.

Turning to face Wyatt, Ryan leaned back against the door, bringing his knee up onto the car seat. "The best burgers anywhere, just you wait and see. Hey! You're kind of quiet all of a sudden, everything okay?"

Wyatt was a bundle of nervous energy. He blushed, aware of Ryan staring at him. His body trembled with excitement. "Have you ever felt like you were exactly in the right place at exactly the right time?" he asked.

Ryan reached over and put his hand around Wyatt's neck and confessed, "I have to say something, and I can't stop myself. I'll apologize now in case I stick my foot in my mouth or what I'm about to say comes out wrong."

Wyatt waited, unsure where this was going. His stomach did a few flips before Ryan leaned in closer and continued. "I'm falling in love with you. It has to be love. I've never felt this way about anyone in my life. Like you, I felt something special from the moment you got in my car at the airport, and it's continued to grow inside of me ever since. My mind is consumed with thoughts of you. I want to make love to you so bad I can't stand it. But it's more than that. I don't want to be away from you. Not for a minute."

Wyatt blinked a few times, maybe to make sure he wasn't dreaming, or maybe he just needed a second to catch his breath and make sure his heart was still beating. Had Ryan just confessed his love for him? If so, it was the very thing he had hoped for. He was feeling the same way. He never wanted to be apart from this man. It felt so right.

Touched deeply by what Ryan had just said, Wyatt was about to pledge his undying love back when he heard the familiar sound of tennis shoes on gravel. Their food was loaded on a tray the girl attached to the side of Ryan's window.

"That'll be thirteen dollars and forty-seven cents," she announced.

"I got this." Wyatt dug into his pocket and handed a twenty to the girl. "Keep the change... ah... Andrea," he said with a smile after spotting her name tag. "We've decided to take the food with us."

Wyatt reached over and snatched the two burgers off the tray. He was hungry for food and starved for Ryan. Whatever he could do to speed up the process of eliminating one before the other was at the top of his agenda.

"Whoa," Ryan laughed as he handed Wyatt the order of fries and milk shakes. When the tray had been emptied, Ryan lifted it off the window and, with a wink and a thank you, put the car in reverse and barreled out of the parking lot, leaving Andrea in the dust. The radio blared an unrecognizable version of the Patsy Cline hit *Crazy* as they sped down the highway.

"Here," Wyatt unwrapped Ryan's burger, sprinkled some fries over it, and placed the whole thing on his lap. "Do you want your shake?" he asked, the model of efficiency.

"I want you, but for now, I'll settle for that shake you've got going on," Ryan said with a wink.

Wyatt handed the cup over and organized his own burger on his lap. The food tasted wonderful. He forced himself to slow down and enjoy it.

RYAN struggled to navigate the car while attempting to eat his food without appearing out of control, which was exactly how he felt. His mind raced a mile a minute from the present to the bedroom. His entire body begged for Wyatt. *Easy, Ryan! Just a few more miles and you'll get what you've been waiting for.* The connection he felt with Wyatt was unlike anything he had ever experienced before. It was at once consuming and its power humbling.

Pulling up to the house, he leaned over and forced himself to ask, "Are you sure this is the right thing to do?" He bit his lip as he waited for Wyatt to respond.

"I've made a few very wrong decisions in my life, but this isn't going to be one of them. I hope you enjoy this as much as I'm going to." Wyatt's eyes sparkled.

Is it possible this guy doesn't have a clue how hot he is? Ryan wasn't sure how to respond to Wyatt. Having sex with Wyatt had been a fantasy from the minute he'd laid eyes on him. He'd never met anyone as charismatic and good-looking as Wyatt Stark. He was mature, successful, incredibly funny, and a man who knew what he wanted out of life. Everything about Wyatt was sexy. Ryan had plotted over and over how such a night like this would play out. It was time to put his plan in action.

"I've been waiting for this from the moment we met." *Why not try the truth for a change,* Ryan thought.

Wyatt leaned over to kiss, but Ryan stopped him by pressing his finger to Wyatt's lips.

"Not here. I won't be able to stop myself," Ryan confessed. "Let's go in."

Wyatt nodded and led the way into the house.

Ryan was surprised to find his palms sweating. "I'll put some music on," he said as he took in a few deep breaths in an attempt to calm himself.

"Perfect," Wyatt said. "I'll open some wine."

Ryan wasn't sure what kind of music to choose. The music had to be perfect, and yet, he reassured himself, it didn't. He forced himself to make a choice. Seconds later, the sound of a sexy saxophone filled the room.

Wyatt entered the living room and handed Ryan a glass.

"Here's to you," Wyatt toasted. "Here's to an incredible summer made better than perfect because of you."

Ryan blushed as he took a sip of his wine. How could he express what he was feeling right now? He wanted to say so much, and yet he knew he needed to caution himself. *Don't go there, not yet. You'll know when the time is right.* Wyatt removed the glass Ryan was holding and placed it along with his own on a nearby table. Ryan opened his arms and Wyatt melted into them, resting his head on Ryan's chest. They swayed back and forth. The music teased and taunted.

"I'm nervous," Wyatt said, looking up. "I want this to be so special."

"It already is," Ryan said, kissing the top of Wyatt's head. "May I take the lead?"

"By all means."

Reaching out for Wyatt's hand, the two made their way to the bedroom. The only light came from the bright summer moon and its reflection off the water of the cove, dancing on the walls around them. Ryan began to undress Wyatt. He savored the slow removal of each article of clothing until Wyatt stood naked.

"You're so beautiful," Ryan said, kissing his way down Wyatt's chest until he was on his knees. Reaching around, he placed his hands on Wyatt's muscled buttocks, drawing him closer. Wyatt's body quivered as Ryan took him into his mouth. Motionless, he held onto Wyatt until he was swollen and pulsating.

Easing off, Ryan stood and began to undress. Wyatt moved to help, but Ryan halted his attempts. "I'm leading, remember?" he whispered.

Wyatt let out a nervous laugh as Ryan darted out of the room, returning seconds later with the wine and their glasses. He promptly took Wyatt into his arms, kissing him as he maneuvered them over to the bed.

"Relax," Ryan whispered in Wyatt's ear. "You'll know when it's your turn."

Chapter 9

WYATT opened his eyes to discover an arm draped across his chest and a nose snuggled up against his neck. The light in the room was muted. A cool breeze blew in from the cove, bringing with it the sound of seagulls far off in the distance. It took him a minute to get his bearings, and when he did, he realized a soft, steady rain was falling outside. *What time is it?* He turned his head to view the clock on the bookcase. Ten twenty-seven.

Last night was amazing. Incredible! Out of this world! Extraordinary! Choosing the right superlative would be a challenge. For the first time in his life, Wyatt had discovered the difference between having sex and being made love to. There wasn't a spot on his body Ryan hadn't visited at least twice. In his wildest dreams, he couldn't have anticipated a more intensely pleasurable sexual experience. The man sleeping next to him had very special talents.

Not wanting to wake his passionate new love, Wyatt raised Ryan's arm and, moving out from under it, gently placed it back down behind him. He glanced over at the sleeping figure in hopes he hadn't disturbed him. The angelic face remained in the same position. Even with the window open, and the cool breeze moving about the room, he could smell last night's adventures. The smell was glorious. What wasn't quite as glorious were the aches and pains he was discovering as he tiptoed out of the bedroom and into the living room. The assault on his body had been relentless, and the areas of particular tenderness were making themselves known, begging for some soothing attention. It was a kind of pain he could handle. Like dancing, the pain went with the territory and he wore his aches as a badge of pride. In this case, exaltation. He had a new lover. *Let the world rejoice!*

Wyatt lumbered through a couple of the rooms that had hosted last night's mischief. A few lights had been left on, and he moved about turning these off. He collected an odd glass here and there, eventually working his way into the kitchen. Opening the cupboard, he took out a couple of tea bags. He couldn't remember if Ryan had said he liked tea or not. He'd give it a shot.

As he poured water into a kettle, Wyatt heard footsteps approaching. He turned and watched as Ryan came plodding around the corner, wiping the sleep from his eyes.

"So this is where you're hiding. I got lonely. Come back to bed and snuggle with me."

The natural light pouring into the room accentuated the dark areas of hair on Ryan's body. "You are the sexiest man alive, you know that, right?" Wyatt sat the kettle onto the stovetop and adjusted the heat.

Approaching him from behind, Ryan's warm, strong arms wrapped around his waist, holding him tight against his body while he planted a series of lazy, snuggle kisses all over Wyatt's shoulders and neck. The hardness he felt growing against the back of his leg told him Ryan wasn't about to take no for an answer.

"Mmm… I can't wait to crawl back into bed with you. I'll bring you a cup of tea and I have some melon too."

"Perfect," Ryan whispered into his ear. "I'll be waiting, so hurry." Before returning to the bedroom, he gave Wyatt's butt an authoritative slap. "Make it snappy, Mr. Stark!"

A feeling of contentment caused Wyatt to smile. While the tea brewed, images of the night before popped up in his mind like special valentines. In bed, Ryan had proven himself wise beyond his years. He was attentive, so patient and giving. There wasn't a hint of selfishness to his lovemaking and nothing about his approach was rushed in any way. The only hint of urgency made itself known at the appropriate time, when Ryan's body was no longer able to resist the powerful forces he had so carefully and expertly cultivated. He coaxed and teased until he and Wyatt crossed the point of no return together.

The results of Ryan's skillful actions had been thunderous. Any control Wyatt might have hoped to hang on to had been destroyed. Annihilated on several occasions, he had been so overwhelmed by the intense sensations of pleasure rocking and racing through his body that he had whimpered as he struggled to ride them out. Each time after, he had been left with chest heaving and his body dripping from every pore.

Perhaps the most amazing thing of all, Ryan made him feel like an equal. He wasn't the old guy who got lucky with the younger guy. He was Ryan's guy.

Wyatt hurried in the kitchen and came back to the bedroom with tea and a bowl full of melon chunks. "Here," he said, popping a chunk of honeydew into Ryan's mouth.

"Mmm, sweet… just like you."

"The weather is perfect, rainy and cool. Perfect for snuggling and…."

"What time is it?" Ryan sat up suddenly.

"It's just after eleven o'clock. Why? Oh no, tell me you don't have to work today. You have to work, don't you?" Wyatt couldn't mask his disappointment.

"Not if I get to my phone and make a call." Ryan jumped out of bed and after a brief search located his cell phone in the pocket of his jeans, which had somehow found their way under the bed. "Hang on. Don't go anywhere. I'll be back in two seconds."

Wyatt listened as Ryan informed his father he would not be making it in. Something told Wyatt this last-minute change in plans might have been worked out in advance. There didn't seem to be much resistance from the other end and the call only lasted for a minute or so.

"I'm all yours," Ryan said with a sexy smile as he climbed back into bed.

Wyatt waited for him to get under the covers before he pounced.

An adventure-filled day gave way to evening. The rain stopped and the sun broke through the clouds, causing everything around them to glisten. Steam, rising up from the surrounding forest, drifted lazily over the cove. The unexpected warmth beckoned them out from the bedroom and onto the porch, where they sat on the sofa, soaking in the lush scenery.

"So… what's your schedule like for the next couple days?" Wyatt asked after heading into the house and bringing back a bottle of wine.

"Why? You tired of me? You want me to pack up and head out?" Ryan asked, looking over with concern as he watched Wyatt fill their glasses.

"No, silly man, I want you to stay with me forever. And if that isn't possible, I want to know how long I can have you on a temporary basis." He took a sip of his wine and rested his head on Ryan's shoulder. Both had stretched their feet out on the table in front of them.

Ryan didn't answer. *What's he thinking right now?* Hesitation was never good in these situations. Wyatt waited, forcing his breathing to remain steady.

"Here's the deal," Ryan said as he looked over and ran his fingers through Wyatt's hair. "I need a break from the store. I've been hitting it pretty hard since the beginning of the season. I'm going to talk to Dad and let him know I'm going to take a breather. Someone else can fill in for me for the next couple of days. It shouldn't be a big deal."

"There's the answer I was waiting for. Call now," Wyatt teased as he tried to push Ryan off the couch.

"Easy there. You're dangerously close to earning yourself a spanking, little mister," Ryan threatened as he got up.

Wyatt wanted Ryan all to himself. Today had spoiled him, and he prayed Ryan's father would give in to his request. He sipped his wine and waited.

A couple minutes later, Ryan came back with a look on his face that needed no explanation. His father had refused. Ryan sat down and stared out at the cove.

Wyatt didn't want to ask, but his curiosity got the best of him. "That didn't go too well, I take it." He reached over and rubbed Ryan's shoulder in hopes of offering some consolation.

Ryan continued to look away. Just as Wyatt was about to say something else he hoped would be of comfort, Ryan whirled around with a devilish grin and proclaimed, "Dad was great! He gave me three days off."

Wyatt sat back in disbelief. Ryan had played him and he had fallen for it.

Ryan bolted up and ran out of the porch and onto the sand, squealing with delight. Wyatt was up and after him.

"You little fucker," he hollered out, "I almost started to cry, I was so bummed. Shame on you!"

"You should... Oh my God, I'm dying...." Ryan could barely talk because he was laughing so hard. "You should have seen the look on your face," he hollered over his shoulder, aware Wyatt was hot on his heels. "You looked like a little kid who was just told his birthday had been cancelled. It was priceless."

"I'll show you priceless," Wyatt shouted as he chased Ryan into the water, overtaking him and dunking him until he came up gasping and begging for Wyatt to stop.

"I have to admit, you got me good with that one," Wyatt confessed once they had settled down.

"It was mean, but so worth it."

"The water feels good on my battered body. Do you want to swim around for a while?" Wyatt asked, moving in closer for a kiss.

"Sure," Ryan said after breaking away from the kiss. "I feel like a sex pig."

The cool day of rain left the water chilly, but invigorating. Wyatt kept his pace relaxed as he swam next to Ryan for a half dozen laps before they called it quits and headed back into the house.

They shared a warm shower, which was uneventful given the potential.

"I'm starving," Ryan confessed as Wyatt toweled him off.

"Me too." Wyatt bit Ryan's ear and then took him by the hand, leading him into the kitchen.

"Wyatt, I have something I have to tell you."

Wyatt looked over skeptically while he cut off a large chunk of meat. "Don't even think of trying another one on me."

"No, and by the way, I'm sorry I did that to you. I have this quirky sense of humor that gets me into big trouble every now and then. I promise I won't do anything to you like that again for at least a couple of days."

"How generous of you. What's up, Casanova?"

"I was waiting for the right moment today, and now I'm realizing quickly there isn't going to be a right moment."

Wyatt took a pull from his glass of Pinot Noir and carefully set it back down. *This is it. This is the part where he tells me he's seeing someone else.* It was in his nature to prepare for the worse. Under the table, Wyatt's feet twisted together like a pretzel.

"Stop with the face already," Ryan said with all the gentleness of a parent comforting a frightened child. Removing his napkin from his lap and setting it on the table, he continued. "Things are moving very fast for me right now, and don't get me wrong, I'm not at all wanting any part of this, us, to stop. I'm serious. Please know...." Ryan paused for a moment as he struggled for the right words. "Wyatt, I can't even imagine what life would be like now, in the short time we have known each other, if you were out of the picture."

Wyatt nodded back in acknowledgment. He wasn't out of the woods yet. The impending lump in his throat sat poised, ready at a moment's notice to launch into action.

"On Saturday morning I have to go to Boston. I have to register for school and look into housing. I know it's presumptuous for me to even think you would ask me to make changes to my life, but I tend to operate with the cart always before the horse. So... I have to share this worry with you. I need time to get my head in the right place. Shit, I'm really turning a good time into a fucking mess. Sorry. What I'm doing such a miserable job of saying is that I don't want you to think there's something wrong. I couldn't be happier. I need to organize my mind for you."

This all worked for Wyatt. As compulsive as he could be about the things he wanted, he understood Ryan's concerns. If he hadn't been so love-struck himself, he'd have understood or recognized he, too, might need some time to sort all of this out. After all, they were traveling at breakneck speed. And he was being presumptuous, entertaining the idea Ryan would drop everything and join his life, his friends and family, his world! This was not the bad news he had dreaded. It was good news. It showed Ryan had good common sense. It confirmed he was mature and his decisions were well thought out. As much as anyone's could be given the situation.

"I completely understand," Wyatt said. He needed a minute to think before he continued, and indicated this to Ryan by holding up a finger. After several moments, he had what he wanted to say. Lifting his wineglass to toast, he winked at Ryan and said, "Here's to the time we have together now. Here's to the future, whatever we decide it to be."

"Everything feels so comfortable with you," Ryan said, returning the toast. "You just get it. So many people out there don't get it. Everyone seems to be out for themselves these days. I don't sense that with you at all."

"Have I got you fooled," Wyatt said. "Repeat what you just said to friends who know me well and you'll get an earful. I've always been driven… it's all been about me and my career for as long as I can remember." Wyatt corrected himself. "In show business, it almost has to be that way if you want to get anywhere."

Sipping his wine, he thought about something else. "I really want us to work out, Ryan. You have no idea. It wasn't until I met you I realized how lonely I was. I'll do anything to make sure we have the best shot. If I can help you in any way, just let me know. I know people."

Wyatt knew the minute those words came out his mouth he'd made a tragic error in timing.

Ryan, catching the twinkle in Wyatt's eye, was the first to explode in fits of laughter, with Wyatt erupting just seconds later. The words "I know people" effectively ended any further heart-to-heart discussions for the remainder of the evening.

The rest of the night was all about cuddling, giggling, and sharing each other's secrets. Ryan was deathly afraid of snakes and bats. Wyatt's first crush was on a boy who only had one eye. Ryan shit his pants in an elevator on a family vacation to Washington, D.C. He was fifteen. Wyatt threw up in a taxicab on the way home from his first

Broadway opening night party. Ryan's favorite food was hot dogs, which sent them both into another extended fit of laughter.

The next couple of days flew by. For Wyatt, it was like being on a vacation you never wanted to end, but knew in the back of your mind it would, at some point, no matter what you tried to do. He couldn't keep his hands off of Ryan and at one point, caught himself following him into the bathroom.

The last night before Ryan headed off to Boston for his week of school business, they spent very much like their first. Neither of them seemed to be able to get enough of the other.

"Don't take any more time away than you have to. I'll be counting the minutes."

"Trust me, if I could avoid this trip altogether, I would." Ryan reached over and pulled Wyatt on top of him. "I know how to make good use of the time we have." Ryan's hands slid under Wyatt's ass, lifting him up while he repositioned himself.

"You certainly do." Wyatt leaned forward and kissed Ryan on the nose as he eased himself back down. "I like it better when you take the lead."

RYAN placed the pencil back in the drawer and read over what he'd written. This was probably not the best way to leave things, but it was the only way. Saying good-bye to Wyatt in person would be next to impossible. He didn't trust himself to keep it together. This was the best. Wyatt would no doubt wake up a little miffed, but that would be okay. *Leave them wanting more. That was an old showbiz saying, wasn't it?* Ryan thought as he placed the note in the center of the counter. The last few days had been incredible. Perfection. And unless Ryan had misjudged him, Wyatt felt the same way. Looking back through the house, he paused, listening for any new sounds from deep inside the house. Certain the coast was clear, he walked down the hall and out the door.

He'd come so close to telling Wyatt the truth. So close. During that first morning together, Ryan had teetered back and forth, drifting in and out of the moment as he contemplated what would be best. In the end, his fears had gotten the best of him. In defiance, he'd made a last minute pact with himself: He'd tell Wyatt he was going to Boston to register for school and find another place to live. *I thought you weren't going to tell any more lies!* Having the week away from Wyatt after spending so many wonderful days together was by far the best plan, given what he had to work with. At first he'd thought about asking Wyatt to call him, but thought better of it when he realized how damaging it would be to tell even more lies as he faked his way through a trip to school. Even though it made him feel like shit to do it, giving the wrong cell phone number to Wyatt was for the best.

In a week's time, when he did come back, Ryan placed his bets on the fact that Wyatt would be starving for more time together. *This need to have me around,* he rationalized, *would act in my favor.* When he did sit Wyatt down to tell him the truth, Wyatt might be more forgiving. He might be.

Ryan pulled onto the highway and headed for his hotel. He needed to sleep. After deciding to make a quiet exit, he had forced himself to stay awake, with Wyatt in his arms, until he was certain he could slip away unnoticed. He and Wyatt had gone for broke, refusing to call it a night until the light of dawn signaled to them that night had the good common sense to give it up and so should they. Wyatt, Ryan thought as he tooled down the road, was an extraordinary man. Complex, yet simple. He was loving and warm and so responsive during their lovemaking. Ryan was surprised at how hungry Wyatt was for sex. How unwilling Wyatt was to waste even a single moment. It was thrilling and exhilarating and Ryan had never experienced anything like it before.

This was best, Ryan reconfirmed. *In a week, I can come up with something.*

WYATT opened his eyes to discover the other side of the bed empty. Searching the house in hopes of finding Ryan before he departed, he found a note on the counter in the kitchen.

Wyatt,

Thank you for the most marvelous days of my life. You have no idea how happy it makes me feel, being with you. Take this time we are away from each other to give me some serious thought. I can tell you right now… I'm a goner. You have my heart… so please be careful. I will stop by the moment I'm back. Have a good week and be safe.

Love ya like no other ever,

Ryan

Wyatt read Ryan's note over and over until he forced himself to put it away. After a cup of tea on the porch where he sat staring out onto the cove, an idea came to him. It seemed the right thing to do. Strolling into the house, he grabbed the phone and called his parents.

"So I think you'd really enjoy it here." Wyatt waited for his mother's response. Over the last few years, his success had severely limited the time he had available to spend with his parents.

"We'd love to come. I can't wait to see what Murphy's done to the house. What? Hang on, honey."

Wyatt waited for his mother to come back on the line. He was thankful his parents were still adventurous. Times like this made him think of the alternatives. Because they were so mobile, he felt blessed.

"Your dad wants to know if Murphy is going to be there."

"Nope." For the life of him, Wyatt couldn't figure out why it pissed him off so much that his parents continued to rely on Murphy for so much.

"He's not going to be there," Wyatt heard his mother reply to his father.

"Ah, shit," Wyatt heard his father answer, even though he knew his mother had attempted to muffle their exchange by misplacing a hand over the wrong part of the phone.

"Your father is thinking about buying stock in a pharmaceutical company. He wants to talk it over with Murphy before he does anything."

"Tell him to give Murphy a call." Wyatt felt shamed he was jealous of his business partner and best friend. A part of him understood, but there was still a part of Wyatt that wanted to scream to the world that these were *his* parents. They should be focused on him, not Murphy.

"We can't wait to see you, honey. Take care!"

"I love you, Mom. Tell Dad hi for me."

Looking around the house, Wyatt realized he hadn't done much cleaning since he had arrived. He hadn't done *any* cleaning except to pick up after himself, run a load of laundry here and there, and keep the kitchen organized. There was work to be done. His mother was coming. Ms. Neatnik USA. Wyatt smiled, remembering Murphy's arsenal of cleaning products. There still was the challenge for him to read all the labels so he could figure out what they were all used for.

Taking one room at a time, he painstakingly cleaned, polished, and sanitized every inch of every nook and cranny, including the furniture. Even though he despised house cleaning, he enjoyed readying the place for his parents' visit. Loud music was a great motivator and he had figured out the intricacies of Murphy's extensive sound system. He was thrilled to discover he could have public radio yakking in the bathroom while at the same time Mozart was waltzing his ass off in the living room. Amazing.

It took the better part of three days to get the house in order. When he had finished, Wyatt celebrated with a wine-infused inspection tour. *I think you can safely let Ms. Neatnik through the door now.*

Next on the list, sightseeing. Wyatt didn't want to hurry or stress his parents out, and yet he wanted them to have a good time and experience the beauty of the area. It would have been nice to wait until Ryan returned for his opinion on what would be fun, but he wanted a plan put in place and figured it could be tweaked along the way. He found a tourist outfit in the tiny local phone directory and decided to pay them a visit.

Wyatt parked the Jeep in front of a Laundromat. To the right, he spotted a street number matching the one in the directory. A sign hanging over the doorway read "Lutz Travel."

"I know you!"

Wyatt wasn't sure how to respond. Having climbed a narrow flight of stairs to the second floor, he had opened the door to the travel agency and found himself standing in a tiny, one-room office containing a very large man, a desk, two chairs, presumably for customers, a wire rack of brochures, and a ceiling fan with a faded cardboard jetliner dangling below it.

"I know you because I go to New York a couple times a year to see theater. I love your shows. They're always very good. I've seen *Dress Up* twice. And you know what? I'd see it again. I tell all my friends to go see it when they go to New York. Go see *Dress Up*! You'll love it. That's exactly what I tell them."

"Thank you! I'm so glad you enjoyed it." *I deserve this. I've wronged someone, somewhere at some point, and this is my payback. I know I deserve this.*

The man stood, extending his hand to Wyatt, and in the process sent the massive wooden chair he had been seated on crashing with a loud bang against the wall in back of him. Wyatt was overwhelmed by the vision of this poor guy navigating his large butt up and down the narrow stairway.

"I'm Jerrold Lutz. The owner," he announced with pride.

Jerrold wore a short-sleeved shirt buttoned only in the center, leaving the top and bottom buttons undone to accommodate his large neck and huge stomach. A family-size bag of cheese curls lay open next to the biggest soft-drink container Wyatt had ever seen. He stepped forward and shook Jerrold's hand. "Wyatt Stark." Jerrold's hand was warm and sticky. And now, so was his.

"Never in my wildest dreams would I have thought one day *The* Wyatt Stark from Broadway would be standing in my office. My office! Gee!"

Wyatt decided to let Jerrold's comment hang. There was an appropriate response, but to save his soul, he couldn't pull anything up.

He used the time to nonchalantly wipe his hand on the side of his shorts. *I can burn these when I get home.*

"What brings you to these parts?" Jerrold motioned for Wyatt to sit, while retrieving his chair and wedging his enormous ass back down onto it.

As a preventative measure, Wyatt shot a glance down to both chairs before sitting in the one positioned farthest from Jerrold. It would be just his luck to leave with a Twinkie stain on the seat of his cargos.

"I'm going to have guests staying with me next week, and I'm interested in finding out what kind of local sightseeing tours might be available."

"Are you living in the area?" Jerrold asked. "How exciting for us if you are."

"I'm staying with a friend." There was no way in hell Wyatt was going to offer up any more information than he had to. Jerrold was a little too excited by his presence, which made Wyatt nervous.

"Well, two of our more popular local tours are the carriage ride through Acadia Park and a whale watching excursion. Do either tours sound like something you might be interested in? We also have kayaking... there's bus service to the casino, bicycle rentals, lobster trapping...."

"The first two sound perfect!" Wyatt didn't care that he had cut Jerrold off. The least amount of time he could spend with this man was his new goal. Why hadn't he gone with his first instinct after opening the door, which had been to turn right around and walk down the stairs as if he'd never been there.

"The carriage ride through Acadia and the whale thingy, let's go with those."

"Lovely choices."

Wyatt watched as Jerrold opened a desk drawer and took out a binder with laminated inserts. "Here's some information on some of the other excursions we offer."

"Nope. I'm good.," Wyatt answered while motioning with his hand for Jerrold to keep the binder. *Like I'm going to touch that?*

"How many people are we talking about?" Jerrold asked.

"Four."

"Four. For both tours?"

"Yes."

"Four for both tours," Jerrold confirmed as he picked up a pen and scribbled something down on a piece of paper. "What dates did you have in mind?"

Shit! Wyatt had to think about this. "Acadia is near Bar Harbor, right? How far do we have to drive for the whale excursion?"

"Yes, you're right. Acadia is just outside of Bar Harbor and the whale excursion leaves from there too. Not far at all." Jerrold sat back with a smile, no doubt thrilled he'd been able to provide such welcoming information.

Wyatt did the math in his head. *They come in on Friday... spend Saturday hanging out around Murphy's. Sunday. Do the whale watch on Sunday, and then the carriage trip later in the week. Tuesday.* Wyatt communicated his plan, including start times, to Jerrold, who wrote it all down on his piece of paper.

Wyatt sat staring at his knees while Jerrold made a couple of calls to confirm availability. Where to rest his eyes had been a problem. He couldn't stand looking at Jerrold, and he was frightened to look around the office for fear he might spot something nasty. His knees seemed like the safest bet.

"Okay, here's a confirmation for you to take with. I've written down the dates and times for your events. And then... let's see, we're almost finished. Just the icky part left. How do you want to pay for this?"

The icky part? Wyatt was overwhelmed with icky. *Trust me, the icky has nothing to do with money.* "Cash okay?" Wyatt reached into his pocket praying he had enough cash along. He couldn't bear the thought of having to wait around for a credit card transaction.

"Well... I don't have any way to make change...."

"Let's see how close we can get," Wyatt insisted. "How much do I owe you?"

Jerrold returned to the paper in front of him and began adding up the total. Wyatt reached into his pocket and pulled out his wad of cash.

"With tax… three hundred and twelve dollars."

"Very good!" Wyatt counted his money, all the while praying he'd have enough. With a sigh of relief, he realized he had it and then some. He peeled off six fifty-dollar bills from the back and added a twenty.

Standing, he placed the money in front of Jerrold on the desk. "Close enough." He retreated back to the door in case Jerrold initiated a pleasure-doing-business-with-you handshake.

"It was an honor meeting you, Mr. Stark. Just show up with your party on time. I'll have taken care of everything else. Stop by again if I can help you with anything else?"

"Will do," Wyatt said with a salute while opening the door to leave. *Christ, even the doorknob feels greasy.* Bounding down the stairs, three at a time, he didn't waste a second getting into the Jeep and pulling out of his parking space. He drove directly to a gas station on the edge of town where he washed his hands with hot water. Twice.

Wyatt made two more stops on the way home. Taylor's, to pick up the ingredients his mother would need to whip up a batch of her scrumptious lasagna, and a flower stand a mile or two before the turnoff to Murphy's. Being in Taylor's again wasn't as strange as he had thought it would be. He smiled to himself as he revisited Ryan's explanation regarding his previous visit.

When he got home, it took him several trips to carry everything inside. He scurried about, putting away all the groceries first. When he had finished, he poured himself a glass of wine and started organizing the flowers into groups. He never thought to check if Murphy had any vases before he had left the house. He checked a few likely spots but came up empty-handed. Always resourceful, he selected some glasses, a pitcher, and retrieved a few art glass pieces that had the right height and depth to accommodate his creations. By the time he had finished his second glass of wine, the counter was filled with beautiful masterpieces of various colors and size. He was immensely proud of his efforts.

On the way to the bedroom to shed his clothes, he entered the living room to pick out music. His choice was an easy one; Miles Davis, in honor of Ryan, whom he missed terribly. Naked, he headed back to the kitchen, poured a third glass of wine, and with the help of Miles, distributed the flowers around the house.

Hoping for a call from Ryan, he checked the machine, but there were no messages. Horny beyond words, Wyatt strolled into the bedroom with the note Ryan had left with his new cell phone number. Ryan mentioned he had lost his phone and had borrowed a friend's for the trip. Wyatt made a couple of quick preparations and plopped back down on the bed.

He bit his lower lip as he dialed the number. *Oh please, pick up.*

Wyatt hoped Ryan was in his hotel, or apartment, or wherever it was he was staying and could talk. Really, really talk. Wyatt had to do something or he'd explode, and if he couldn't be with Ryan, he'd go for the next best thing, his voice. He and Murphy used to have phone sex occasionally when they were lovers and forced apart. There was something so sexy about an urgent voice on the other end of the line describing in explicit detail what their tongue would be doing if only they were together. It never failed to bring results.

He pushed the call button and waited. He heard the familiar ring tone. Once, twice and then, "I'm sorry," a mechanical voice said into his ear, "The number you are calling is no longer in service. Please check the number and redial." *Ah fuck.* In his heightened state of horniness, he must have entered the number wrong. Reaching over the bedside table, he grabbed Ryan's note and compared the number written on it to the one he had just called. They matched. He tried entering the number again just to make sure. Maybe there was something screwy with the phone system right now. Once again, the phone rang twice before the shitty, fucking, goddamn voice on the other end told him the number was no longer in service.

Frustrated and no longer interested in sex of any kind because of the shitty, fucking, goddamn mood he was in, he buried himself under the duvet and fell asleep.

RYAN walked into the restaurant, and after pausing for a moment to decide if it was food he needed, walked right back out. His remorse, for all the lies he had told Wyatt, was getting stronger by the minute. Even though he knew he should try and eat something, nothing appealed to him. Soon the headache would set in. It always did.

All he'd been able to think about the last several days was Wyatt. Walking across the hotel lobby, he tried to imagine what Wyatt was doing. Was he watching a movie? Eating dinner? Was he alone?

Of course he's alone, you asshole. He thinks you're a nice guy. He's waiting for you to call. Call him! Call him and explain. He can't call you because you gave him a bogus number.

No, no, he couldn't do that. Rounding the corner, past three huge marble planters filled with palm trees stretching up to the skylights, Ryan hit a stretch of thick, ornate carpet leading into the small, dark bar. He'd give the bar another chance. At this point his options were limited. Squinting to acclimate himself to the dimmed lighting, he chose a stool at the end of the bar. Taking a quick glance around, he was relieved to discover he was the only patron, which was exactly what he was hoping for.

He sat for several minutes before the bartender, dressed in a black bow tie, white tux shirt, and black vest, came darting around the corner with a large bucket of ice.

"Sorry, man, you been waiting long?" The guy emptied the ice into a stainless steel compartment next to the glass washer. Setting the bucket down, he grabbed a small square napkin, placed it in front of Ryan, and waited.

"I'll take a dark beer. If you have something on tap, great. If not, give me a bottle of something. I don't care." He was miserable. This bar sucked. His room sucked, and he hated himself. It was despicable what he was doing and he knew it.

"Here," the bartender said, placing a glass in front of him. "It's a dark made locally called Whale Bone."

Whale Bone? Are you fuckin' shittin' me? I'm so sick of all this nautical bullshit.

Ryan closed his eyes and took a sip, allowing the creamy, rich liquid to roll around in his mouth before gulping and sending it on its journey to his stomach. It tasted great. Opening his eyes, he was surprised to see the bartender still standing directly in front of him.

"Well, whatcha think?"

"It's good. Hits the spot," Ryan said.

"Alright! You want to settle up or should I start a tab?"

"I'll charge it to my room, four-thirty-two." Ryan closed his eyes and took another sip.

"Got it! I'm gonna grab another bucket of ice. Be right back."

Ryan was thankful to be on his own once again. It didn't matter how friendly anyone was to him, he wasn't in the mood. The bar was dreary, but comforting. It didn't expect anything out of him, and Ryan wasn't expecting anything back. They made a perfect pair.

The first lie had come so effortlessly. It had taken him by surprise. He couldn't believe what a cornerstone that first one had become. It was the foundation for one of the most stupid, idiotic messes he had ever gotten himself into. And now look where he was. He'd gone past the point of return.

"No matter what you say, it's going to be too little, too late. If it were me, I'd fucking rip your balls off."

Wyatt was such a great guy. There had been a connection, something Ryan couldn't explain, from the moment their eyes first met. The physical attraction was immediate, and once he'd gotten a flavor of Wyatt's personality, he was hooked. It had nothing to do with Wyatt being famous. Oh fuck, the man could dance. Could anyone be that talented? Ryan took another sip of his beer and closed his eyes. There had to be a way out of this.

The sound of footsteps from behind brought Ryan out of his trance. A well-dressed older gentleman took a seat several down from him. Ryan noticed the large, jeweled rings on both of his hands. His body tensed as he waited for the inevitable. *I must be a fucking troll magnet. Look all you want, buddy, but it ain't gonna happen.*

"Anyone around here resemble a bartender?" the man asked.

"He's around. He went for more ice." Ryan hoped his answer would suffice. The beer tasted good, and for now, his headache was manageable. If he was forced into engaging in a conversation, he'd have to think about heading back to his room. He took another sip, careful to avoid giving off any signals he was open to conversation. A sliver of tension lifted when he saw the bartender emerge from the backroom with another bucket of ice.

Ryan eased back onto his chair. What sense did it make to run through his options again? There wouldn't be any new changes in the lineup. What he should be concentrating on was how he was going to break the truth to Wyatt. Was there any chance in hell Wyatt might be forgiving?

"Nothing ever tastes as good as the evening's first Martini. And trust me, this one has been well earned."

Ryan looked over as the man sipped from the stemmed glass and then returned it to the cushion of its napkin without spilling a drop.

"You know, I'm no expert, but from the looks of it, you've either lost in love, lost your job, or you're just plain sad you're sitting in this godforsaken hotel bar with an old-timer like me and not out somewhere else revving your engine. Am I right?"

Here we go. Ryan reached for his glass and downed a third of it as he contemplated how to not answer. He didn't want to be rude. The guy seemed nice enough, but he sure as hell didn't feel like talking.

"I'm a pretty good listener. You should give it a shot. After I'm finished with this one," the man pointed to his drink, "I'm going to order another, and then I'm going to grab some dinner before I go up to my room and finish my invoices. It never changes. This is what I do three nights out of the week when I'm on the road. The other four nights I'm back home, working from the office. That's my story. You've heard enough, I'm sure. I'm in listening mode now, if you feel like it."

Ryan couldn't help smiling. This guy hadn't wasted a word. He signaled the bartender for a refill.

"I've still got a job," Ryan said, managing a slight grin.

"Ah, so there's somebody out there getting in your way. I'm only halfway through my first, if you care to elaborate." The guy pointed again to his glass and gave Ryan a wink.

Go for it. You've got nothing to lose.

Ryan downed the last from his glass just as its replacement was set down.

"I'm a lying sack of shit. I never intended to be a liar, but unfortunately, it turns out I have a talent for it."

"You mean you told a lie, and then you told another lie, and now you're up to your elbows in alligators, right?"

The analogy took Ryan from a smile to a light chuckle. "I've never heard that one. I like it."

"You have to be a member of AARP to get the list."

Ryan chuckled, although he had no idea what AARP was.

"So you lied," the gentleman continued after a moment. Ryan was sure the old gent was investing some serious thought toward a solution to his dilemma, "and now, you've painted yourself into a corner. Okay, not the best place to be in, but not the worst either. Can I ask you a question?"

"Sure." Ryan was surprised at how good this felt. It felt good to share his misery. *This feels like I'm sitting across from a shrink.*

"Did you lie to cover up something bad, something mean or awful you've done to this person?"

Ryan thought for a second and then said, "Naw, nothing like that." There was an unexpected positive. He didn't purposely set out to be mean-spirited or hurtful. It was something at least.

"The mean lies, those are hard to extricate yourself from. The other lies, the little ones people tell for no reason, those are much easier to fix."

The man reached for his swizzle stick and bit off the olive. "Another, please," he said, waving at the bartender, who was in the corner looking up at the basketball game on television.

"Look, let's cut to the chase. About the lie or lies, assuming you have a couple here to deal with. I'm confident you only have one choice to make at this point."

"I know what you're going to say. I keep coming back to that one too," Ryan said, his smile fading. "You're going to tell me I have to confess. I have to tell the truth. I was hoping for something a little more creative."

Ryan was surprised he wasn't more bummed out with the outcome of their discussion. In a way, it was liberating to admit out loud what he already knew.

"You got it. Now I'm not a prophet, so I'm not about to even discuss the odds with you that once you tell the truth, you're going to get out of this mess. I will tell you, however, and I know this from experience, you've got no other choice unless you want to keep on walking and never look back. I guess that's the question you're going to have to ask yourself."

"Thank you. I'm Ryan, by the way." Ryan stood and leaned over to the man and shook his hand.

"Pleased to meet you, Ryan, I'm Harold."

Ryan spent the next few minutes shooting the breeze with Harold as he nursed his beer. The two left the bar together, and before parting ways, Ryan once again thanked him.

"Listen, Harold, thanks again for turning a really shitty night into a nice time. You really did help. Best of luck!"

"Don't mention it."

Walking back to his room, Ryan was amazed to notice his headache had, at least for the moment, vanished.

Chapter 10

WYATT parked as close as he could to the terminal and walked to the baggage claim area where he had agreed to meet his parents. Checking the large built-in arrival screen, he was relieved to see Flight Z417, arriving from Minneapolis, was on time. He hadn't even thought to check on the flight before leaving.

With less than fifteen minutes to kill before his parents' plane landed, Wyatt took a seat on a bench and began observing the activity around him. Over to his left, he watched with wonder as a young mother tried to keep her two small sons corralled until their luggage came down the chute. Where had they arrived from? What was their story?

She looks like she was rolled somewhere between seat 57D and the baggage area. I could never handle traveling with kids. Absolutely not!

All of a sudden he had it, her whole story. The woman and her kids had left her husband of almost eight years, and they were coming home to spend time with her parents until they could regroup. She had caught her husband, a handsome doctor in the city, screwing one of his patients. Although he had pleaded for a second chance, she told him no. He was scum, she had screamed in his face, and while he was out of the house, grabbed the kids, a few handfuls of clothing, and marched right out of his life, leaving him alone to wallow in disgrace.

Good for her! Once a pig, always a pig.

Soon the light on the carousel began flashing, followed by a loud buzz. Bags began to tumble down onto the rotating conveyer belt. It wasn't long before they spotted their luggage. He watched as Mom and her big rolling bag led the way toward the exit. The two boys and their smaller versions followed close behind.

I wonder how Ryan feels about having kids?

Wyatt hoped the best for Mom as he watched them head out the door.

There was a pop machine at the far end of the baggage area. He was kind of thirsty, but was it worth the walk all the way down and back? While he was making up his mind, a couple of handsome young men convinced him to stay put.

Now what could these guys be up to?

Wyatt sensed a comfortable, relaxed nature in how the men interacted with each other. Was it because of the way they were dressed? Possibly. Maybe they were business partners, business travelers.

No, that's not it. It's the way they look at each other. They're a couple. Had they just been on vacation? *Look, it's me and Ryan returning from a week in Paris.* No, that wasn't it. They looked exhausted.

And now they're looking at me, looking at them.

Wyatt casually turned away. Alex and Stephen were their names, he decided. But it was Stephen with a P, he was sure, partly because he had always preferred that spelling. He loved the sound of those names together. Alex and Stephen. Maybe someday he would create a musical comedy called Alex and Stephen.

Loud coughing from behind distracted him. Wyatt turned around to watch a heavyset woman dressed from head to toe in baggy denim waddle past him. She reeked of cigarettes. *Enjoy your time here, honey. You ain't got long if you keep poisoning yourself like that.*

Christ, the only person who looks happy around here is the nun waiting for her luggage over at the next carousel.

She looked a little too happy. Who could blame her? Somehow, she'd found a way to break out of the convent. Chances are, she wasn't wearing any underwear either. Wyatt laughed out loud when the nun looked in his direction and smiled.

Cautiously, he stole another glance in the direction of Alex and Stephen.

Why were they at the Bangor airport in the middle of the day on a Friday? Hmm... I know, I know!

Wyatt tapped his foot as his mind whirled into action. Alex, a bartender at the local gay watering hole, met Stephen during Stephen's final year of graduate school at the University of Maine. Alex had tried school, but it wasn't for him. He liked to write, but at this point in his life, wasn't sure what he wanted to do. With his good looks, tending bar earned him a respectable living. Stephen was dirt-poor and would occasionally treat himself to a night out, choosing Alex's bar to hang and relax after finals, or some other intense period of school. Stephen was shy and always came into the bar alone. Alex thought he was adorable, in that preppy, graduate student way and started picking up his drinks whenever he would pop in. Before long, they were fucking and fucking hard. Hard fucking!

Wyatt smiled. Before he was caught looking like a stalker, he turned away. *The younger guy looks like Ryan. Well, he has Ryan's bedroom eyes. I'll stop there. Nobody looks as hot as Ryan. Are they capable of hard fucking?*

Wyatt nonchalantly looked their direction to confirm they had hard fucking capabilities.

Oh sure they do. Get a couple of glasses of wine in the tall guy, and he'll have his ass in the air faster than you can Google butt plug.

Wyatt checked his watch. There were still a couple of minutes to go before his parent's plane would land.

Where was I?

After graduate school was over....

What did Stephen graduate in... engineering? That's it!

Engineering, a manly, hard-fucking business. After graduate school was over, Stephen accepted a position with a large engineering firm in... oh what the hell, Boston. Alex quit his job and they moved in together. They had a great life in Boston, meeting friends together, enjoying the culture of the big city, and of course, fucking hard whenever possible. Really hard fucking. Alex eventually took a job as a librarian.

Wait... was that right? Sure... that works.

Librarians could be very sexy in a quiet, confident way. Life for Alex and Stephen went along smoothly. Reading, designing big buildings, and hard fucking until Stephen got a call in the middle of the night.

Oh, this is really good!

Stephen's mother was involved in a tragic car accident. Since Stephen's father had flown the coop when he was only seven years old, after the accident it was left up to her only son to sell her house of thirty years and move her into an assisted care facility. Alex and Stephen had just finished this massive project, which had put their lives—and for the most part, their hard fucking—on hold for several weeks. Finally they were headed....

"Wyatt honey!"

Wyatt turned away from Alex and Stephen to see his mother Mindy storming down the corridor toward him in a sensible floral print dress and flats. His father, Ted, dressed in khakis and a polo shirt, followed several paces behind. The story of his life, Wyatt thought as he jumped up to greet them.

"Hi, you guys! Oh it's so nice to see you! I'm so glad you could come!" Wyatt hugged and kissed his mother. "Dad, it's great to see you. You look good." Wyatt hugged and kissed his dad.

"You know, I try. Your mother keeps me on my toes," Ted said, with a familiarity that made Wyatt smile.

They celebrated their togetherness with an awkward group hug. Wyatt fought back the urge to introduce them to Stephen and Alex, whom by now, he felt like he had known forever. The nun was trouble. There would be no heartfelt introduction for her.

The wait for his parent's luggage was short. Wyatt snared the largest piece and his father followed several paces behind, hauling a matching companion piece.

"What are you driving these days?" his dad asked from a few paces behind as they left the terminal and headed out into the parking lot.

"Nothing but the best for you two," Wyatt said, suppressing a snicker as he stopped in front of Murphy's Jeep.

"Oh my," Mindy said. "Where did this come from?"

Wyatt detected a slight uneasiness in his mother's voice. He knew just how to handle it.

"It's Murphy's. It's what he drives when he stays here."

"Oh, I love it," Mindy said.

Of course you do! If I had shown up with a camel that Murphy insisted you ride bareback, you'd love that too! Geez, give me a break!

"Here Dad, let me do that," Wyatt said as he took his father's bag and piled it into the back of the Jeep.

"Oh my, this is so exciting," Mindy said as Wyatt helped her up into her seat. His dad took his assumed place in the back.

The conversation was lively driving back to the house. Mindy couldn't get over how beautiful it was. Each bend in the road evoked a similar comment on how lush it was compared to back home.

"The Gordons next door send their love. I can't believe how lush it is." Mindy loved going places and Wyatt loved how she was enjoying herself.

"Oh, say hi back for me. Is Nancy Gordon still planning on going to NYU next year?" Wyatt hoped she wasn't. The last thing on earth he wanted was to be saddled with the responsibility of looking out for her. The Gordons were good family friends, and there would be no getting out of it if that was her plan.

"Well, I don't think there's much chance of that happening," Mindy said, adding in a whisper, "Dale's business isn't doing very well. She'd have to have a pretty good scholarship if she was still planning on going. Gee… there's so many trees."

Praise the Lord!

"Nobody's buying cars these days," Ted piped in from the back seat. "I'm sure as hell glad I'm retired. Crazy time to be doing business."

"Dad, how's Uncle Simon's pacemaker working out?" *This should be good.*

"Oh for Christ's sake, he'll live to be a hundred. Now he's going to Mayo because he thinks his goddamn feet are swelling and he's going to have to have his foot amputated. I think they otta amputate his head and be done with it."

"Ted, how can you say such a thing?" Mindy snapped. "He's your brother. Hypochondria is a disease, you know. So many shades of green... I've never seen anything like it."

"So, what's this place like Murphy's got? I bet it's pretty impressive," Ted asked after a sufficient amount of time had lapsed after his comment about Simon.

Murphy held a post higher than any other mortal in his parents' eyes.

"Well, you're just about to find out." Wyatt pulled off the highway and onto the dirt road leading back to the house.

"Oh my goodness," Mindy giggled as she bounced back and forth in her seat. "It's as green as all get-out here too."

Wyatt eased the Jeep around the last curve. "Well, we're here!"

"Is this really Murphy's place?" Mindy asked with a nervous twitter as Wyatt pulled up to the back door.

This is great. Mom has the same reaction I did when I first saw the place from the outside.

"Yep! This is it. The outhouse is in the back so it can drain right into the water."

Wyatt hopped out of the Jeep and went around back to haul out the luggage. He couldn't resist the chance to tease. Deep down, it was the payoff for playing second fiddle to the god named Murphy.

"Pretty nifty, huh?" Wyatt asked when they had made their way inside the house. Both parents had nothing but oohs and awws as he took them on a tour of the house. He could see how happy they were to be here, and that made him happy. He couldn't wait to take them on the sightseeing adventures he had planned.

Even with all the distraction and activity over the last couple of days, Ryan was never far from Wyatt's thoughts. Wyatt wished like mad he was there with them as they all sat down to dinner. According to his voicemail, Ryan would be back tomorrow.

"So, Wyatt announced as he navigated a fork full of salad to his mouth, "I have an announcement to make."

"Oh Wyatt, is it about the movie? Have you decided whose going to play the lead yet? I'm just dying to know. It's Meryl, isn't it? Oh please tell me it's going to be Meryl. She would be so perfect."

"Mom, I'm not sure Meryl would be the best choice. Remember, this is a dancing role."

"Mindy, let the boy talk, for Christ's sake." This was a constant problem for his dad, who disliked anyone interrupting or preventing the news from flowing from one source to the other.

Mindy didn't honor her husband with a reply, but simply bit her lip and gave him that disappointed look she had honed to perfection over the years. Wyatt had secretly stolen her look and had used it to great effect on many occasions.

"This isn't about the movie, Mom. It's about someone I've met. His name is Ryan. He's in Boston right now, registering for school." Wyatt paused as he watched his parent's faces for a reaction. They appeared stunned.

"Registering for school?" his father asked after they had all sat in silence for what seemed to Wyatt like a decade. "That means he's pretty young then."

"Oh, he's in graduate school," Wyatt added, understanding his father's concern. After all, registering for college as a freshman would put many more years between them than already existed.

Wyatt could tell by the expression on his face, his father wasn't much interested in hearing more. "Graduate school, I see. So… any chance Murphy might show up during the week?"

Wyatt shook his head in response. He knew if he vocalized his feelings, he'd end up putting much more emotion into his response than was needed.

"We really miss seeing him."

"I know you do, Dad." Unable to mask his disappointment in his parent's reaction to the news about Ryan, Wyatt concentrated on his plate, reorganizing the arrangement of food groups with his fork.

"Well," his mother forged on with considerable effort, "when can we meet him? This… Ryan."

"He's flying back tomorrow. He'll be here sometime in the afternoon." Wyatt forced himself to nibble on his food before deciding how to segue from Ryan into more amicable territory.

"Mom, I have a favor to ask." Wyatt applied his trademark "oh pretty please" look. "Can I coax you into making your killer lasagna for dinner tomorrow night? I think I have all the ingredients you need."

She didn't disappoint. It was as if someone had just informed her that she had won the lottery. "Oh honey, I love to cook for you, you know that. Tomorrow you can show me what you have for ingredients and if we're missing anything, we can send your father out for it."

Ah, the payback. There it was. His father would be tasked with running out if needed because of his snippy remark earlier. There was always a payback, never spiteful or mean, but there was always some form of retribution and it usually came in the way of an additional chore or responsibility. Growing up, Wyatt had spent time visiting his grandmother in the nursing home, shopping for produce at the local farmer's market, and accompanying his mother on furniture-buying trips, just to name a few, all as part of his penance for something he had said. Her strategy was brilliant.

"You didn't forget the noodles, did you?"

The table was quiet for a brief moment until both Wyatt and his father realized they had just witnessed one of Mindy's rare attempts at humor. Wyatt exploded in laughter first, followed by his father and finally his mother, who always seemed so surprised at what she had triggered. Wyatt never wanted to know if she really had no idea how funny she could be, or if she did it on purpose. It was part of her charm.

Despite their reluctance to put Murphy on the back burner, they were the very best parents in the world and he loved them to death. He knew Ryan would feel comfortable and enjoy them as well, and as far his parents accepting Ryan, well, how could they not? Ryan was a charmer.

WYATT stretched his arms out wide, and releasing an enormous yawn, he stumbled out of the bedroom to the kitchen. The sun was already beginning to creep over the trees.

What time was it?

The clock on the microwave display read 8:12. Wow, he had really slept in. Neither he nor his parents had wanted to give up on their first evening together. After dinner, they retreated to the porch, where they talked and listened to the nighttime sounds coming from the cove. It had been a beautiful evening and he had used the opportunity to tell his parents more about Ryan. He loved how he could share his thoughts and feelings with them. Their style of parenting had more to do with patience. To sit back and allow life to happen. Wyatt respected them for this and hoped he had acquired similar qualities. He was sure he had not, but would continue to strive in that direction. It was well past midnight by the time they had emptied their glasses and cleaned up the porch.

Still half asleep, he opened a cupboard and began to contemplate the task of making coffee.

"Morning, sport! You didn't tell me this was going to be a clothing-optional vacation."

Startled, Wyatt whirled around to see his dad enter the kitchen, looking understandably perplexed. "Dad! Geez! Shit! Sorry!"

Bolting from the kitchen at the speed of light, he hustled back to his bedroom, where he quickly threw on a pair of shorts and stood panting, his face burning with embarrassment. Pausing a minute to catch his breath, a quick glance in the mirror confirmed how he felt. His face was as red as an apple.

Wyatt had never been comfortable naked around his father. For as long as he could remember, he'd felt uncomfortable naked in front of him. With anyone. Well, until he hooked up with Murphy, who broke him of his shyness.

Thankfully it was Dad that walked in on me. Thank you, thank you, thank you a hundred times it was Dad and not Mom. Oh my god, I would have died if it had been Mom. Holy crap! The thought of his mother seeing him naked caused a shiver to rock through his body.

It's not because he didn't feel comfortable with his body. It wasn't that at all. He knew he was in good shape, and for some time he had been aware that, in matters of most importance, he measured up far better than most. No, he had nothing to be ashamed of there. *They're my parents for God's sake!*

"Geez Dad," Wyatt said sheepishly as he reentered the kitchen. "Sorry about that. I wake up and the first thing I do is wander out here for some tea before heading out to the cove for a swim. That's pretty much how my mornings have started since I arrived. It's so private here. I haven't been wearing clothes much." He forced himself to make eye contact with his dad, but no matter how hard he tried, traces of his embarrassment still lingered.

"This is probably too much information for you, but I guess I owe you one. Your mother and I have been doing the same thing lately. It's kind of fun. Sexy too, if you know what I mean," his dad added with a devilish display of rapid eyebrow-rising.

Yikes! There's a visual he needed like a hole in the head. "You're right about that one Dad, way more than I needed to know." He and his dad chuckled as Wyatt came up to his father and put his arm around him. "I'm so glad you and Mom are here. I miss you so, but my schedule, you know...."

"We miss you too," his dad said, returning the embrace, "but we understand. The last thing we want to do is stand in the way of you achieving your goals. Besides, we know where to find you, and if we don't...."

"We call Murphy," they both said in unison, laughing at how obvious it was.

And that's what they did. Both parents considered Murphy one of their own. It wasn't out of the ordinary for them to call him for an update, or for Murphy to pick up the phone on his own and chat them up. In fact, there had been times when Wyatt found out information from Murphy regarding his family, which either comforted him or pissed him off, depending on the nature of the news.

"Hey, Dad, feel like joining me for a swim in the cove this morning?" Wyatt asked as he pulled out Murphy's elaborate coffee contraption from one of the shelves below the counter. "If you didn't bring a suit, I know Murph has a bunch of styles and colors to select from."

"How cold is the water?" his dad asked as he watched his son fill the coffeemaker with beans.

"Depends. Sometimes it's on the cool side, sometimes it's warm. Yesterday it was very warm. Just beautiful."

"I'm pretty sure your mom packed a suit. If not, I'll give you a shout. I better go check on her to make sure she didn't sneak back into bed. Last night was the latest she'd been up in at least a year. Keep moving along with the coffee. We both could use a little of that."

Wyatt struggled with the coffeemaker but got it running after realizing he had to grind the beans first. *What a mess! I'll stick with a tea bag any day.*

When he was sure the whole process was underway, he went back into the bedroom and dug out a pair of Murphy's baggy swimming trunks. He couldn't suppress a chuckle at the thought of his dad walking in on him naked.

He returned to find both his mom and dad seated at the counter. His mom had already showered and had on a pastel pantsuit displaying a North woods theme Wyatt was sure had been purchased special for this trip. His dad, who still sported the whitest legs on the planet, had on plaid swimming trunks. Not unlike his own.

"Very stylin' Dad." Wyatt strolled over to his mother and planted a loud good morning smooch on her cheek. "You'll dazzle the sharks in that number," he joked.

"Sharks? You're kidding, right?" A real look of horror crossed his father's face.

"Yes! I'm kidding," Wyatt promised with a wink.

Why did I just say that? You idiot! You know better and besides, who's the scaredy-cat when it comes to sharks?

Eager to make amends for his thoughtlessness, he asked his dad, "Do you think there would be any chance in hell I would get into water if I thought I was sharing it with a shark? Come on, Dad. Jaws, when I was finally allowed to see it,"—Wyatt couldn't resist a look over to his mother, who had been the official censor when he was growing up—"scared the bejesus out of me. Now that I think about it," he added, "I've never noticed any fish when I've swam. Well, you'll see some minnows in the shallows. Little guys, that's about it."

"Wyatt honey," his mom said, getting up from her stool and pouring a cup of coffee, "why don't you show me what you picked up for lasagna? I can start organizing while you and your dad swim."

While Mindy poured her husband a cup of coffee, Wyatt dug out the lasagna ingredients from the refrigerator.

Did I forget the ricotta cheese?

After taking a second look, he located it in the back. Mindy spied over his shoulder as he spread the ingredients out on the counter.

"Why, my lord, I think you did exactly right. How did you ever remember what all went into it," she wondered out loud. "Wait! Eggs, that's the one thing I don't see. Eggs, and maybe some parsley."

Wyatt went back to the fridge and produced a half carton of eggs. "No parsley, Mom, sorry," he informed her.

"That's okay, sugar, parsley we can work around. You boys go swimming now and let me get acquainted with Murphy's kitchen. Knowing the boy as well as I do, I'm sure he's got it very well organized. I'll have some breakfast ready for you when you get back."

That was their cue. They knew better than to hang around. The kitchen had always been Mindy's domain, and unless you were helping, she preferred her privacy.

Wyatt and his dad headed to the beach. It had been a long time since Wyatt had seen his father in a bathing suit. The old man was holding up pretty damn well.

Wyatt was pleased; the water in the cove was like the day before, warm. His father had been a regular swimmer at the local YMCA, but that had been years ago and he no longer swam with any regularity. Wyatt adjusted his powerful stroke to swim alongside his father. Together, they zigzagged back and forth until his dad became noticeably tired.

Wyatt broke out of his lap and guided them back onto shore. The midsummer sun evaporated the water from their bodies. He used this opportunity to inquire about his mother, who looked fabulous.

"So Dad, tell me, how's Mom been doing lately? She still involved with all those groups, church, book club, and the garden stuff?"

"Oh hell, yeah," his dad confirmed. "If anything, it's gotten worse. Last week, she asked me if I thought we could handle adopting a couple of golden retrievers. Seems one of her girlfriends told her about this group that saves dogs from going to the pound. Christ, I told her, why not bring in some chimpanzees and a few horses too. We can open our own zoo."

This made Wyatt laugh. His dad's response had been a classic. The type of response he had heard all his life from his father. He could be sarcastic as hell, but if Mindy had insisted they take in the dogs, he'd have dog-walking on his list of daily chores. It was clear who wore the pants in his family.

"Well, she looks good. She looks happy," Wyatt offered. "I don't suppose she's ever going to lose the need to be joining things. She's sure helped a lot of people over the years. I'm proud of her for all the volunteering she does. Both of you—you're almost as involved as she is but you won't admit it."

"Oh, don't get me wrong, son, I'm still proud as can be she married a hooligan like me. Hell, most people these days don't give a rat's butt about anyone else but themselves. It's terrible to say, but when she kicks the bucket, and I hope it isn't for a hundred years, the entire town's going to turn out. She's got friends everywhere. Oh, and everyone always asks about you too. You're a celebrity to those folks back there."

"I've been very lucky, Dad," Wyatt admitted.

"Listen son," Ted said as he used his towel to dry off his hair. "I could lie and tell you that your mother wanted me to ask you this, but I'm not going to lie to you."

"You can ask me anything, you know that." The muscles in Wyatt's neck began to tense up. He was sure he knew what his father was going to ask.

"We love you so much, your mother and I, and we want to make sure you're happy. This Ryan fella... I mean, do you think...."

"Come on, Dad, we've been through this one before. What you want to ask is do I think there's a chance Murphy and I could get back together, as a couple."

"You guys made such a great team," Ted said, patting Wyatt on the shoulder.

"Well, we still are a team. Maybe more than we've ever been," Wyatt assured his father once again. "Look, I love Murphy and I always will. I know he loves me. He's the brother I never had. Wait...." Wyatt took a second to think about what he was going to say next. Even though he understood his parents' concern, he was growing tired of this. They needed to move on too.

"Dad, I need for you and Mom to give this new guy a chance. He's something special and I'm falling in love with him. If this helps you any, Murphy would approve. I know he would."

Wyatt searched his father's face to see if what he said had registered. A flock of gulls squawked and they both looked up as they passed over, landing in the middle of the cove.

"I hear you," Ted said, looking back at his son. "We get set in our ways sometimes and it gets worse the older you get. Your happiness is what counts. If this Ryan makes you happy, then we'll be happy. I'll set your mother straight when the time is right."

"Thanks, Dad. Before we go in, let me ask, you doing okay?"

"Oh sure. I'm slowing down some. Don't seem to have the energy I once had. My doctor tells me I'm in good shape, though. I guess I need to come to terms with growing older is all. Happens to everyone, so brace yourself—although I have to say, you look great. I don't think I've ever seen you look healthier." Changing the subject wasn't unusual for Ted. He never wanted to spend much time on himself, talking about himself.

Wyatt shot his dad a puzzled look as they approached the porch steps. Mindy, who they had left all alone in the kitchen, was chatting up a storm with someone. Wyatt squealed with delight when he spotted Ryan hunkering over the counter, lining a casserole dish with lasagna noodles.

"So the sharks didn't get you after all," Mindy joked, flavoring her voice with mock disappointment.

"Hey handsome," Wyatt hollered, bolting over to Ryan and throwing his arms around his new beau.

"I missed you powerful bad," Ryan laughed as he returned the hug and planted a loud smack on Wyatt's cheek.

"Welcome to the Stark Lasagna Factory," Wyatt joked, gesturing around the kitchen. "I see you've already met Mindy the foreman. I'd like to introduce you to the CEO, my father, Ted Stark. Dad, meet Ryan Taylor."

"A pleasure to meet you, Ryan. Our boy hasn't stopped talking about you since we arrived." Ted stepped forward and pumped Ryan's hand.

"Before you think I'm some kind of slave driver," Mindy chirped in, "it was Ryan who offered to help me. I told him to consider this Lasagna 101." Another joke from Mom, Wyatt observed. She's on a real roll this trip.

"I finished all my stuff yesterday afternoon and found an earlier flight. I couldn't wait to get back here."

Wyatt was surprised to hear Ryan had flown to Boston. For some reason, he had it in his mind he was driving. Oh well, he had his wires crossed, as usual.

"Well, I'm sure you boys have plenty to talk about. You leave Dad and I here in the kitchen to finish up. We'll join you out on the porch when we're done."

"Oh gosh, no," Ryan protested as he sat back on his stool. "I wouldn't miss this opportunity for the world. Lasagna is one of my favorites and my mother never seemed to get the hang of it. Wyatt, you don't mind if I help, do you? That is, if your mother can put up with me for a while longer."

It was Mindy's turn to blush. Ryan had just made her day. Imagine, a young, handsome man wanting to spend time with her in the kitchen. She was in paradise.

"Let me tell you, Ryan, you'll be twice the help I'd ever manage to squeeze out of these two," she twittered, shoving her mixing bowl closer to her new pal, who had resumed his noodle responsibilities.

"Well, how about this?" Wyatt suggested. "When you're all done with Lasagna 101, perhaps we can talk Ryan into being our tour guide for the rest of the day. There's tons of beautiful areas close by. We can grab lunch at one of the local diners.

"I'd be honored," Ryan chirped. "Oh… I've got the perfect place to take you for lunch. We can tour a couple of the inlets close by too. You'll get a flavor of the area."

Wyatt couldn't contain his happiness. How terrific it felt having someone like Ryan here with his parents. Mindy was vibrating, she was so excited at the prospect of spending the day sightseeing. What a wonderful tableau; his mom and Ryan, already thick as thieves, and his father, comfortable as always traveling through life in the backseat. Everyone was so happy and he was the happiest of them all.

He and his dad enjoyed a cup of coffee out on the porch after showering. Soon they were joined by Mindy and Ryan, who had finished constructing the lasagna.

"It sure was nice having a helper who jumps right in there," Mindy said, looking over to Ryan with a smile. "You'd better be careful, Wyatt," she cautioned, "I might have to take him home with me."

"Oh no you don't," Wyatt said, walking over and putting his arm around Ryan. "He's all mine."

"Hey, let's go sightseeing," Ryan said planting a kiss on Wyatt's cheek. "Is everyone ready?"

Ryan, acting as if he had been a family friend for years instead of merely hours, assumed the role of host and tour guide with ease. Wyatt, who typically had issues relinquishing control in any situation, felt calmed by Ryan's take-charge manner. Having Ryan's comfortable SUV to tour around instead of Murphy's Jeep was another plus. Not wanting to disturb their newly formed bond, Mindy sat up front with Ryan. Wyatt and his father took their seats in back.

Dense canopies of trees covered narrow country roads as they toured some of the quaint inlets along the coast. Wyatt fought the urge to laugh out loud at his mother, who had fallen into a pattern of repeating almost every word of Ryan's tour narration. It was more comical than irritating.

"The mayor of this little village," Ryan informed them, "recently drowned hauling up lobster pots in the middle of the night. His body washed up on shore several days after he was reported missing."

"Drowned hauling up lobster pots in the middle of the night," Mindy echoed. "Oh my," she improvised, wrapping her observation up with, "washed up on shore several days after he was missing. Oh my, can you imagine?"

Wyatt and Ryan would laugh about this later, he was sure. It was possible Ryan was baiting her for his own enjoyment, making it all the more funny.

Rounding a bend and crossing yet another single-lane bridge, Ryan pulled the car into the parking lot of Sammy's Seaside Snack Shack, a little lobster hut like scores of others dotting the coast.

"You've got to try the local specialty everyone around here calls a lobster roll," Ryan suggested after putting the car in park.

"The local specialty around here is called a lobster roll," Mindy repeated while at the same time opening her car door and hopping out excitedly.

"Nobody makes 'em better than they do here at Sammy's. Freshest you'll find anywhere," Ryan quipped like a used car salesman making his pitch.

Each of them took Ryan's recommendation and returned from the order window with a gigantic lobster roll loaded onto a double paper plate and a huge plastic glass filled with iced tea. Ryan guided them to a seating area in back of the shack overlooking a bay filled with colored markers.

"Oh my, aren't those pretty," Mindy commented at all the buoys in the bay as they took their seats at the picnic table.

"Those are markers for the lobster pots." Ryan informed them, pointing out to the bay. Before Mindy had a chance to repeat, he added, "Each lobster pot has its own marker. The different color combinations are registered and belong exclusively to an individual or company. That's how everyone keeps from mixing up each other's pots." Ryan took the seat with his back to the water.

"You must have loved growing up here, Ryan," Mindy said before taking an ample bite of her sandwich. "Oh my... Ted... you're just gonna die when you taste this. It's fabulous."

Wyatt smiled over at his parents, who truly seemed to be enjoying themselves. Reaching down under the table, he squeezed Ryan's hand. Ryan squeezed back and winked knowingly. Wyatt had to fight to keep his emotions in check. This whole visit with his parents, and having Ryan here, was making him emotional. He was cry-happy.

Thank you, Ryan, for being you. They're falling in love with you too.

Without any instruction from Wyatt, Ryan seemed to understand what kind of day this would be. He was making Mindy and Ted feel special, which of course, they were.

After lunch, they continued their drive along the coast. Now and then, Ryan would stop at an antique store or local shop to break up the time in the car. On the very first of such stops, Mindy insisted on buying "her boys," as she was now calling the three men along with her, T-shirts displaying large red lobsters waving from the inside of a boiling pot.

Are lobsters really that stupid?

"What the hell are we going to do with that?" Ted asked in alarm at another stop. Wyatt looked over to see Mindy holding an old wooden oar.

"Well I thought it might look good out in the screened porch back home. We could start a nautical theme out there, Dad."

Ted just shook his head and walked away. Arguing at this point would be senseless.

"I guess… this would be a nightmare to take back on the plane. Shoot… I'd better pass." Mindy never gave up easily on one of her ideas. To leave the oar behind had been an extraordinary struggle between want and plain old practicality.

Sensing his mother's disappointment, Wyatt stepped up and offered, "No need to think that way, Mom, I can have anything you want shipped back for you. If you want the oar, it's yours."

This sent his father fleeing to the opposite side of the shop in disgust. In the end, Mindy settled for a brass clock shaped like a clam.

It was going on late afternoon when Ryan turned off of the highway and onto the road leading back to the house. Silent contentment had now replaced the lively banter. Ted and Mindy were snuggled together in the back seat like teenagers when Ryan pulled the car up in front of the house.

"I'm going to run home for a minute before dinner," Ryan said as he watched everyone stumble out of the car.

"You're coming back to spend the night, I hope?" Mindy asked, turning and patting Ryan on the arm through the open car window.

"I wouldn't miss it for the world," Ryan assured her.

"I'll wait until you get back before I stick the lasagna in the oven," she promised. "So hurry back!"

"See you sooner than later," Wyatt said, leaning forward and giving Ryan a smooch.

"I'll only be a minute. I need to check in with the parents. Whatever you have planned, I should be able to work around it. I love your parents," Ryan whispered. "You're so much like your mother. It cracks me up."

"What?" Wyatt asked, feigning shock. He knew Ryan was right. Before following his parents into the house, he turned and mouthed an oversized "Thank you" as Ryan smiled and pulled away.

As soon as they were inside, his parents retreated to their end of the house to regroup. Wyatt wouldn't have been surprised if it was nap-time. It had already been a very full day and after being up so late last night, he expected them to seek out some downtime.

Turned out he was wrong. Wyatt had just sat down on the porch with a glass of wine when they both came back to join him. He ran back to the kitchen and grabbed a wineglass for his mother, a beer for his dad, and a small plate of cheese and crackers. Music floated out from the house as the three sat looking out on the cove.

"Ryan's a real nice guy, Wyatt," his father offered, reaching down and snagging a cracker and some cheese. "Have you guys talked about how you're going to operate apart? He's going to school in Boston, right?"

This was a conversation Wyatt needed to have very soon with Ryan. He didn't doubt Ryan would follow through with attending school. He had accepted this. He needed to discuss expectations, how each envisioned this relationship progressing. He was curious what a relationship meant to Ryan. How were they going to work out time together when they were forced apart? With the movie cranking up very soon, life would be crazy. In his mind, he tried to picture Ryan's life at school. He suspected it would be crazy too, what with all the necessary studying, not to mention all the papers and tests. Somehow though, they would make it all work. He felt confident about this. Hopefully, at some point, their lives would weave together. The distance they both had to deal with would be eliminated. For one of the first times in his life, Wyatt prepared himself to wait for something he wanted. He needed to be patient with this one. Ryan was worth the wait and he deserved Wyatt's respect.

"Truthfully Dad, we haven't talked about that one yet," Wyatt confessed. "Of course I need to get this movie off the ground and out of my hair. Murphy tells me we are talking about a couple of years before it's all said and done. I'll be more than ready for a break after that."

Wyatt would have a hard time honoring his last comment. It was true, he'd be ready for a break, but finding the time to enjoy one was another thing altogether. After the movie, he would have to focus his energies on developing his next project, a stage musical based on teens coming of age. Wyatt had spent a considerable amount of time last winter working with a development group that was expecting, and even more importantly, relying on his involvement. An ever-popular topic these days, he had noticed most projects tackling this subject lacked real grit and honesty, which he would focus on. He'd even had a few opportunities this summer to make some of his own character sketches and to outline a few story ideas. He made a mental note to share his work with the rest of his collaborators before he left for the west coast. It was important for the development of a new project to proceed with everyone on the same page, working toward the same goals.

"Honey, I'm sure you two will work something out. I mean, he can't stay in school forever," Mindy added with a reassuring smile.

"Oh for Christ's sake, Mindy, the boy isn't going to stay in school forever. It takes longer these days, what with all the specializing and the competition," Ted barked out, attempting to set her straight.

You'll never learn, Dad.

Wyatt sat back and sipped his wine. He had a front-row seat for the Ted and Mindy show. He had always thought the majority of their disagreements could be avoided if they just listened to each other. They pretended to listen, but didn't.

"We'll figure something out, I'm sure. I'm just so happy you both like him. I mean, well... I haven't come right out and asked, but you do like him, right?" He had been so encouraged with how well his parents interacted with Ryan, and he with them, he had failed to officially get their blessing. He waited for their response.

"He's a darling," Mindy answered.

"He seems like a very nice young man," his dad added with a hint of fatherly caution. "I can't wait to get to know him better. I mean... I want to get to know him better."

"Oh, me too," his mother added, as if she hadn't said enough the first time. "I can't wait to spend more time in the kitchen with him. He's so helpful."

"He'd enjoy that, Mom, I'm sure he would." Wyatt had their blessing, no doubt about it. If they had disapproved of Ryan for any reason, they would have found a way to let him know. This was despite the fact, Wyatt could tell from the looks on their faces they both would have preferred this discussion be about Murphy. But they were trying, and this pleased him.

Antsy and unable to control her need to be productive, Mindy stood, patted her hand on the thighs of her pantsuit, and declared, "I'd better put the lasagna in or we'll be eating at midnight. Ryan should be here any minute, right, honey? I want him to have time to relax and enjoy a glass of wine, or two," she added with a giggle.

It was clear to both Wyatt and his dad that Mindy had her sights set on another glass of wine after she had her kitchen under control, which was paramount to her at the moment.

"I'm back!" Ryan announced, bounding out onto the porch, a bundle of hottie energy.

"Ryan! Perfect timing! I was just headed into the kitchen to put our creation in the oven." Mindy squeezed Ryan's arm as she made her way into the house. "Make sure you get this boy a glass of wine," she ordered over her shoulder.

"I'd be glad to help you, Mrs. Stark," Ryan hollered after her.

"You sit and don't ever call me Mrs. Stark again. I'm Mindy, or Mom," she hollered back.

"I'm Mr. Stark, though," Ted deadpanned, and after Wyatt shot him a concerned look, added a chuckle and a wink to reinforce the notion he was joking all along.

The conversation remained playful, and soon Mindy, empty wineglass in hand, waltzed back onto the porch, thirsty and hungry for chat. Wyatt filled her glass and she was out the gate. As a mother, it was her official duty, she would argue if pressed, to fill in any gaps Ryan might have regarding Wyatt's past. Nothing was sacred when she got herself wound up. His childhood. Dancing. His move to New York, and of course, his success. After all, her son had made her proud beyond her wildest dreams.

Wyatt blushed profusely and literally begged for her to stop, eliciting giggles from Ryan, who soaked it all up like a sponge. Ted chimed in occasionally, lest Ryan would come away with any doubt of how proud Dad was as well. They emptied a second bottle of wine before the aroma of lasagna began to make its way out onto the porch. Mindy excused herself and headed off to finalize dinner.

Tonight's meal, they decided, would be casual, eating at the counter in the kitchen. The house was filled with the powerful scent of garlic. Wyatt recalled how fond he had been of the smell, growing up. Lasagna, because of the work it took, was a special treat.

Responding to Mindy's vocal dinner bell, her boys entered the kitchen and took their seats.

"Anyone care for wine with dinner?" Wyatt asked.

"Me," Ryan said.

"Dad, you want wine?" Mindy asked.

"Nope! I'd like a glass of milk.

"Mindy?" Ryan asked.

Wyatt watched in fascination as his mother teetered on the fence. He knew she wanted to keep the buzz going, but he couldn't remember a time when she'd had "another" when Ted had passed.

"We have a big day tomorrow," she said after a tremendous internal battle. "Milk for me and Dad."

Wyatt opened a bottle of wine while Ryan poured milk for his parents.

"Yummy!" Wyatt said after he had taken a bite. He had been waiting all day for this. "Mom, thank you so much for making dinner."

"Excuse me," his mother corrected, wiping her mouth. "You better not forget to compliment my helper or you'll be going to bed without desert. Ryan was a huge help."

"Oh fuck...." With all the excitement, Wyatt had forgotten to make his cobbler.

"Excuse me," his mother said, disappointed by her son's language.

"I'm sorry," Wyatt apologized, embarrassed he'd dropped the f-bomb. "Chef Ryan," he corrected himself, "thank you for such a fabulous dinner."

"You're welcome… potty mouth," Ryan added with a smirk.

"I'm sorry, it's just that I had found this great recipe for blueberry cobbler and I forgot about making it."

"Blueberries and ice cream? Lord knows we'll need something to sweeten up that mouth of yours," Mindy teased, making Wyatt feel like he was ten years old.

"That we can do," Wyatt said. "And I'm sorry for swearing."

Wyatt sent his parents off to their guest room for the night while he and Ryan picked up the last of the dinner dishes and cleaned up the kitchen.

"Wow, I love your parents," Ryan confessed, handing plates over to Wyatt, who loaded them into the dishwasher. "They're so warm and loving. They made me feel welcome. I don't know what I was expecting, I guess, but whatever it was, they far exceeded it."

"I could tell the second I walked into the kitchen and spotted you with Mom… I could tell by the look on her face you were going to be a hit. College boy, you've got them under your spell."

Wyatt wiped his hands on a towel and then wrapped them around Ryan's lean, muscular waist. "If anything, I was more concerned you would find them bothersome. The wine sort of fuels them on. My mother can talk up a storm when she gets going."

"Speaking of that…."

Wyatt put his finger to Ryan's lips, gently silencing him before replacing his finger with his mouth. Together, they gently rocked back and forth, nibbling and kissing.

"Sweetie, let's not talk now," Wyatt begged, sensing Ryan was gearing up to lay something heavy on him. "Is that okay? I've only got so much energy left tonight and I can think of much better ways to deplete it. Okay?"

"Wyatt, I really need to talk to you."

"Whatever it is, can't it wait until later? You haven't grown tired of me, have you?"

"Oh my gosh, no, of course not. It's nothing like that."

"Well, then, I'm thinking it can wait. But I know what can't wait a minute longer...." Wyatt took Ryan's hand and placed it on his burgeoning crotch.

"Mmm... okay," Ryan purred, pulling Wyatt back into an embrace. "Okay, you win. But we have to talk soon. It's important to me."

"Yikes, that doesn't sound good." Wyatt buried his head into the crook of Ryan's neck.

"No... no worries, I love you. I thought about you day and night while I was away. And you're right," Ryan whispered into Wyatt's ear, "there're much better ways to spend our energy other than talking. Come with me, handsome."

Ryan took Wyatt by the hand and led the way out of the kitchen and into the bedroom. "I've got plans for you, Mr. Stark."

Wyatt had plans of his own. Ryan had surprised Wyatt with the depth of his experience and his intuitiveness in the bedroom. It was time for Wyatt to step up to the plate, as he very much wanted to be an equal partner.

With plenty of kisses in between, Wyatt slowly removed Ryan's clothes. The almost full moon shining in from the bedroom windows lit Ryan's body in a way that robbed Wyatt of his breath.

"You're so beautiful," Wyatt said as he kissed each of Ryan's nipples before dragging his tongue down the chiseled chest until he was on his knees, lazily circling Ryan's navel.

Wyatt paused, inhaling the exotic aroma coming from the vicinity of Ryan's cock and balls. His own cock was dripping with excitement and begging for release. Cradling Ryan's hefty ball sac in one hand, Wyatt licked his finger and went after the prize. Inching up closer, allowing Ryan's cock to paint his eyelids and his face, Wyatt located what he'd been looking for and as his warm, wet mouth opened to engulf the throbbing dick before him, Wyatt inserted his finger into Ryan.

"Oh yes…." Ryan moaned as Wyatt began his dual assault.

Wyatt felt Ryan's hands on his shoulders as he found his stride. Working both his mouth and his finger, he played his handsome partner until it was obvious the time had come to slow things down.

Wyatt stood and guided Ryan over to the bed, where he positioned him on his hands and knees. He removed his shorts and T-shirt and scooted up behind Ryan. With his hands, he pried the man's muscled ass apart and began feasting on Ryan.

"Oh… Wyatt! That feels *so good*," Ryan gushed as he buried his head into the pillow.

Wyatt felt a strand of his own pre-cum drip onto his thigh as his tongue darted eagerly. It was time.

"Don't move," Wyatt said softly as he crawled over to the side of the bed and opened the top drawer of the bedside table. When he returned to Ryan, he was ready and wasted no time positioning himself on his knees. As he glided slowly into Ryan, Wyatt leaned down and rested his chest on his lover's back. Taking Ryan's cock into his warm hand, he began making long, slow, deliberate thrusts in and out.

Ryan welcomed Wyatt's newfound confidence, and together, they humped and bucked their way into the night. Exhausted and spent, they cuddled under the duvet like human pretzels before falling fast asleep in each other's arms.

Chapter 11

A COOL breeze swept across his face, coaxing Wyatt out of a deep slumber. Dreams gradually gave way to reality as he surfaced. Unwilling yet to open his eyes, the official beginning of the day, he stretched his long body to its full, impressive length. In hopes of spooning Ryan, he stretched over to discover cold, empty sheets.

Where is he? Wyatt wondered, his eyes popping open. He listened in the direction of the master bath, but heard nothing to indicate Ryan was there. With the relationship so new, he fought off a wave of panic as he hopped out of bed. Remembering to throw on shorts, he bolted out of the bedroom in search of his new love. Soft voices guided him to the kitchen, and Ryan.

Showered and dressed for the day, Ryan stood behind the counter, ever so handsome, hauling a spoon lazily around a large mixing bowl. Next to him, like a female version of Tonto, stood his mother, who also appeared ready and raring to go. A happy vibe filled the room as Ryan stirred and Mindy chopped.

"Hey, sleepyhead," Ryan called out as he cocked his head over to Mindy, aware of how darling the two of them must appear together.

"Hi, sweetie," his mother chimed after a rather aggressive chop. "Meet the new cooking sensation, Ryan and Mindy."

"Wait! No, no, no," Ryan protested. Halting the stirring process, he turned to address Mindy. "That's just not right. It's the new cooking sensation, Mindy and her *helper*, Ryan. There's no way I can share top billing on this one."

Mindy giggled as she returned to her work.

"You have plenty of time for a swim. I'm helping your mom throw together some breakfast before we have to leave for the whale watch excursion."

"You guys are starting to scare me. I'm just saying." Wyatt couldn't have been happier to see his mother and Ryan hitting it off so well. "Is Dad up yet?" Wyatt asked as he poured himself a glass of orange juice.

"He's in the shower," his mother answered, transferring chopped fruit into a bowl.

"Well, it looks like I'm swimming alone. Just my luck, today will be the day the shark decides to pay a visit," Wyatt mumbled, but unfortunately not soft enough to prevent his mother from overhearing.

"Wyatt Patrick Stark," she scolded, "You should be ashamed of yourself for worrying me with comments like that."

Her use of his full name brought him racing back to his childhood. *What was it about being with your parents,* he asked himself. It's like he'd never grown up or left home.

"I'm sorry, Mother," he apologized, walking over and kissing her on the cheek. "I made a stupid joke about a shark swimming in the cove," he confessed to Ryan, who was clueless. "It scared the crap out of Dad yesterday and alarmed my mother today. How stupid is that?" he asked, kissing Ryan.

"Geez, Wyatt, that is stupid. I might have to rethink this relationship thing," Ryan cautioned, earning a disapproving elbow jab from Tonto.

"Careful, she's already starting to treat you like one of her own."

Wyatt left the adorable cooking duo, changed into his swimming trunks, and sprinted into the cove at full speed. The water was much colder this morning, causing him to jump up and gasp. In an attempt to take away the chill. He pushed himself harder than usual, forcing his arms to extend their full length, cupping the water with powerful strokes.

That was a good workout! Feeling fatigued, he slowed his pace. Raising his head above the surface, he caught a glimpse of his father, who had strolled out on the sand with a cup of coffee. Wyatt smiled. He envisioned his dad standing out on the beach, squinting across the bright surface on the lookout for a single fin, signaling danger.

By the time he had hauled himself out of the water, his father had retreated back into the house. He stopped for a few moments on the warm sand, facing into the sun. His chest was still heaving from the effort put into his laps. Would he ever enjoy swimming in a city pool again after having this wonderful cove to himself? Murphy really had a piece of paradise here. Down the road, he could see himself with a similar setup. *To hell with nonstop work!* The summer here was causing him to reevaluate the way he thought about his career and his priorities.

Ryan poked his handsome head out of the screen door and hollered, "Breakfast is ready, Flipper. Don't dawdle," he yelled.

Flipper and dawdle? Wyatt hurried into the house.

Taking advantage of the remaining berries, Mindy and Ryan had made his all-time breakfast favorite, blueberry pancakes. He and his father were served plates heaping with warm cakes, smoked bacon, and a fresh fruit compote that either Mindy or Ryan—it was anyone's guess at this point—had garnished with a sprig of fresh mint.

After they finished eating, he jumped into the shower while Ryan and his parents cleaned up breakfast and organized for the day's activities. Squeaky clean and ready to roll, he returned to find the whole gang seated at the counter, patiently waiting. Mindy was beside herself at the prospect of spotting a whale. Ted, not one to show emotion of any kind, was also antsy to get the show on the road.

This is going to be a fun day for them. Years of watching the Discovery Channel would be trumped by today's adventure. It could be worse, Wyatt speculated; instead of shark specials on television, they could be sucking down bourbon sevens at the local Elk's club.

"You guys head out to the car. I'm going to grab a bottle of water and make sure the house is all locked up. I'll be out in a minute."

Checking the entrance to the house from the beach was locked, he stopped off at the refrigerator and grabbed a water. Confident all the appliances were shut off, he turned, but was stopped by the telephone ringing.

"Hey, Wyatt, it's Murph! Glad I caught you near the phone. Everything going okay? Ted and Mindy enjoying themselves?"

"How did you know they were here?" Wyatt asked, not surprised Murphy was up to speed with the current events.

"Mindy called me after you invited them to ask what they needed to bring."

"Naturally," Wyatt said dryly. "Anyway, it's going great."

"That's good. Hey, I miss you, pal!"

It suddenly dawned on Wyatt this was the longest stretch of time he and Murphy had ever been apart. Even now, with a majority of Murphy's business out on the West Coast, they still managed dinner on the fly at least a couple times a month.

"I miss you too," Wyatt said. "Hey, we're just about to head out for a whale-watching tour."

"No shit! Mindy must be moist with excitement. Ted too."

"Quit," Wyatt scolded while at the same time laughing at Murphy's irreverence.

"Listen, Wy, I know you're in a hurry, but I have a couple things I have to cover with you. If you refrain from interrupting me, it'll go fast."

"Well… okay," Wyatt leaned into the counter. "They're already in the car waiting."

"Yep, yep."

Wyatt relaxed and listened.

"First, and this is probably going to come as a relief to you, I need you out here no later than next weekend. Everything is developing as expected, but we're getting to the point where we can't go forward without your creative input and approval. I'd limit your involvement to teleconferences if I thought it would be effective, but I think it's time all these movie folk met their new boss."

"Wow! Okay, I guess…."

He can't be serious. Next week? I don't want to go. What about Ryan? Maybe he can join me for a couple weeks before his school starts up. This really sucks. I thought I had at least another month here.

"Call me next week and let me know when you're coming. I've spoken to Linda and she is already starting to organize you for the coast. You won't believe this, but I think I've talked her into coming out here. You don't know it now, but trust me, you'll need her here. I think it's the idea she might get to meet movie stars is why she's even considering it. She might give you some shit when you talk to her, but she'll come out."

"Linda? Who's never been outside of the five boroughs, that Linda? Amazing! You're a miracle worker," Wyatt said, impressed.

"Yeah, I know I am. Anyway, that's the two big pieces of news. Before I forget, my assistant, Ryan, the guy I stuck out there to keep an eye on you, he'll take care of putting the house away before coming back to join us in LA. You don't need to worry about any of that stuff. That's what I pay him to do."

Huh? Did he just say Ryan?

Wyatt removed the phone from his ear and shook his head several times. Squinting, he attempted to comprehend what Murphy had just said. He'd probably heard wrong.

"Say the last part again?" Wyatt asked evenly. "Who's closing up the house, your assistant?"

"Yep," Murphy confirmed. "Ryan's been working remotely from a hotel in Bangor. Have you guys gotten to know each other at all? He's a sweetheart, a really dedicated worker. You'll enjoy working with him out here if you don't already know him."

Breathe.

"No!" Stunned, Wyatt sat on the closest stool and stared at the wall.

"Ryan is your assistant?" he asked, realizing he had been holding the phone so tight to his ear it had begun to ache.

"I hired him this spring when I was putting together my team for the movie," Murphy explained. "When you agreed to spend your summer there, never being one to take a chance with my prize cash cow—which would be you, honey—I asked him to keep close in case you needed anything. You know, as kind of a safety net. I didn't want anything to jeopardize your summer. Wait... you're not interrupting. Hey... he hasn't been in your face all the time, has he? I told him to stay out of your hair so you could relax and be on your own. I'll kick his ass if he's been a pest, I swear to God."

Before Wyatt could answer, Ryan came bolting in the door.

No! This can't be happening. Take deep breaths!

"We're waiting for you, sweetie. Anything wrong?"

"Who was that? It didn't sound like Ted. Wyatt, you there? Look, you're not tracking right now, so I'll give you a call early next week to finalize the details. Have a whale of a time today. Bye!"

Trembling, Wyatt placed the phone back in its holder. *This can't be happening. Ryan....*

"What's happened, Wyatt?" Ryan asked with concern as he walked over and placed a hand on Wyatt's shoulder.

"Get away from me!"

Feeling Ryan's touch triggered an explosion. Jumping up off his stool, Wyatt bolted to the opposite side of the room, where he began to pace back and forth.

"How was your trip to Boston?" Wyatt shouted while pausing long enough to make eye contact. "Let's start by hearing a little bit about your trip to Boston, and then we can talk about your growing up here in Maine. That should be a fascinating tale."

Keep breathing, Wyatt!

Wyatt wasn't even sure what was coming out of his mouth. His mind was going a mile a minute as he attempted to process what had just happened. He froze in his tracks, staring at Ryan who hadn't moved an inch. "I'm waiting, tell me right now? How was Boston?"

"Wyatt!" Ryan took a couple steps forward. "I was going to talk to you. Please, believe me...." Ryan implored. "Please believe I was going to talk to you when I got back yesterday, but your parents... your parents were here, so I didn't have a chance."

"Talk to me about what?" Wyatt screamed back. "Talk to me about how fucking fun it was to fuck with me this summer? Fuck you, Ryan! How could you fuck with me like that? I believed we had something. How could you fuck with me like that?"

Wyatt was hollering across the room while at the same time struggling to keep his knees from buckling.

"Wyatt... we do have something. I love you!" Ryan cautiously inched further into the room. "I was going to tell you everything once your parents had left."

What have I done to deserve this? What is it that I've done....

"You know what...." Wyatt stepped forward defiantly. "You need to leave. You need to get your lying ass out of here *now*."

"Wyatt, please...."

"Fuck you! Leave... leave right now. I'll get my parents out of your car and then you can leave. I never want to see your lying, fucking face again. Is that understood?"

Wyatt didn't wait for a response. He charged past Ryan out the door to the SUV, where his parents sat smiling, waiting patiently for their trip to get underway.

"Grab everything. Ryan has to leave," Wyatt announced through clenched teeth as he reached for his mother's day bag.

"What's wrong, honey?" Mindy asked Ryan, who now stood slightly behind Wyatt, watching in horror as she and Ted scurried out of his car. "Is there anything we can do to help?"

Both parents looked over to Ryan, who shook his head sadly as he watched them amble up the pathway to the house.

"Leave," Wyatt barked.

RYAN was paralyzed. Wyatt's reaction to finding out the truth was much worse than he could have ever imagined. When his pleading for Wyatt to believe that he'd planned on telling him of his lies failed,

Ryan had no other defense than to just stand there and take the full brunt of Wyatt's fury.

What else did you expect to happen? You deserve this!

Hearing Wyatt scream at him with such anger and contempt paralyzed him. He watched, helpless, as this promising relationship with this wonderful person unraveled before his eyes. He watched in horror as Wyatt came unglued.

You're losing the love of your life, and you should! When this gets back to Murphy, and it will, you'll lose the job you love. Nice work, Ryan! You fucking JERK-OFF!

He had stumbled out of the house after Wyatt. Frantic, he watched Wyatt hustle his parents out of his car. There was no appropriate time for good-byes.

You hurt their son. You will forever be scum in their eyes.

Between the car and the house, Wyatt doubled over and wailed. Mindy, looking around in a panic, rushed to her son. Ted was right behind her and, together, they stood on either side of Wyatt, who was having a full-fledged panic attack.

You're responsible for this, Ryan.

It took several minutes before Wyatt was able to gain control and continue up the steps and into the house. When they were all inside, the door was slammed so hard it sounded like a gunshot. Ryan was left standing in a daze.

Several minutes passed and he still hadn't moved. Staring at the door, he had thought briefly about knocking and making one last attempt at getting Wyatt to listen to him.

Grow up, Ryan! When are you going to learn? You blew it! Last night was magical. This, right now, could have been so different if you had insisted on talking to Wyatt. Instead, you let your dick make a decision for you. Stupid ass!

Tears poured down his face. *It's too late.*

Turning his back to the door, Ryan got into his car. The lingering scent of Mindy Stark's perfume fueled his despair. There was little doubt in Ryan's mind as he headed down the bumpy road that what had just taken place, the loss of Wyatt Stark, would be mourned by him for the rest of his life.

WYATT knew he owed his parents an explanation. "Wait here. I have to use the bathroom. We'll take the Jeep. I'll explain it all in a minute." Wyatt didn't wait for a reply. He stormed through the house to his bedroom and into the adjoining bathroom.

What the fuck am I supposed to tell them? You're right, Mom and Dad. You're absolutely right. I'll never find anyone like Murphy again, and I'm an idiot because we aren't still together.

Splashing water on his face, Wyatt peered into the large mirror hanging over the vanity.

I can't tell them the truth. I don't even know what the truth is.

Wiping his face, he forced himself to take deep, deliberate breaths.

This is unbelievable. Unbelievable!

Wyatt closed his eyes and concentrated on keeping himself together. He felt like a live wire, emotions jolting him from every direction. His parents were waiting for him. He needed to call on his acting skills and forget the enormous blow he'd just taken. He needed to keep the day moving forward. Splashing his face again, he dried off with a towel and bravely began his performance.

"I'm sorry for being so abrupt earlier," Wyatt said, reentering the kitchen. Neither of his parents had moved. "Ryan...."

"Honey, is there something wrong with Ryan?" his mother asked, taking his hand in hers. "Is he all right?"

Jesus! He's fine, Mom. It's me that isn't all right. "Ryan... Ryan has some issues... we... he and I are going to have to deal with them on our own. It's nothing to worry about. I'd tell you if it was. A disagreement, that's all. You know how that can happen."

Please buy into this and let it pass. I can't say anything more or I'll come undone. I'm dying.

Wyatt was too devastated to move on. Sitting down on one of the stools, the warmth of his mother's hand on his back opened the floodgates. Wyatt buried his head in his hands and wept.

"There, there...." he heard his mother's attempt to comfort.

"Just let it go, son," his father advised from the stool next to him.

Wyatt, through huge sobs, attempted to tell his parents what had happened. Neither of them asked a single question or commented on what he was telling them. Instead, they stood close and did their best to comfort. When he couldn't cry anymore, he stood up and grabbed a wad of paper towels.

Wyatt wiped the tears away and sat back down between his parents. "Thanks, you guys, for listening. I know how fortunate I am to have you both. I guess I'm destined to be unlucky in love."

"Oh, you boys," his mother said, waving her hand in the air. "Honestly, I can't believe how worked up you get sometimes. Life is too short to put yourself through all of this." Typical Mom, Wyatt thought. It made him smile to think how resilient she was. *She is trying to tell you shit happens.*

"I agree," Wyatt said with a nod. "Life is too damn short to put myself through all of that. Let's not say another word about it, okay? Come on, we've got whales to see." He grabbed the keys off their hook and led the way to the Jeep.

The whale watch was everything Wyatt could have hoped for, providing at least a momentary diversion from the ugly scene earlier with Ryan. After an initial high-speed journey out past the islands, the catamaran-style boat slowed to a crawl and within minutes, huge blasts of water high into the air announced the presence of the enormous whales that swam only a few hundred feet in front of the boat. Whale after whale breached the surface to the thunderous click of camera shutters, eliciting oohs and awws from the captivated spectators. The young staff onboard did an exceptional job of narrating the activity.

"I never thought I'd see anything like this in person," Ted commented, amazed, as he watched a baby whale and its mother twist and turn in the water. "It's like being seated right in the middle of a nature show. You enjoying this, Mindy?"

"Oh my gosh, yes," Mindy replied, her cheeks flush with excitement. "I sure hope my pictures turn out. Your dad gave me this camera for Christmas last year and I'm still learning how to use the darn thing. I don't know why they make these things so difficult."

Back on shore, they agreed to grab something to eat. One of the crew suggested a seafood restaurant near the boat dock that, according to his parents, turned out to be quite good. Wyatt could only manage a few bites. With the diversion the whales had provided gone, anger and sadness over Ryan came creeping back even stronger than before. He was sure they couldn't possibly understand the hurt he was experiencing. The fact they had so quickly, and completely, embraced Ryan as one of their own made it even worse.

The banter in the car was subdued. Wyatt navigated the Jeep back home. Kissing his parents good night, Wyatt closed the door to his bedroom and collapsed on the bed.

How could you do this to me? I was so happy. How could you... the depth of your lie... it was so complete. I'm never going to find someone to spend my life with. Never...."

Wyatt buried his head in his pillow and cried himself to sleep.

Ted and Mindy stayed on for a couple more days, but no matter what he tried to do, Wyatt couldn't stop himself from falling into a deep, sorrowful funk. His time at the beach house was ruined. No amount of distraction was capable of mending his broken heart. Now, all he wanted was to leave.

So many questions revolved around Ryan's decision to portray himself as someone he was not, Wyatt didn't know where to begin. The lies, the extent to which he had lied to keep his real identity from Wyatt was staggering. The fake parents, the fake friends at the fair, the list went on and on. What saddened him most: the powerful feeling of betrayal he felt from someone he had begun to love and trust. He was devastated.

Of course it wasn't Murphy's fault. Murphy had tried to ensure Wyatt's summer went off without a hitch by assigning his assistant the task of keeping watch. Murphy would have had no idea what Ryan was up to. Wyatt chose to keep his relationship with Ryan private until he was confident it had a future. There was no way Murphy could have seen this one coming.

Ryan had attempted to call Wyatt several times, but Wyatt ignored his calls, his voice-mails deleted without being played back. There was nothing left to say at this point. No excuse would have been good enough.

After sticking his parents on the plane for home, Wyatt decided to give Murphy a call to explain what had happened. No doubt, Ryan had already gotten to him.

"Hey it's me."

"What's wrong, where are you?" Murphy asked.

"I'm lying on your bed, wishing you were here right now." Wyatt fought hard to keep his emotions in check.

Murphy, hold me.

"You sound like shit. Talk to me."

"Ryan's an asshole," Wyatt offered without thinking.

"Excuse me? Are you talking about my assistant, Ryan?" Murphy asked with concern.

"Yes! It turns out he's a lying sack of shit." Wyatt knew he had to start making some sense, but for now, it felt really good to just babble. "He lied to me."

"I need more to go on here," Murphy prodded.

Wyatt detailed for Murphy exactly what had happened. Murphy hadn't heard anything from Ryan for a couple of days and was at a loss to explain his bizarre behavior. Murphy didn't offer to fire Ryan, and Wyatt stopped short of requesting it.

"I don't want to tell you how to run your side of the business or who you work with, but please believe me when I tell you I'd better not set an eye on him ever again—are we clear on that?"

"We're clear," Murphy said. "I'm sorry. I'm stunned by what you've just told me. Can I do anything for you right now?"

Wyatt couldn't keep it together any longer. The tone of Murphy's voice, his sincerity, triggered another round of devastating sobs.

"I'm here, Wyatt, I'm here."

"It hurt so bad," Wyatt said after several attempts at getting himself back in control. "I was in love with him. I thought he was the one...."

"I have to get you out of there. I'll deal with Ryan later. You don't need to pack or do anything, I'll have a driver there in an hour and you'll be here by dinner. I promise."

"Okay...." Wyatt sat up on the bed and wiped his face on his sleeve.

God, I hate it that I'm such a fucking baby.

On the way to the airport, Wyatt let his thoughts drift back to Ryan. He focused on the lies. Now that he had had his big cry with Murphy, he was starting to get hold of himself. He'd wasted too much time in "poor me" land. Enough was enough.

Ryan lied and deceived me. Sure, it's true he may have attempted to come clean. He told me he needed to talk. Who's to say whatever he was planning on telling me wouldn't have just been another lie? How would I know?

Wyatt sat back and closed his eyes as his car sped down the freeway to the airport.

No, it's best... no matter how painful... to push him away and out of my life forever. I'm not overreacting. I'm glad this happened now and not further down the road, when more people and more baggage would make calling it quits even that much harder. It's all for the best.

Chapter 12

"SO, WHAT do you think? Does the movie *Sunset Boulevard* come to mind?" Murphy ushered Wyatt further into the house. "Before I show you anything else, you have to see this view."

Murphy lead Wyatt through the tiled hallway leading into what could have been a ballroom at one time.

"I feel like I'm in a movie." Wyatt was impressed. An unexpected bright moment to a day he knew would be burdened by thoughts of Ryan. "I've always wondered what it would be like to live in a house like this. I don't even want to know what this is costing us."

"You're right," Murphy said with a wink. "You don't. The owners are in real estate. They're on a world cruise or some silly-ass thing like that. You can stay here for an entire year if you want. We have a lease."

Murphy opened the huge double doors at the back of the room. Sunlight came rushing in. "This is going to blow you away."

The villa was located in the hills. The view, with the city and the ocean beyond, was breathtaking. Like the *Sunset Boulevard* mansion, the back of the house was home to a pool with an adjacent Jacuzzi and a gazebo from which you could gaze out at the city far below.

"This is spectacular. I mean really, truly, spectacular," Wyatt said as he soaked it all in. The prospect of living here comforted him. Wyatt blew out a huge sigh, in hopes it would carry away some of his hurt.

"Let's hope it chases the blues away, my friend,"

It's scary how well he can read me.

"Come on, let's take a look at more of the inside."

The lower portion of the house was designed for entertaining. The front door opened into a black-and-white tiled hallway leading to the ballroom they had just walked through. An enormous pair of stairs, framing the room on both sides, wound up majestically to the second floor.

"It's kind of spooky, if you think about it," Wyatt walked up the huge stairway. "The parties, can you imagine? Think of all the stars who are dead that might have danced down there. It blows my mind."

"Welcome to Wyatt's world," Murphy said when they had reached the top of the landing.

The whole second floor was a master suite, complete with a small kitchen, workout room, entertainment room, and of course, a huge bedroom with a walk-in closet and a bathroom resembling a roman spa.

"Are you going to have enough space up here?" Murphy joked.

"Hell, yeah," Wyatt said laughing. "I could share it with the Chippendales and I'd still have enough space. So, is there somewhere up here for Linda?"

"Linda's quarters are downstairs. Come on, let's finish the tour."

Murphy led Wyatt back down the marble stairs to the entryway and through a door to the right of one of the massive stairways.

"Look, she's got her own bedroom, kitchen, entertainment room, she'll be happy as a clam. This is part of the reason I think this place is so perfect. When she wants to get away from you and the world, she's got this great apartment to retreat to. Hell, I'd be happy down here."

"When is she getting in, I miss the old sourpuss." Wyatt hadn't spoken to her for a couple of weeks.

"She's flying out tomorrow afternoon. I have to warn you, she's dangerously close to snapping. She'll be okay once she gets settled in. I'm sure it's the uncertainty of what to expect that's making her whacky."

"I can imagine. Coming out here is like relocating on the edge of the world," Wyatt added with a laugh.

"God bless her, she's doing this because she loves the crap out of you and wants the movie to be a success. She's a team player," Murphy reminded Wyatt.

"She's a mouthy old bitch who has had my ticket from day one. It's a two-way street. I wouldn't want her to back off for the world. She's like an annoyingly long chest hair you don't want to pluck out because, for some unexplainable reason, you're proud of it."

"That's the best you can do?" Murphy asked, raising an eyebrow.

"That was lame," Wyatt had to admit. "I'm fatigued from the trip. Look, I'll get real needy right off the bat and she'll feel right at home." Wyatt laughed at his own plan.

"You do that. Hey," Murphy said, glancing down at his watch, "I've got a meeting in a few, so I'm going to have to head out. Make yourself at home and I'll pick you up later for dinner. I'll take you to someplace fun. We can talk about what happened with Ryan if you want."

"I'd rather drag my dick through cut glass."

"Okay...."

"I'm not sure I'm up to schmoozing with anyone tonight," Wyatt confessed. He hoped Murphy would let the comment about Ryan disappear and die.

"Schmoozers can't even get into this place, it's so hot. Don't worry, I'm not up for that either. I'll pick you up at eight. Call me on my cell if you need anything."

Wyatt kissed Murphy good-bye. Walking back to the stairs, he began peeling off his clothes.

OVER the course of the following week, Wyatt had very little opportunity to think about Ryan. He was swept up in the process of making movies. Meeting after meeting kept him hopping from dawn to dusk as all the elements of *Dress Up* began to materialize and come to life. Casting the picture—which had started out a nightmare with the studio insisting he use Lana Melville in the lead role—had, for the most part, been ironed out. The lead had been offered to a very talented Broadway star who was thrilled to get her feet wet in pictures. To appease Ms. Melville and the studio, with Wyatt's blessing, Murphy had offered her a nonsinging, nondancing supporting role that had the possibility of stealing the show if she played her cards right. Wyatt was excited to see what she could do with the part. God willing, she'd see the potential and give it her all. He was apprehensive about meeting her for the first time, but Murphy, who had brokered the supporting role offer, accompanied the two to lunch prior to filming.

"Wyatt, I must confess, I've not seen any of your Broadway shows, but I hear from absolutely everyone how talented and creative you are. I'm excited to be part of your movie. I wouldn't say that unless I meant it."

Wyatt found himself captivated by Lana. Her warm, bright personality allowed him to feel at once relaxed and comfortable in her presence. Already he could sense her professionalism and he knew he wouldn't have a problem directing her. She was lovelier in person than he'd remembered from her movies.

"I'm excited for you. There are some wonderful moments throughout the movie for you to sink your teeth into. I'm very much a collaborator, Lana. I'm going to be disappointed if you don't come up with some ideas of your own for the part." Wyatt hoped she would roll up her sleeves and dig in.

"Funny you should mention that," Lana said, with a hearty laugh that was immediately recognizable. "I *do* have some ideas. And please, don't be afraid to bat them down if you don't like them. I'm not that kind of an actress. I take direction well and when I have the opportunity, I throw in a little extra along the way."

"Sounds perfect! I wish we could start filming tomorrow," Wyatt said, looking over to Murphy. Any anxiety he felt about the start of filming was outweighed by his need to keep his mind off the Ryan ordeal. *I'd start filming after this lunch.*

"We're a couple months away from filming. You still have to finalize your ensemble," Murphy pointed out.

Wyatt could tell by the look on Lana's face that he needed to explain what Murphy was talking about. "I work with a corps of dancer-singers when I work on stage, and for continuity reasons, I'm planning on using a similar concept in the movie. In some respects, if it plays out the way I intend it to, the movie will resemble the stage version," Wyatt explained for Lana's benefit. "I don't want to change the flavor of the piece, I want to grow it and make it bigger."

Murphy had argued with the studio heads over who to cast in the ensemble. After a few tense meetings, he won them over. Strong singers and dancers from the east coast would be cast in many of the supporting roles. If this had been done before, it hadn't to the extent he had proposed. Wyatt and Murphy both held strong feelings of fairness regarding who would be cast in these breakout roles. Bottom line, as they saw it, the Broadway talent had put the show on the map. Without their previous hard work, this movie wouldn't be possible. They wanted to give back to those who had been so instrumental in the success of *Dress Up*. A screen credit in a large-scale movie like this would be a huge addition to anyone's resume. Ultimately, it would be the audience who validated this decision. Wyatt had vowed from the start to always have talent win out over name recognition, which is why the Lana issue would have become a showstopper if it hadn't been successfully resolved.

"MURPHY wants to see you," Zoe said from outside the office.

"Huh?" Ryan stared across his desk at Murphy's receptionist.

"Murphy wants to see you," she repeated, leaning into the doorjamb.

"Tell him I'll have his production notes on his desk before lunch." Ryan rubbed his eyes and resumed typing from the yellow legal pages she'd given him earlier that morning.

"Ryan, go see what he wants. He asked me to walk down here and get you."

"Fuck! Okay! I'll be there in a minute."

"Ryan, please...."

Ryan stopped typing and placed his head in his hands. He could feel a deep ache beginning behind his eyes. Today, if it was possible, was going to suck even worse than yesterday. Without saying anything else, he got up and followed the receptionist down the hall to Murphy's office. *This is it! He's going to fire me.*

"Boss man," Ryan said, forcing a smile as he entered the handsomely appointed office. It even smelled good in here, he noticed. Behind the huge oval desk, Murphy sat looking off to the side at two large computer screens.

"These set renderings are incredible," Murphy said as he gestured for Ryan to sit on one of the soft leather club chairs. "You look like shit, what's going on?"

"No, I don't," Ryan answered defensively as he plopped himself down in the chair.

"True, but you don't look as good as you usually do."

Ryan couldn't resist Murphy's charm and his comment made him smile.

"Spill. I know something's bothering you and it's starting to bother me." Murphy leaned back in his chair and bit down on his pen.

I'm afraid to tell you. I'm scared of what you might say.

"I hired a happy Ryan who loves to laugh and does outstanding work. Now I have a mopy-dopy Ryan who still does good work but is bugging the crap out of me because he's not happy anymore. Ah come on… if you tell me, I'll show you my appendix scar."

Ryan was no match for the evil forces of Murphy's odd and zany sense of humor. "God, you're sick," Ryan said, stifling a laugh.

"You smiled. That means you're sick too."

"I don't feel like laughing." Ryan looked away from his boss.

"I know you don't." Murphy reached over to the credenza in back of him and picked up a box of tissues, setting it down in front of Ryan. "We're going to do this whether you like it or not. Tell me the Wyatt story, from the beginning."

Murphy's blunt request caught Ryan by surprise. After the blowup with Wyatt, he had expected Murphy to fire him. To his surprise, nothing had been said. The subject of Wyatt hadn't been brought up. He wasn't sure where or how to begin. He was a bundle of emotion and incapable of hiding his fragile state. "I miss him so much." Ryan could feel his eyes grow moist and his lower lip began trembling. He felt powerless. "I fucked this up...." He couldn't hold it back any longer. Tears began rolling down his cheeks.

"Let it go. It's not good to internalize your feelings." Murphy got up from behind his desk and sat in the chair next to him. "Come on, let it all out." Ryan crumbled and Murphy comforted him, holding his head to his chest.

"Sorry," Ryan said several minutes later as his sobs began to diminish.

"Hey... we all need to have a good cry now and then. Wyatt cries almost every day. It's in his DNA."

"Why didn't you fire me?" Ryan asked, lifting his head off Murphy and accepting a handful of tissues.

"It's obvious," Murphy said, getting up and sitting back down behind his desk, "you didn't cut your teeth in the Broadway community. If I had to fire everyone who had a love affair sour, there wouldn't be anybody left to work with."

"I thought maybe...." Ryan blew his nose and looked around for a wastebasket.

"Here, I got it," Murphy pressed a button on his desk. "Zoe, could you please come in here and remove some snot-filled tissues from Ryan? They're really gooey and gross. Thanks, love!"

"You are so sick," Ryan said, unable to keep from laughing. Wiping the tears from his face, he stood up and threw the tissues into the trash bin on the side of Murphy's desk.

"To answer your question, Wyatt never asked me to fire you. If he had asked, I would have refused. You do good work... and I enjoy working with you."

How did I get so lucky to end up with you for a boss?

"Thanks," Ryan said. "I love my job."

"You feel like telling me what happened?" Murphy pushed back his chair and put his feet up on the desk.

"I don't know where to start."

"Oh, sure you do. Why Wyatt?"

Ryan took a few moments to think about the question before answering. "There was this guy I met in college. We dated a couple times and then he vanished. I never did find out what happened. I felt this incredible... attraction to him. I haven't felt anything like it until Wyatt got in my car at the airport. It was instant. He was handsome. I'd seen pictures of him...." Ryan glanced over to the portrait of Wyatt and Murphy on the bookshelf.

"It's okay, what we had... what we have," Murphy corrected himself, "is different than what you're talking about. We've moved on to a different level. Go on."

Ryan smiled. "He's so damn handsome. And... he was nice. For some reason, I thought he might be full of himself. He wasn't. And, I guess... I was in awe of his success. Wyatt has it all going on."

"Wyatt is a good guy. Most people have no idea just how good of a guy he is. I'm not surprised you had your doubts, given the nature of this business and the huge percentage of assholes that inhabit it."

"It happened... so suddenly," Ryan continued. "I was driving him from the airport to your house, and when we passed through town, he asked me if the grocery store, Taylor's, was any relation to me. Murphy, you have to believe this, I have no idea why, but for some reason I said yes." Ryan felt his face redden.

"That's kind of strange, but I've heard stranger things." Murphy laughed.

"I know it's strange. It was like I was possessed or something. From the moment I spotted him, I knew I wanted Wyatt. In the back of my mind, I mean... now that I've had a chance to analyze it, I think I thought that if Wyatt knew I was working for you, he'd never even give me the time of day, you know—in that way, I mean. He'd be cautious and stuff and I would have never stood a chance with him."

"Now that's some interesting shit," Murphy said, removing his feet from the desk. "You made a very correct assumption. Wyatt, unless I'm mistaken, would have engaged with you in an entirely different manner if he knew you were working for me. I'm sure of it. Despite what other people say about you, you're pretty damn intuitive."

"The next part is kind of creepy." Ryan couldn't sit any longer. Standing, he began to pace. "I was so bored at my hotel I started driving around, and more than once found myself turning off the highway onto your road. One time I parked the car and hiked around back of the house to the end of the cove."

"Wow, that is creepy," Murphy joked.

"It *is* creepy. In a way I was stalking him. Anyway, it was warm out and I had on shorts so I thought I'd take a dip. Climbing over the rocks, I spotted Wyatt on the beach and he was naked. I just about shit my pants."

"This naked thing with Wyatt has gotten to be a problem. You have no idea."

"Seeing him naked was like offering candy to a kid, I couldn't stop myself. I spied on him a couple more times. He'd swim at about the same time every day and I made sure I was there for the show. One time I slipped up, and I thought he saw me. I wasn't sure, and I got scared. I was afraid he'd call you and you'd think I was a freak and pull me off of the job. So, I decided to approach him to let him know I was not spying on him when, in fact, I was."

"Hey, don't worry if I'm with you or not, because I'm not."

"I thought I'd—"

"Oh for Christ's sake, lighten up." Murphy put his feet back up on the desk. "I get it. You made yourself known to Wyatt so he wouldn't freak out and call me. Makes sense."

"I hate myself for being so sneaky."

"Nothing seems weird to me… yet," Murphy said with grin.

"Thanks for making this so easy," Ryan jousted back.

"It's the least I can do. So… you watched him romp around the beach naked, and then you outed yourself, and then you fucked him?"

"Murphy!" Ryan gasped, mildly appalled.

"Well, I have to admit, I'm starting to get bored. Pick up the pace or I'm turning the channel."

"Okay. We started hanging out together and because I had lied about being a local, I had to continue to lie to keep it all working in my favor. I could tell he liked me and it was intoxicating. I had to have more."

"Sure, that makes sense." Murphy reached into a bowl of candy on his desk and popped one in his mouth, passing it to Ryan.

"No, thanks! I started falling in love with him. He danced for me and it was so incredible, it made me cry. I mean it was awesome."

"He's got a gift, I'll say that."

"One day, he went to the store looking for me, and of course they had no idea who I was. I had to invent more lies to get out of that one. We had a date to go to the county fair, and before I picked him up, I paid some local to pretend he knew me and my parents. That worked pretty well."

"That's genius, but weird."

"I started to feel like a lying sack of shit and after staying away from him for a while to sort out my head, I decided I had to tell him the truth. I was all prepared to do this, but when I showed up at his house, his parents were there and he had told them all about me, about us as a new couple, and of course, without him knowing it, almost everything he told them was a lie."

Ryan looked over at Murphy, who sat quietly behind his desk, rubbing his chin with his thumb.

"Actually, that explains a lot. I love his parents and, for whatever reason, they love me, even though Wyatt and I aren't lovers any longer. They're like my family. It's not my fault, and I certainly don't promote this, but they still harbor some kind of hope we will eventually come together again. To them, and especially Ted, the fact you lied about who you were is more ammunition he can use down the road to support his argument for us to get back together."

"Wow!" Ryan was beside himself. The fact that what he had done could have in some way hurt Wyatt even more than he had originally thought sucked the life right out of him.

"Oh, don't worry, I can fix all of that." Murphy stood and walked over to Ryan. "Listen, go back and finish those production notes. In the next few days, if you think you're up to it, go over to the auditions and flail yourself at Wyatt. He usually hangs back and makes notes on his cast. He has some great talent auditioning and he should be in a good mood. The timing is the best it's ever going to get."

"Really?" Ryan asked.

"I wish I could predict the outcome, but unfortunately, I can't. Wyatt can take an eternity to bury the hatchet if he's been injured. However—and this I can tell you for fact—you got to him. I would never tell you that or advise a meeting with him if I didn't think you at least had a chance.

"I don't know if I can...."

"Ryan, listen to me. Give this a shot. If it doesn't work, you did what you could, and you'll just have to move on. Life is going to get even crazier as we begin filming and there will be plenty of work to keep your mind off of Wyatt, if for some reason it doesn't work out. But... I think there's at least a chance."

"I can't go on like this, I'm miserable." Ryan admitted as he walked over to the door.

"It's now or never. Confronting him will only get harder as more water passes under the bridge. Wyatt likes to move on. Hopefully, you can catch him in time. Be yourself. You have hurt and agony written all over yourself."

"Thanks for taking the time." Ryan was beginning to think he could do this.

"We all fuck up. You're cool, you're not a freak."

"Hey, thanks," Ryan said, shaking his head as he left the office.

He was several feet down the hall when he heard Murphy holler, "Ryan!"

Ryan turned around and poked his head back into Murphy's office. "What now?"

"Don't even *think* about fibbing when you talk to him. If you feel like telling even an itsy-bitsy squeaker, for heaven's sake, don't do it."

EARLY one evening, after a day jam-packed with production meetings, Murphy drove Wyatt home and the two enjoyed some rare time alone together. Linda whipped up a light dinner before retreating into her own part of the house.

A couple glasses of wine later, Wyatt and Murphy found themselves soaking, naked, in the Jacuzzi as the lights of the city began to shine below them. Wyatt couldn't be sure about Murphy, but for his part, he hadn't allowed himself to think of the two of them sexually since they had agreed to end that aspect of their relationship. Seeing his ex-lover naked still aroused him.

In their early days together, Murphy had been so skinny, he looked emaciated. Together they hadn't had two cents to their name after rent was paid. Back then, when they were first starting out, food was delegated to the bottom of the list. As long as they had coffee, they could survive. Coffee and handouts.

The last few years had been very kind to Murphy. He had some meat on his bones, and what's more, he was toned. Wyatt had always had the muscle tone because of his dancing. Murphy had to work hard to achieve any visible results. His role as manager, and more recently producer, had for the most part kept his ass chained to a desk chair. Whatever he did to make the recent physical improvements had to have included countless hours in the gym.

"I gotta tell ya, if you'd been in the shape you are now way back when, I might've toughed it out a little longer," Wyatt quipped as Murphy eased his body back into the water after stepping briefly into the brisk night air to grab their bottle of wine and put it within closer reach.

Murphy appeared to ignore his comment, but seconds later, Wyatt felt one of Murphy's toes attempt access to an area on his body it had no business being near.

"You perve! Stop it," Wyatt squealed, while at the same time beating the intrusive toe away.

"You're absolutely despicable, and you know something, Wy my boy, it's what I love about you the most," Murphy said with a grin, raising his glass in toast.

We're more like brothers than most real brothers. There's no way anyone—with the exception of maybe my parents, Linda, and a few close friends like Sandy—there's no way they could ever understand the depth of this friendship. Is he lonely? Go for it, ask him.

"So… you seeing anyone these days, studly?" Wyatt asked, relaxing back into the steaming water. An unwritten law had developed between them, forbidding the solicitation of any information on current boyfriends, sexual escapades, or anything of a similar nature. He knew he was flirting with danger, as another attack by Murphy's big toe could happen without the slightest warning.

"I think it's time we talked about Ryan," Murphy said, ignoring Wyatt's personal inquiry.

Wyatt knew this was coming and dreaded it more than anything. Murphy had made little comments here and there to get him to open up on the subject, but so far he had avoided an all-out detailed account.

"There's nothing to talk about."

"Of course there is. You're internalizing this and it's going to take its toll. I think it's time we worked through it."

That did it. The anger that had been rumbling and brewing under the surface exploded. "Why, so you can exonerate yourself?" The accusation flew out of Wyatt's mouth before he could call it back. The moment lingered like the stench at a dump.

Murphy reached over for his glass, took a sip, and placed it back on the ledge. "Is that what you think?" he asked without the slightest hint of emotion.

Wyatt was furious with himself. When he had replayed the events surrounding Ryan, all the lies, and was feeling sorry for himself, he had assigned a small percentage of blame to Murphy. There wasn't a single part of him that believed Murphy was responsible for anything Ryan did, but it made him feel good.

"No, I'm sorry." Wyatt felt his face flush from shame. *How could you say that?*

"No worries," Murphy said with a smirk. "That doesn't even come close to making the top ten list of shitty things you've said to me over the years."

"I can't talk about Ryan right now."

Wyatt looked over to his partner, who once again, reached for his glass, sipped, and placed it back on the side of the Jacuzzi.

"I'm fucking my trainer, Rafael," Murphy volunteered without emotion.

"What?"

"You'd asked me if I was seeing anyone. I'm fucking my trainer. He came onto me one day when I was feeling a bit... what's the word I'm looking for?"

"Hungover?"

"I was feeling a bit... randy, that's it. So I decided to let it just happen. It turns out he's a sweetheart and smart as a whip. We've grown quite fond of each other and the sex continues to be phenomenal. I'm cut-glass hard right now just thinking about him. Wanna see?"

Wyatt managed a smile. He was relieved. They were over the hurdle.

"Sorry, I left my magnifying glass in the house. Another time, perhaps?" Wyatt's body was on full alert for any sign of a naughty toe inching its way toward his bat cave. It would be uncharacteristic of Murphy to let Wyatt's jab go away without some form of retribution.

"What are you doing to make sure I have strong talent auditioning for the ensemble?" Wyatt asked, changing the subject as he shifted his body to shield himself from Murphy's annoying probing.

"About a week…" Murphy leaned his head back, "after I placed an ad in *Variety*…."

The light, steady breeze coming from the ocean had calmed, allowing clouds of steam to rise into the clear night sky. Wyatt's view of Murphy was momentarily lost behind a plume of vapor.

Here comes that fucking toe again, I can sense it.

"I had Sandy start contacting our usual cream of the crop folks," a familiar voice continued from the opposite side of the tub. "Sandy, by the way, and I don't think I've told you this yet, is in the process of replacing herself as dance captain and will join us out here in a week."

"I can't wait for her to get out here, but please… please make sure she's got somebody replacing her we can count on," Wyatt begged. "The last thing I want is New York to suffer because we've spread ourselves too thin."

"We've got it covered. Don't you fret none, Ms. Pickle. Christ, you can be a pill sometimes," Murphy added with a frown as his image reappeared out of the mist.

"Sorry."

"We need her as soon as we can free her up. I don't think you understand yet how much people want to be a part of this project. It's looney tunes. People we haven't worked with in years are crawling out of the woodwork. The talent I've spoken to, without exception, act like you just informed them they've won the lottery. They're pumped. You should be proud *Dress Up* is causing so much excitement. It's all because of you, little Hitler."

"You're purposely baiting me," Wyatt said with a smirk.

"I'm not. I'm not baiting you and I don't even know what you're inferring, so there."

"Keep that toe to yourself… I mean that." Wyatt sensed another stealth attack was imminent.

"I wasn't going to do anything," Murphy lied, displaying a smirk on his face he couldn't hide.

"You want me to say something like, let's see… You can have all the talent in the world, but without funding, backers, and a heaping amount of charisma, you could be the best damn talent in the world working on a cruise ship for your entire life. It's my bad that I don't recognize your efforts more often. I mean that. Nobody can do what you do." Wyatt couldn't have been more sincere.

"You're right. I'm the best." Murphy agreed with a forced sense of self-worth.

"You joke, but it's true. You are the best." Wyatt said, lifting his glass.

"Next subject," Murphy countered, more than satisfied his efforts were being appreciated.

"I *miss* working with my babies," Wyatt said after a few calm moments had passed. "Isn't it wild how much like family they become? Just think how much of our lives we spend together. Do you realize some of those people have been dancing for me since the beginning?"

"What you do," Murphy said, sitting up and pouring Wyatt more wine, "and this is why you have the following you do, by the way, you accommodate people who are loyal to you. You may not know you do this, but I've seen you take a dancer who is past their prime, and when possible, you find a home for them. More importantly, you fit them in without sacrificing quality. It's like you continue to play to their strengths. I hear it all the time about you. That's extremely rare in this business. I'm serious."

"You're so adorable when you idolize me," Wyatt said with an exaggerated wink, prompting Murphy to lunge at him.

"Stop it, you butt-head, Wyatt gasped as Murphy submerged his head, causing him to thrash and splash like a mad man while searching for an opportunity to squirm out of Murphy's grip.

Free again, Wyatt hastily made a retreat to the safety of the other side of the tub, where he sat for several minutes gasping to catch his breath.

"Well, that was fun," Murphy said flatly.

"Enormous fun. Thanks so much for giving me the opportunity to suck in water through my nose. I never tire of that, never ever. You're the life of the party and don't let anyone tell you differently," Wyatt added sarcastically.

"Okay, pumpkin, here's the deal," Murphy said after they had sat for several minutes. "I'll have Sandy draw up a list of the talent we've heard back from. From there, you can determine how many more singer-dancers you'll need. Galaxy, by the way, has a great facility for auditions. You give me the specifics and we'll put it all together."

In addition to being the current dance captain for *Dress Up* in New York, Sandy Tipple had the rare distinction of being employed by both Wyatt and Murphy. It all depended on what stage of development their project was in. Early on, she spent more time with Murphy, planning, arranging talent, and organizing auditions. Once the production was past planning and into development, she acted as an advisor to Wyatt. If asked, she'd tell you her preference would be dancing in the show every night. Dancing would always remain her first love.

"Pumpkin, kitten, honestly, you're just too...."

"Too handsome and debonair for most?" Murphy answered for Wyatt.

"Well, there's that," Wyatt said with a devilish grin before lunging at Murphy and repaying him for his earlier shenanigans by submerging his head in the steaming water.

Murphy, no longer the gangly stick man he once was, wiggled his way out of Wyatt's grip, springing out of the water with a powerful surge, gasping and spitting into the air. Pounding his manly chest like Tarzan, he waded to the side of the tub and hoisted his now-muscular frame out into the cool night air, and in the process offered up a splendid view of his sculpted, wet, meaty butt for Wyatt's enjoyment.

"On that note, I bid you adieu," Murphy said when he was out of the water and heading for the comfort of his warm towel.

"Hey," Wyatt said as he climbed out of the pool.

Murphy picked up a towel and handed it to him.

"We've got a winner here, don't we?" Wyatt asked, drying off his face. "Let's go there for minute and never go there again until it's all said and done. Do you think this is going to be the big one we've always fantasized about?"

"How many times do I have to remind you, this…" Murphy stopped drying off his junk to thrust it out for Wyatt's benefit. "is the only big one you've ever fantasized about."

"Get that thing away from me," Wyatt teased, threatening to snap it off at the root with his towel.

"This movie is going to be bigger than either one of us could have ever imagined," Murphy confirmed, stepping into his underwear for protection. "All we have to do is make sure we don't lose control, and the world will be ours. Come to daddy, poopsie." Murphy motioned for Wyatt to come into his arms.

Still naked, Wyatt did as he was commanded. Murphy enveloped him in a huge bear hug.

You have no idea how much I miss being in your arms.

Wyatt rested his head on his friend's chest.

"Wyatt, no matter what goes on in our separate lives, I want you to know how much I love you. My life would be slimy shit without you, I swear."

"Mmm…." Wyatt purred while Murphy dried off his back.

"I can't imagine anyone in my life who will ever mean as much to me as you do."

Wyatt felt Murphy plant a kiss on the top of his head.

Never let me go.

"Hey," Murphy said, breaking off the embrace and pulling a shirt over his head, "how long does it take for that fucking chlorine smell to get out of my nose?"

"Less than a week," Wyatt replied, turning away to wipe the moisture that had magically appeared in his eyes.

Chapter 13

"THERE isn't a single part of me that doesn't want to freak out right now," Wyatt said, glancing out the window of Murphy's SUV as they drove down Le Brea to the studio. "It doesn't help to have palm trees jutting out everywhere you look either. They're freaky."

"Look, you've got auditions coming up and you know how much you enjoy those. For now, let me worry about everything else. I promise you I have it all under control. I'd tell you if I didn't."

"Oh right! How stupid do you think I am?" Wyatt knew better. Murphy would shield him from the painful reality of defeat right up until they were forced to jump into the lifeboat to escape the sinking ship. "All I ask is that you give me a warning if we start getting into trouble so I can at least prepare myself."

"We're fine. There's no trouble yet and I don't foresee any in the future. Okay, dumpling?" Wyatt could feel Murphy looking over his way, but refused to acknowledge him.

"What I can't wrap my mind around is how many people are connected with making this film. It makes me nervous. People are everywhere doing… who knows what the hell they're all doing." Wyatt needed this opportunity to expose his worry list to Murphy.

"I know what they're doing."

They sat in silence for a good block before Murphy added, "If you keep this up, I'm going to get pissed off. You're not trusting me to keep it all together. I'm in the front lines daily, trying valiantly to keep as much of the everyday bullshit as I can away from you so you can concentrate on what you do brilliantly, which is create a musical hit. Cut me some fucking slack."

"I'm sorry." Wyatt rarely angered Murphy to this degree. They sat in silence.

"You know, it's like babysitting a horde of unruly children," Murphy added after a couple blocks had passed by.

"I didn't mean to doubt you," Wyatt said, reaching over and rubbing Murphy's shoulder. "You're as tough as anyone in the business. You're amazingly smart and you're not easily influenced. However, I am my mother, and because of this, I worry."

"I know, I know," Murphy said, smiling over at Wyatt. "You know, it's always been my philosophy… there are others who know the entertainment business better than I do, but there aren't many, if any, who know what it takes to put together a hit musical better than we do. We have that part nailed. I don't give a rat's ass if we're talking film or stage."

"I'd like to think so," Wyatt added, looking out the window.

Without warning, Wyatt's thoughts shifted to Ryan. Falling asleep last night had been a struggle. He was very lonely. More so, he realized, than before his time spent in Maine. A taste of Ryan, how right and good it once felt, left him with an even bigger deficit in the "somebody please love me department" than he'd ever experienced before. For the first time since the blowup, Wyatt entertained the thought of reconciling with Ryan. This notion was squashed as soon as the memory of Ryan's lies worked their way back into the forefront of his thoughts.

WHILE Murphy was out slaying the studio dragons, Wyatt worked with Sandy, his assistant, to set up auditions for the twenty or so dancer-singers that would make up the film's ensemble. Many of his favorite people were on board, and even though he would audition them just to make sure there weren't any surprises or conditions he wasn't aware of, for the most part, their auditions would be a formality.

Sandy had put out an open casting call a few weeks earlier. Resumes arrived in such abundance she was forced to bring in two temporary employees to keep track of all of them. She narrowed the prospects down to a couple dozen who, at least on paper, had what they were looking for.

Wyatt glanced around the theater while Sandy shuffled through a stack of resumes. When Murphy had mentioned Galaxy Studios had a space to hold auditions, he had failed to elaborate on the fact that the space was a mini replica of a Broadway theater. It was a perfect space, and the best part about it—the setting would make his talent who traveled here from New York feel comfortable and welcomed. "You've got to love Hollywood money. Makes you feel right at home, doesn't it?" Wyatt asked.

"I was floored when I walked in here the first time. You know, this reminds me of the Henderson on Forty-fifth," Sandy said, glancing over her glasses at Wyatt. "I love that theater. It has so much character. Remember the old doorman, Gus? He used to bring me flowers. He wanted me."

"You mean he didn't have you?" Wyatt asked, raising a provocative eyebrow.

"In his dreams! Stripping a man before hot sex doesn't involve a diaper. What's that like, anyway?"

Sandy's barb cracked Wyatt up. He had to be at the top of his game to keep up with her, and that was one of the things he loved about her the most. She could hold her ground and her scathingly brilliant wit had gotten him through some very challenging times. Like right now.

Several days before the auditions, Sandy had met with the studio carpenters to have a series of seats removed from the center section for tables she and Wyatt could sit at and make notes. She had been through the audition process so many times she didn't need to trouble him with any of the logistics. Lighting, music, it all had been set up in advance. All he had to do was show up and select his talent.

"So, is this list final?" Wyatt asked, looking over the names.

"Yeah. What do you think?" Sandy asked.

"Wow, lots of new names. I hope there's a Casey hiding somewhere in here."

"Yeah, me too. He's going to be a tough one to cast. Here, take a look at these headshots. They're the potential Caseys I've singled out for you." Sandy handed Wyatt a stack of resumes. "I went over our notes from the original casting in New York. I hope I'm on the right track."

Wyatt sifted through the stack of young hopefuls. "Noah Renville, adorable," he commented. "There's a great vulnerability in his look. I think that's key to this role working the way it's supposed to. Lets hope he can carry a tune and dance."

"A little hottie. He definitely looks the part."

Auditions were scheduled to extend over two days. Wyatt used the first day to weed out those who, for whatever reason, either weren't of the caliber required or physically didn't complement the rest of the ensemble. From all of their years of experience they could spot a clinker a mile away. Sandy had a talent for noticing discrepancies and inaccuracies while they were still on paper. Sometimes it was style, or attitude, that emerged from the headshot and flagged trouble. This prescreening task had long been removed from Wyatt's list of responsibilities.

The two of them had gotten so efficient with this first day of the audition process, they were able to find time during breaks to discuss those who showed potential and make notes about how they would audition these individuals on the following day. Again, they were able to minimize the time wasted sorting out the good from the fabulous.

Dress Up altered their process slightly. It was a different style of show, requiring a wider range of types. As long as the singing and dancing talent of an actor was strong, Wyatt could have fun playing around with type. Sometimes he even changed dialogue around or made notes to make script changes based on ideas he had while casting. This flexibility was unique in that most directors had a preconceived idea of what type of actor should play a specific role. By keeping things loose, Wyatt was able to cash in on some stronger, more interesting casting that translated to a more interesting production.

"Wyatt, what the hell happened to Rosemary Troussant? She has no voice." Sandy had already delegated her resume to the pile of rejects.

"She looks terrible too. Seems to me I heard something about drugs a long time ago, maybe she's having issues again." Wyatt was disappointed Rosemary wasn't making the cut. They had a long history of working together. It frustrated him he no longer had the time to look into situations like this. To some extent, he felt he owed that to his actors. "Let's move on," he said with a sigh.

"Drugs... I'd never heard that about her." Picking up another resume, Sandy shoved it over to him. "What about Patsy Joas?"

"I *love* her look! She screams sassy!" Wyatt said, laughing. "What planet did she drop down from?"

"She's been working in Toronto for the last several years. Trade shows, some commercial work. This is her first trip to Hollywood. She's a powerhouse. I was thinking she might work as the photographer's assistant. Wait until you talk to her, she has this built-in comedic thing going on. Very fresh."

"Great. Yeah... the assistant. That could work out very well. Good work, Sandra."

Both Wyatt and Sandy were pumped as the first day wound itself down. They could easily fill most of their vacancies in the cast with, in some cases, a variety of options.

"Thank you, my dear. Are you ready for the boys?" Sandy asked.

"More than you know," Wyatt shot back. "Let's keep our fingers crossed we have at least one good Casey in the bunch."

Wyatt expressed a huge sigh of relief once they had finished looking over the men. They had a couple of strong Casey candidates to put through their paces the following day. Noah Renville had, in Wyatt's mind everything the role required. Vocally, he was a ten. Dancing, a ten. He was as charming as his photograph had promised. Noah's closest competitor for the role, a young man from the Detroit area, was almost as strong in the singing and dancing areas, but lacked the sparkle Noah brought to the stage. Sparkle was important.

"Are you ready for me to bring them out?" Sandy asked after flipping through the stack of resumes on the table in front of her.

"Let's do it." Wyatt said, standing up and stretching.

The flip side to finding the talent they needed was saying good-bye to those they didn't need. It didn't matter how many times Wyatt was put in this situation, sending someone away, especially someone talented but not right for the show, was painful for him. There were always a few tears. Wyatt worked hard to be fair and encouraging. He insisted his staff follow his lead to ensure each actor who auditioned was treated with dignity and respect.

Occasionally, egos got the best of an individual. Instead of accepting their defeat, they made the very wrong decision to attempt to argue their way into a show. Wyatt had a reliable way of dealing with these situations. A few exceedingly personal, and absolutely spot-on criticisms, tailored specifically to the individual and voiced loud enough for anyone in the vicinity to hear, were tough to argue with and, typically, all it took for the disgruntled actor or actress to pack up and leave the audition area. "Leslie Frank," Wyatt would offer when the situation warranted it. "She's great at reintroducing a dancer to the *basics*." It worked like a charm.

On the morning of the second day of auditions, Wyatt met Sandy for an early breakfast at the studio commissary. It was crucial they were both on the same page going into this final phase. It was rare they weren't, but if needed, Sandy could argue for or against an actor, and in most cases she won the argument. He never took offense to these discussions, which at times could become quite heated. It was all good.

"Look who I ran into," Sandy said, walking up to Wyatt's table with Murphy right behind her.

"Hi, snotty," Murphy said with a grin. "Sandy said you guys had a good day yesterday."

"Hey, Murph!" Wyatt said, smiling back. "Yep, we sure did. I've been here since five, trying to organize myself. Sandy, the other guy for Casey... um... Matt Perkman, I can't remember our final thought on him. What did we think?"

"Well, I can see I'm just going to be in the way here. You guys have a great day," Murphy said, giving Sandy a peck on the cheek.

"No," Wyatt said, standing, "You don't have to go."

"Yes, I do," Murphy said, moving over to Wyatt and giving him a hug. "I've got a meeting with Stilton over on stage two in a few minutes. He's concerned we're getting too dark with the interior of the ad agency."

"What do you think?" Wyatt asked.

"I think he may be right," Murphy said. "We need the agency bright to mirror the energy during the photo shoot number. On the sketches we approved it didn't seem that dark. I'll take a look, and if it's a close call, I'll send for you. Could you step away from auditions for a few minutes this morning if I need you?"

"Mom, can I go with Murphy later and play?" Wyatt asked Sandy.

"Okay, but I'll want you home by lunch. I'm going to need some additional time with the dance captain. I want her to teach both of the potential Caseys as much of the solo as possible. They worked on it yesterday afternoon, but in all fairness, they need more time with it."

"Call me on my cell," Wyatt said, sitting back down. "I'll get over there as quickly as I can."

"Okeydokey! Play nice today, kids," Murphy said as he squeezed Sandy's arm.

"Bye, Murph," Wyatt and Sandy said in unison as she plopped her notes down on the table and sat next to Wyatt.

"I'm glad you brought Casey up," Sandy said as she opened her notebook and glanced over her notes. "I woke up in the middle of the night and I couldn't get back to sleep."

Wyatt was gunning for Noah Renville to have the role but he could tell by the tone in Sandy's voice she had reservations. "What are you thinking?" he asked, hoping she hadn't closed the door on Noah.

"I know you like Noah, and I like him too. But he might not have the depth we need. That's what I liked about Matt Perkman. He brings this edgy quality in with him. We could use that to our advantage."

Shit! Wyatt saw where she was headed with this, and to some extent she was right. He had one chance to verbalize why he thought the role could work a different way. Sucking air through his teeth, he quickly framed up his defense.

"Conceptually, I think we are looking at this role from two different places," Wyatt began.

"Could be," Sandy said. "Go on."

"I see Casey as being more of a free spirit and I think Noah plays stronger into that aspect. Don't get me wrong—if pressed, I'd take Matt in heartbeat. He's going to be noticed no matter where he ends up. But I think he's too, well, like the agency set, too dark. Here...."

Wyatt paused for a minute, to make sure he had his thoughts in order. "Look at it this way. If someone told Matt he wasn't ever going to be good enough to be a top model, he'd probably agree. And that's why, as an actor dancing Casey, he would have to work harder at overcoming that instinct. Noah, on the other hand, has this crazy kind of unbridled enthusiasm that, well, right or wrong, he's going to go for it anyway. Does that make any sense? There's a quality about him that tells us he doesn't give a shit. He's going to prove everyone wrong."

Wyatt gave Sandy a few moments to mull this over. He could see her attempting to visualize his argument.

"What I think Noah brings to the role," Wyatt continued, "and this to me is *so* important, is his wonderful, careless energy. It's an innocence, a real sense that, despite just having his entire career, his ambitions chopped off and handed to him on a platter by someone who knows the business, he's hurt, yes, but he knows deep down they're wrong. It's about an actor's instinct. I think he can play this more honestly than Matt can. I mean, we're talking a very subtle difference in the two."

"You're right, Wy," Sandy said with a smile. "I see it now."

"Huh? Did you just agree with me?" Wyatt was surprised his assistant was throwing in the towel without more of a fight. "Is there a catch?"

"No catch," Sandy said, taking a sip of her coffee. "I haven't progressed as far with the part since New York as you have. I agree Casey should be more like Noah. That was a great point."

"Did you hear that, everyone?" Wyatt shouted as he stood up, throwing his hands in the air. "She agrees with me."

"Shush! There's a little baby sleeping behind you, you dummy." Sandy pointed in back of Wyatt as he sheepishly sat back in his chair.

"There's a little baby sleeping behind me?" he mouthed.

"Yes, so stop being such an asshead. And you know I've agreed with you in the past, so stuff it." Sandy picked up a piece a paper and began ignoring Wyatt.

"Is it a little cocktail wiener or a mini donut?" Wyatt whispered.

"What are you talking about?" Sandy asked, looking over her notes at Wyatt.

"The baby, is it a wiener or a mini donut?"

"You're very sick," Sandy said, laughing now that she finally picked up on Wyatt's sophomoric humor. "It appears to be dressed in yellow, so maybe it's a little cheese curd."

Just as she finished, they heard a wail originating from behind Wyatt.

"See what you did!"

"I didn't do a thing," Wyatt hissed over the table before turning around to catch the attention of the mother seated behind him. "I'm sorry I was so loud before. I didn't know there was a little one behind me. I'm usually not this rude."

"Oh, don't worry about it, Mr. Stark," the woman answered. "She's letting me know she's hungry."

Wyatt turned back with a look of horror on his face.

"Wyatt, stop that. She has a bottle in her hand," Sandy assured him before returning to her notes.

"It's too early for bare boobies," Wyatt said with a twinkle in his eye.

"Honey, is there ever a good time for you and bare boobies?" Sandy inquired with more than a hint of frustration. "I think not. Now, can you focus so we can get through these notes before we have to head over to the theater?"

"Yes, ma'am." Wyatt put on his glasses, signaling he was back to work. "Wait."

"What?"

"Do you want a little one of your own some day? I've always wanted to ask you." Wyatt was serious. He'd often wondered if Sandy had any desire to act on her maternal instincts.

"God damn it, Wyatt. We have so much work to do here." Sandy put down her notes and stared across at her boss. "I'm going to answer this, and then you're going to stop with this shit and get back to work. Deal?"

"Deal," Wyatt answered, leaning into the table.

"A part of me, I'm not sure where this comes from, but a part of me would like my body to experience the act of childbirth. I'm not sure I want to go through life missing out on that. However, I don't see that happening because I have absolutely no desire to parent. None. Zero. Have you ever wished your dick had two heads?"

"Huh?" Wyatt asked confused.

"Back to work!"

Wyatt typically joined the dancers on stage during a portion of the auditions. Today wasn't any different. He was a show-off at heart. Because he no longer performed, dancing at auditions was a real kick for him. Dressed in loose sweats and a sleeveless T-shirt, he rehearsed Casey's solo with both Noah and Matt together. He believed that to get the best out of a dancer during auditions, you had to provide them with the best foundation possible. Oftentimes he would stop the audition process to take time to ensure what he was asking for was clearly understood. The payoff was well worth the time spent.

"Take a ten-minute break and then I'll have you run the combination on your own. You guys are dancing great, so start having fun with it. Show me some personality."

With a towel wrapped around his neck, Wyatt walked down the stairs and sat next to Sandy at the audition table.

"What do you think?" she asked, handing Wyatt a chilled bottle of water.

"Matt's got it nailed. Noah, not so much. Something isn't right with him. Did you pick up on anything when you were talking to him earlier?" Wyatt sipped his water and wiped the sweat off of his neck with his towel.

"No, but he's definitely not the same performer we had in here yesterday, that's for sure. I'm sure they're nervous. What are you thinking?"

"His dancing isn't confident and the charm I saw yesterday seems to be missing. He's hitting the moves, but he isn't owning any of it. He's tentative. I don't see the strength either." Wyatt couldn't hide his disappointment.

"I'm sorry," Sandy said, reaching over and patting Wyatt on the arm. "I know how excited you were for today to work out for him."

Wyatt sat sipping his water until the two dancers had returned to the stage.

"You want them together, right?" Sandy asked, looking over to Wyatt to make sure he hadn't changed his mind.

"Wait, I have an idea." Wyatt got up and walked down to the stage. "Matt, Noah, I'm changing the game plan. I'm going to see you guys separately. Matt, let's start with you. Noah, you can hang out in the wings."

Wyatt waited for Noah to exit before he continued. "You're doing a great job, Matt. You should feel very good about your work today. Now what I need from you is to sell this character. Show me his feelings. If the dancing slides a little, don't worry about it. I know you can move. Any questions?"

"No. I'm ready."

Wyatt headed back to the table and took his seat. "I have a plan," he whispered to Sandy.

"No doubt you do," she whispered back.

The music started and Matt began to dance. Wyatt watched for several minutes before standing and signaling for the music to stop. "Matt, you're too concerned with precision. I need to see some personality. Let's try it one more time."

Wyatt sat back down and once again the music started. This time Wyatt allowed the dancer to finish.

"That was nice, Matt. Please send Noah out on the stage, but don't go anywhere."

"Sure thing! Thanks, Mr. Stark."

"What did you think?" Wyatt asked Sandy.

"I caught glimpses of Casey, but I don't think he gets it. I think he's confusing energy for nuance."

"That's what I think too. I'm going to have a little chat with Noah before he dances. I'm not giving up on him… yet."

Wyatt approached the stage. "Noah, how ya doin', hangin' in there?"

"I'm really nervous today, Mr. Stark."

"Were you nervous yesterday too?" Wyatt asked.

"Not so much. I had no idea yesterday until after I had danced that you were interested in me for Casey. That's huge," Noah answered meekly.

"Is there anything you want to tell me, Noah?" Wyatt placed his hand on the stage. "I think there's something you're not telling me."

"I'm not sure what you mean, Mr. Stark."

Wyatt was convinced this all had to do with nerves, but he needed to be certain. "Here's what I think." Wyatt hoisted himself up onto the stage. Putting an arm around the young dancer, he walked Noah over to the opposite side of the proscenium so they could have a private moment together. "I think you're nervous and it's gotten the best of you. Yesterday, before you knew much about Casey, you had it nailed."

"I blew a few steps this morning and—"

"And you were afraid I'd lost interest in you for the part, right?" Wyatt smiled. "You're my Casey, Noah. You were my Casey from the moment I laid eyes on you. I hoped you could sing, you can. I hoped you could dance, you can. However, neither of those talents make you Casey."

"I want this role so bad, Mr. Stark."

"I know you do. Look, today you know much more about Casey than you did yesterday. What I think you'd like to tell me is how much you and Casey have in common. Am I right?"

"I went home last night and I cried because I was so... so happy. Casey feels so right. I know exactly who Casey is, Mr. Stark. He's me."

Wyatt smiled back. He hated the control he had over Noah, but this was business and he needed to be sure.

"I'm so emotional right now, and I'm sorry I can't control it better." Noah wiped the tears from his face. "My family... my friends... there wasn't one person in my life who thought I could do this. I have fought my ass off to be here. You have no idea how much I identify with Casey. He's me, Mr. Stark. Fuck! Oh... I'm so sorry for swearing. I'm just... well... this... you... this is my dream. Right now... this is my dream."

"Noah, you're doing better than fine with me." Wyatt resisted the urge to hug the boy and instead, took his hands into his own. "I had a feeling you and Casey were kindred spirits. Okay... here's the deal. Both Sandy and I are rooting for you. Let's give it another shot, shall we?"

"Yes! Thank you so much!"

"Make this role your own, Noah, and I'll be thanking you. Trust me."

Wyatt jumped off the stage and sauntered back to the table. "I think he's feeling much better about today."

Sandy signaled for the music to start. The familiar strains of Casey's solo flooded the auditorium. Wyatt sat glued to his seat. From the beginning moves, Noah had taken to heart his advice and was now, as Wyatt had hoped, dancing his heart out. Noah was nowhere to be found. It was Casey's turn to shine.

"What did you say to that boy?" Sandy whispered, unable to divert her eyes from the performance she was watching.

"I told him he was good."

Chapter 14

AT THE end of the day, there was only one dancer Wyatt and Sandy differed on. Her name was Molly Wicks. Sandy, too used to looking for lean and sexy, was having a hard time wrapping her mind around Molly, who was a big girl. Wyatt was impressed with her dancing. For a big girl, she moved very well, learned the choreography with lightning speed, and had a very pleasant and strong singing voice. Though typically he would have to pass her up because of how she would stick out in an ensemble, with *Dress Up*, he had the flexibility to cast a Molly if he wanted. He had hoped for a male version of Molly as well, but he hadn't found one yet. Wyatt argued he could have some fun in the background with her, and eventually Sandy agreed.

The dancers were called back. Wyatt delivered a brief speech thanking them all and praising their abilities. The names of those who were not to join the cast were read out. When those dancers had gathered up their belongings and exited the theater, all hell broke loose with whoops and hollers of joy from those who had made the cut.

Wyatt joined his cast on stage and talked briefly about how he worked, what his expectations were, and also made a point to let everyone know he was open to suggestions, as long as they were positive. Looking around at the young faces, how earnest and thrilled they all seemed, it was almost like they had an audience with the Pope. It was easy to see how directors and other people in power could take advantage and become egomaniacs. Thankfully, he had people like Murphy in his life to balance it all out. Murphy would have no problem calling him on any behavior that wasn't one hundred percent professional.

Wyatt finished going over what he had on his list and turned the stage over to Sandy, who discussed the basics, like schedules and contracts. Once she had covered all she had on her list, they opened the floor up for questions. He always thought it was strange his performers didn't have more questions. Many took the opportunity to thank him for bringing them aboard.

"Mr. Stark, are there any major changes planned for the film version?" Patsy Joas from Toronto asked.

"Definitely, you're in it this time," Wyatt joked as he walked over and gave her a hug. "You guys stop calling me Mr. Stark. I keep looking around expecting to see my dad. I'm Wyatt."

Wyatt walked back to where he had been standing. "There is one major change in the movie. Well, it's not really a change, it's an expansion. The role of Casey has been expanded and will now have much more screen time than the character had stage time in the original production. By the way, Noah Renville, the adorably bashful young man hiding in the corner there, is our Casey."

The cast applauded and whistled, causing Noah to turn about as red in the face as humanly possible.

"We will also be looking into expanding the role of the photographer's assistant, and we are lucky enough to have Ms. Patsy Joas devouring that role. Let's here it for Ms. Joas."

This announcement was again met with cheers and well-wishes from the cast.

"Any more questions?" Wyatt asked, looking around the room. "Great! Go home, keep yourselves healthy, and we'll be mailing out contracts and other essentials in the next week. Is that right, Sandy?"

"Yep, that's the goal," Sandy answered.

"You guys are amazing! I can't wait to start working with you. You're all geniuses. Have a good night!"

And with that, the ensemble for the movie version of the hit Broadway musical *Dress Up* was formally dismissed for the day. Wyatt stood on the wings and shook each performer's hand as they gathered up their dance gear and left the stage.

"We're in good shape, don't you think?" Wyatt asked as he plopped down at their table.

"I'm still thunderstruck over Noah. If we can capture even half of what we just saw today on film, he's going to annihilate them."

"It makes you wonder how many kids out there get passed up because they're having a bad day. Matt's a great guy, but I don't think I could have cast him." Wyatt put his elbows on the table and massaged his temples.

"In a strange way, I feel like it's my first show." Sandy curled herself up into a ball on the chair with a smile filling her entire face. "Just like those kids, I'm thrilled to be a part of this. Thank you so much for all the things you've done for me over the years. I know this is going to come back and bite me in the ass, but I adore working with you."

"Hey," Wyatt said, patting her knee. "Do you think for one minute I could do any of this without you?" Wyatt purposely didn't return the smile. He meant what he said. He and Murphy, on a multitude of occasions, had commented on how Sandy really got it. She was almost a third partner.

"Listen, Sandra my dear, it's been a long couple of days, so why don't you pack up and have a big glass of that Chardonnay you like? What's it called, rat's ass or something elegant like that?"

"I'm off white wine these days. Bradley, the guy I was fucking all through last spring, the one nice thing he did for me before he took off with my purse and stole my mother's ring was turn me onto red wine. I'm in the big league now."

"I'd forgotten about him. Did you ever get any of it back?" Wyatt could tell Sandy was still wounded by the whole experience. He hoped by asking about it he wasn't making things worse.

"I did," Sandy answered proudly. "The cops recovered my ring and my purse, but alas, my cash was gone. It could have been worse, I guess. He's doing jail time, which is some consolation."

"Listen, I'm serious. Get the hell out of here. You did an awesome job today. We have an excellent cast and it's all because of you."

Sandy began stuffing her notes into the large tote she took everywhere. Wyatt smiled as he watched her pack up. He'd nicknamed her tote "the well" because the depth of the bag seemed endless to him.

"Do you want to join me for a drink somewhere, Wy?" she asked as she stood, slipping her bare feet back into her flats.

"I'd love to, but I have some ideas I want to jot down before they float into never-never land," Wyatt answered with a deep sigh. "Besides, I'm wiped out after giving birth to Casey through Noah Renville's body. It was truly an experience." Wyatt felt exhausted, but he knew if he worked out what was rolling around in his mind, it would save him a ton of time later trying to recapture his ideas. "I'll call you in the morning and we can go over contract specifics and any other issues you come up with. That girl, Melanie, is it? We should try and find an answer for her about medical. I'll talk to Murphy about it. Have a good night, sweetie!"

"You too! If you want to meet up for lunch or something, let me know."

"Will do!" Wyatt sat back and watched her exit up the stairs.

"Wy?" Sandy asked as she turned back.

"Yeah, babe?"

"Audiences are going to shit in their pants when they see *Dress Up* on the big screen. It's going to be mega. That's it. Good night!"

Wyatt delved into his audition notes and had been working for about an hour when he heard voices coming from backstage. Poking his head up from his notes, he listened as the voices grew louder. He was sure they were coming from somewhere on the left side of the stage. "Auditions are over. I've told you that several times now. If you don't leave this minute, I'm going to have to call security."

He thought he recognized the voice as that of the woman who acted as the receptionist for the front of the building. Besides this theater, there were studio offices both upstairs and down. He had never met her, but she had one of those squeaky voices that, if you heard it once, you knew who it was when you heard it again. He continued to look in the direction of the voice. Suddenly, both the receptionist and Ryan bolted onto the stage at the same time.

"I'm sorry, Mr. Stark," the woman cried out in frustration. "I've tried to tell him auditions were over and you were done for the day. Do you want me to call security?"

Ryan had separated himself from the woman and stood at center stage. He was dressed in a suit and tie. It took Wyatt several seconds to recover from the shock of seeing him before he could answer. "That won't be necessary," he said without emotion, staring down at his notes. "You can leave us now."

"Wyatt, please give me a minute to talk," Ryan asked.

Wyatt continued to stare down at his notes. It had been a good month since leaving Maine, and he was just starting to feel okay about putting the Ryan episode behind him. Taking a deep breath, he looked up. Ryan stood under a soft pool of light with his hands in his pockets.

"What can I do for you, Ryan?" Wyatt asked impatiently. "Oh wait, let me guess. You're an accomplished dancer and you've come to audition for my movie. Is that it?"

Ryan ignored the barb. "I'm a lot of things, Wyatt, but I'm not a dancer. I've come to say… I've come to talk to you, if you'll just give me a minute."

"To talk, is it? Well, I can't imagine what we could have to talk about," Wyatt quipped sarcastically, looking back down at his papers. "Except maybe you're planning on including me in your next deception because you saw how much I enjoyed playing a role in your previous one." Wyatt surprised even himself at how bitter he still felt and sounded.

"Look," Ryan continued, removing his hands from his pants pockets, "I don't blame you one bit for still being angry. I had no idea how foolish I was being this summer by not revealing my identity to you from the very start. Hands down, it was the worst decision I have ever made in my life. But Wyatt…." Ryan stepped forward, his hands reaching out. "I never meant to hurt you. I fell in love with you. I'm in love with you. I want to be part of your life. Please give me a second chance. We can start slow until I've built back some trust. Anything, it's your call. Wyatt… I'll do anything to make this right. Please… please give me a second chance."

Wyatt waited for a moment to make sure Ryan had finished. Folding his arms across his chest, he scrunched up his jaw and looked out over the rows of seats, and finally back up onto the stage. This man, the man standing before him, had hurt him deeply. So deeply, in fact, he was almost debilitated now by the rage he felt building just at the sound of Ryan's voice. Shuffling the papers in front of him, he fought for control before he looked up.

"Ryan, I have a movie to make here," he said as evenly as he could. "I get the part about you being sorry for what you did to me this summer, but I have to tell you...." Wyatt paused to keep his emotions in check. Sweat had broken out on his neck and he was trembling. "I... I just don't have any interest in pursuing anything with you... ever again. Now, if you'll forgive me, I have work to do here. That is, unless you want to continue what you're doing up there so you can fuck with me even more than you already have."

Wyatt froze his stare on Ryan. The two held their gaze for several moments before Ryan, with a shake of his head, turned and walked out.

Wyatt sat back down and put his head in his hands. He was spent.

"Well, that was an impressive piece of drama," a familiar voice called out from the back of the auditorium. Startled, Wyatt turned to see Murphy strolling down the aisle.

"I didn't mean to eavesdrop, but the receptionist called to say there might be some trouble here. I heard the whole thing."

"You have no idea what happened this summer."

"Actually, I do, at least from Ryan's perspective." Murphy took off his coat and threw it over a chair. He sat down a couple feet away. "You're probably not interested, but I'm going to tell you a little bit about who Ryan really is."

Murphy didn't look directly at Wyatt. Instead, he took off his tie and folded it in his hand while he talked. "Ryan," he continued, "comes from very wealthy parents. His mother is a therapist with a bucket full of A-list clients and his father, an investment banker. He grew up differently than you and I. He grew up privileged and didn't want for a single thing. Well, at least nothing money could buy."

"Lovely. Where is this going, Murphy?" Wyatt sat looking forward with his hands once more folded across his chest.

"Ryan did time at a summer camp in northern Maine, and because of that, it made sense to me he should be the one to watch over you. I knew I needed someone close by because, well, you were fragile. I can't tell you why he made the decision to present himself as someone else. As I'm sure you understand, I never asked him to do anything like that. It was a decision, a stupid decision he made on his own. I've got to be honest with you—other than this monumental lapse in good judgment, for a kid who grew up with all the ingredients for a disastrous life, he is remarkably well-grounded and he does a fabulous job for me."

"Murphy, I asked you this before and I don't plan on asking you this again. Where is this going? I have a fucking movie to make here."

"I'm getting off point." Murphy reached over and stuck his tie in the inside pocket of his coat. "When Ryan met you and got to know you, he... well, he wanted you. According to what he's told me, and I believe him, he figured if you knew he was my assistant, as opposed to a local kid I hired to watch over you and the house, you'd have never given him the time of day. So, he devised this alias in hopes you would, well, like you did—fall in love with him."

Murphy sense, here it comes. Breathe!

"Wyatt," Murphy continued, "I know you like the back of my hand. Come off it. Do you want to let this one slip away? He's a terrific guy. He's got looks, he's smart, and I know for a fact those tears he shed in my office were genuine. He loves you more than you'll ever know. And from what I already know by the degree of anger you're displaying right now, you had... wait, that isn't right."

Wyatt looked over at his friend, wondering why he had stopped mid-sentence.

"You have genuine feelings for him still. I know this is true. So I ask you, do you really want to let this one slip away?"

For the first time in two days, Wyatt became aware of the air conditioning system in the auditorium. It purred in a soft, mechanical way. Despite the cool air circulating around the room, beads of sweat broke out on his forehead and rolled down the side of his face. Wyatt slammed his fist down on the table and bolted up the stairs to the stage.

CLUTCHING his hand over his mouth, Ryan ran down the hallway. Frantic, he searched for the exit. Rounding a corner in the hallway behind the stage, he spotted the familiar red sign. He charged at the heavy metal door and threw himself at the release handle. The door banged open and he was thrust out into an asphalt parking lot. Falling back onto the closed door, his knees buckled as he clenched his stomach. He couldn't get air fast enough. Oblivious to his surroundings, he curled into the door and began to cry. Huge sobs racked his body as he squinted into the blinding sun.

"Wyatt... Wyatt... Please! Please, Wyatt!" he called out. "I'm so sorry!"

Unable to stay on his feet, he slid down the door, wincing as his knees came in contact with the hot pavement. Immobilized by the sickening reality that any chance of being forgiven by Wyatt had been swiftly wiped away, his heart bled. A profound feeling of sadness kept him on the ground.

Eventually, a distant siren reminded him he was still on his knees. Wiping the tears from his face, he took a couple of deep breaths and slid his body back up the door until he was back on his feet. Rogue waves of emotion continued to erupt from deep within as he staggered forward.

This is really happening! It's over!

Stopping to get his bearings, Ryan realized he was turned around and his car was parked on the other side of the building. Embarrassed at the thought he might have been watched, he wiped his face once more and began walking. Crossing the entrance to the parking lot, he started down the long sidewalk to the other end of the building.

With his head bowed, he passed a group of men standing near a side door, smoking. Reaching the corner, he looked up and spotted his car at the opposite end of the lot. Weak and spent, he willed himself to his car, hoping to make it inside before the next wave of emotion took control of him.

WYATT flew out a door in the back of the theater and found himself in a brightly lit, white-tiled hallway. He looked left and right. He needed to keep moving. He chose left, which took him around a bank of offices that led to the reception area.

"Mr. Stark?"

Wyatt dismissed the receptionist with a wave of his hand as he flew past her.

"I'm sorry about interrupting you...."

Stepping aside while an elderly couple entered the building, Wyatt marked time as he held the door for them. *Could you move any fucking slower? Giddy up. Come on, FUCKING MOVE IT!* Milliseconds after they had cleared the opening, he was out the door. Rows of cars were spread out before him. *Oh please God, do me a solid. Just this once, please?* Three rows down, a woman was loading a kid into a black Escalade. Wyatt scoured the lot for any other movement. His heart sank.

Near the point of giving up any hope of catching up to Ryan, out of the corner of his eye, he spotted a head. His view was blocked by a van parked between him and the figure. Wyatt stood up on his toes, stretching his body left and right in hopes of catching another glimpse. Seconds later, Ryan emerged from the end of the van.

"Ryan! Ryan! Wait!" he hollered as he ran through the rows of cars. Waving his hands frantically, Wyatt watched as Ryan turned to look in his direction. "Ryan! Wait for me!"

Dodging a car speeding its way through the lot, Wyatt slowed himself as he approached. From twenty feet away, he could tell Ryan had been crying. Wyatt fought a battle with his own emotions as he closed the gap between them.

"You can't just fuck with people and then assume things are going to be okay," Wyatt said when he was within a few feet of Ryan.

"You want me to forgive you, and I'm not sure I can do that. I have feelings, Ryan. I can be hurt."

"What I did to you was very wrong. Trust me, I know that. I've asked myself a million times how I could have possibly been so stupid."

"I trusted you. I trusted you and you betrayed me with your lies. Why would you do such a thing?" Wyatt couldn't hold back. A part of him wanted to hurt Ryan like he had been hurt. "You knew I was falling in love with you and you rewarded me with more lies. Did you honestly think I wasn't going to care? Is it possible you just thought I'd be maybe a little pissed off and I would get over it? Come on, I mean really, what were you thinking?"

"Does it matter what I say to you at this point, Wyatt? Does it really matter what I fucking say to you? Why did you follow me out here?" Ryan moved away from the car. "Come on, this is your chance. Put me in my place. Make me feel like a smaller piece of shit than I do already. Come on, tell me how I'm scum. Say it, Wyatt, and then leave me alone. I can't say I'm sorry any more than I've already said it. I can't hurt anymore than I'm already hurting. Call me a fucking loser and then please... leave me alone. You'll never be bothered by me again."

Ryan stopped and fixed his gaze on Wyatt, as if challenging him. Tears began flowing down his cheeks as he waited for Wyatt to respond.

"What have I done?" Wyatt rubbed his forehead, unsure of what he wanted, what he needed to say. It was his heart that eventually spoke to him. He stepped toward Ryan. "I don't want to leave. I want us to be... like before. I want to hold you again in my arms." Wyatt reached for Ryan, uncertain if he would allow himself to be held. Ryan took a step backward, teetered for a moment, and then collapsed into Wyatt's arms.

"Wyatt...." Ryan threw his arms around Wyatt's waist.

Wyatt struggled to keep them both on their feet.

"I'm so sorry. I'm so fucking sorry," Ryan cried. "I was so stupid. I never wanted to hurt you...."

"I know. I know," Wyatt said as he ran his fingers through Ryan's hair. "I'm sorry too. I love you, Ryan."

"I love you so much. I missed you. I...."

Wyatt waited for Ryan to continue. He held his handsome lover tight to his body as they swayed back and forth.

"Look...." Wyatt stopped himself. Gently, he lifted Ryan's head off his chest and took it into his hands. "I've missed your eyes. I've missed your lips. You're so beautiful, Ryan. I love you."

"Wyatt, I'm so sorry...."

"Mmm." Wyatt pressed his finger to Ryan's lips. He shook his head back and forth as he fought to keep from crying. Using his finger, Wyatt began brushing away Ryan's tears. "I'm as much to blame as you are. I was caught off guard. Someday, we'll talk about the whole thing."

Wyatt felt an enormous wave of relief as he held his lover in his arms. *I don't know how I know this, but we are going to work.*

"Let's give us another try." Wyatt lifted Ryan's face up from his chest.

"I missed you so much, you can't imagine," Ryan gushed as he wiped his face with the sleeve of his shirt.

Smiling, Wyatt tapped Ryan's chest. "You lie to me ever again, and I'll staple your balls to my laundry receipt. Just for starters!" They both exploded in nervous laughter. "I'm totally serious."

Wyatt backed Ryan up against the nearest car. He cupped his hand behind Ryan's head and pulled him forward. His heart soared as their lips met.

Chapter 15

AS OSCAR season approached, Wyatt, with Murphy's help, tried to keep the hype and the buzz surrounding the movie in perspective. He had been involved in scads of award events over the years, including countless Tony celebrations, but the excitement around *Dress Up* was unlike anything he'd ever experienced. The movie had opened just prior to the busy holiday season to unanimously stellar reviews. Critics across the country heralded *Dress Up* as a milestone in how the American musical had previously been approached on film. It ruled the box office for weeks after its release, and he was blown away by how well his baby had been received.

When nominations were announced in early February, the film did extremely well, beating out all of its competitors with eleven nominations. The only disappointment was the exclusion of Abigale Hunter from the lineup of women nominated for best actress. The talented young newcomer from New York had won a fierce battle for the role of Alexis Barron, the iniquitous head of Lockwood and Plum, the ad agency *Dress Up* is centered around. Hollywood had fought hard to cast Lana Melville as Alexis. Outsiders speculated Abigale was being ignored because of her ties with the east coast. Wyatt spent days in a deep funk because her brilliant performance had been slighted. He hated competitions to begin with. He felt her exclusion was petty and unfair.

Two days prior to the big ceremony, Wyatt and company—including his parents and along with Linda and Sandy—moved into the top floor of the luxurious Crawford Hotel in downtown Los Angeles, a few blocks from where the awards were being held. This had been Murphy's idea, and it turned out to be a brilliant one. The press, smelling either a huge win for *Dress Up* or a huge defeat, were relentless in their pursuit of anyone involved with the picture. The hotel, experienced with hosting Oscar participants, added another layer of security to ensure everyone's safety.

On the morning of the big day, Wyatt woke up feeling surprisingly refreshed and calm. "Poopsie, are you awake?"

"Yep!" Ryan answered a mere millisecond later. "I've been awake for hours. I'm not sure I'm ready for this, hon."

"It'll be fine. Maybe even fun." Wyatt snuggled up against his man, planting lazy, early-morning kisses on Ryan's shoulder and neck.

"Who am I sitting with?"

"I'm hoping you'll want to sit with me. Murphy's getting us all together this morning at some point to go over the details," Wyatt said, licking Ryan's neck while at the same time tracing his finger around Ryan's nipple.

"Easy. I get really horny when I'm stressed."

"I get really horny when I'm with you." Wyatt turned over on his side, pushing his body back against Ryan.

"Okay, you asked for it." Ryan turned on his side, providing Wyatt with more than adequate proof of just how horny he was.

"Holy shit! Is that Mr. Ed behind me?" Wyatt giggled.

"Good morning, Wilbur," Ryan whinnied in Wyatt's ear as he pushed his way forward. Gasping from Ryan's swift assault, Wyatt dug his fingers into the side of the mattress to keep from falling off the edge of the bed.

"Oh baby," Wyatt moaned as Ryan began to bang his body against his. *Horny... he wasn't joking. God help me!*

LATER that morning, at Murphy's suggestion, the entire clan met for a brief meeting.

"Okay, is everyone here? Where's Linda?" Murphy asked.

Wyatt looked around the room for his housekeeper. *Where the hell was she?*

"I'm here," a frustrated voice rumbled from outside the room, followed moments later by Linda, who came bulldozing in with her thick black hair piled to the ceiling in large sea-foam-green curlers.

"It's a good thing you're starting early," Murphy joked as she took a seat next to Mindy.

"I'm going to try and outline how today and tonight are going to play out—logistically, that is. This is a huge event, and lord knows anything and everything can happen. Hopefully, our plan is solid enough so we'll be able to keep the surprises to a minimum." Wyatt could tell Murphy was flying by the seat of his pants on this one.

He drifted in and out as his partner detailed the arrival of the stylists, makeup folks, leaving the hotel, arriving at the theater, and the anticipated events following the awards ceremony. Looking down at his palms, Wyatt was surprised to discover he'd broken into a sweat.

Am I ready for this? God I want to win! No! I want the movie to win. I don't care if I win. Yes, I do. Please let me die before Murphy. I don't know what I'd do without him.

After their meeting broke, Wyatt followed his father into the makeup area. Ted was first up.

"So, whataya think?" Wyatt asked after his father was seated and greeted by the young man who would be working on him. His father, quiet by nature, hadn't said a word to anyone all morning. Surprisingly, to Wyatt, he appeared to be the one most likely to implode from all of the excitement.

"Son, do you think I should have him add some color to my hair? Darken it up?"

"Gee, Dad, if you want to. Lewis can probably do anything you ask." Wyatt confirmed this with Lewis by exchanging a knowing wink.

There were only a few times before this Wyatt could remember his father taking any kind of interest in his appearance. No doubt tonight was a really big deal for him. Both his parents had been informed that, in all likelihood, they would have some on-camera time either during the presentation of the awards or leading up to them.

Understandably in this instance, appearances mattered. Broadway success was good, but success in Hollywood was much more interesting to Ted and Mindy's cronies back home.

Flower and gift baskets arrived by the boatload. Murphy assigned Ryan to work with the hotel staff to keep a log of what was received so thank-you notes could be sent out later. Another assistant made several trips to the local hospitals with floral extravaganzas of every shape and size. There wasn't any more space for them at the hotel.

By early afternoon, the activity on the top floor of the Crawford was pumped to a feverish pitch. Wyatt spent much of his time talking on his cell phone, accepting well wishes from his friends and co-workers back east.

"I'm going to hold a strong thought for you tonight," the boozy voice on the other end of the phone slurped.

"Thank you for thinking of me, Bethany," Wyatt said, rolling his eyes while praying for a temporary loss of service.

As Wyatt was ending his call, Mindy, who had finished up with Lewis and the stylist assigned to her, came out into the large living room area looking magnificent. Wyatt walked over to her and, with extreme caution, gave her a hug. The last thing he wanted to do was cause some type of wardrobe malfunction.

"Mother, you look fabulous. I mean, absolutely stunning." And she did. Dressed in a lovely dark green creation by Deonne, Mindy Stark could easily hold her own with the best of them.

"Wyatt? Is there a private place we can go to talk for a minute?" his mother whispered into his ear.

"We can talk in my suite. Is there something wrong?" Wyatt asked, praying that there wasn't.

"WHAT was that all about?" Ryan asked when he had crossed the room to where Murphy was standing. "I'm not aware of any trouble, are you?"

"Don't worry, it's nothing like that. Mindy has a gift for Wyatt." Murphy went back to his clipboard.

He's probably had that clipboard in his hands since he got out of the shower.

"What gift? Do you know what it is?" Ryan couldn't hide his curiosity. Especially if it had anything to do with Wyatt.

"Yes, as a matter of fact, nosey boy, I *do* know what it is. And before you ask me, no, I'm not going to tell you. Wyatt can tell you. He'll be excited to show it off. How's it coming with the deliveries? Are you getting everything routed okay? The hotel cooperating with you?"

"Yes, of course. Everything's fine. How come you know what the present is and I don't?" Ryan knew the answer already but couldn't stop himself from asking. This was going to piss him off, and there was nothing he could do about it.

"Ted told me about it this morning," Murphy answered, absorbed in his notes. "It looks like, after Lewis is finished touching up Ted's hair, you're next."

"Murph?" Ryan was more wounded than pissed off that Murphy's bond with Ted and Mindy was still so strong. He was gaining ground with Mindy, but Ted, that was another story. "Ted… I don't think he likes me very much. I'm trying everything I can to get closer to him, but nothing I do seems to work."

"Give it time. Ted's a great guy, but he's loyal as hell and that's part of the reason he's still treading lightly around you. He likes you, I know he does."

"How do you know that?" This was a glimmer of hope, but Ryan wasn't sure he trusted it.

"I asked him. And after I asked him, I told him you were one of the nicest guys I'd ever met and that Wyatt was lucky to have you in his life. So, in exchange for my heartfelt endorsement, plan on drawing my bathwater for the next month."

"That's right, only real men shower." Ryan was wounded, but he wasn't dead.

"Oh... oh, that hurt. You're so mean. I hope you get really bad diarrhea sometime soon when you're stuck in heavy traffic. Please God, give Ryan the shits when he's least expecting it."

"Shut up," Ryan laughed, thankful for the unexpected silliness.

"Listen to me," Murphy said, looking around to make sure the coast was clear of any unwanted ears. "Ted was the same way with me for years when Wyatt and I first got together. What changed things between us was out of anyone's control. Wyatt was still dancing then and his show was in the final week of previews. Ted's brother thought he was dying, so I took it upon myself to go spend time with him on my own. Ted and I had a couple long nights at the hospital. After that, I was fucking golden. Hang in there, buddy, he really does like you. Oh and Mindy, she adores you. I think you already know that."

"Yeah, she and I got off to a good start right off the bat."

"Listen," Murphy said, reaching into his pocket and pulling out his cell phone. "I have to make a few calls. Do me a favor and check with the stylist assigned to you and Wyatt and make sure your clothes are here and everything is okay. I heard some whispering and I want to make sure there aren't any issues we don't know about."

"Sure," Ryan answered, feeling better now that he'd heard Murphy's story. "Wait!" Ryan had completely forgotten the other thing that he had wanted to ask Murphy. It was part of the concern that had been screwing around with his sleep lately.

"What?" Murphy asked.

"Wyatt, what's he going to be like if he loses tonight?" Ryan hadn't been in a competitive situation like this with Wyatt yet and he was anxious to get Murphy's take on what to expect.

"You won't notice anything different about him at all. He'll party, he'll laugh, he'll schmooze with all the right people, and when he gets home tonight and you guys are finally alone, he'll sob like a baby. He'll be inconsolable. And that could last for days."

"I'll deal with it," Ryan said, knowing somehow, someway, he'd manage it.

"I'm thinkin' you don't need to worry too much about it going that direction. There's a couple of categories that might be close calls.

Editing, we have a run for our money there, but I have a good sense for these things and unless I've completely lost my instinct, tonight is going to be all about *Dress Up*. Remember, these Hollywood folk usually think only their own can make movies. It doesn't matter Wyatt did brilliant work on the stage in New York. They weren't expecting him to adapt as well as he did to film. Wyatt and *Dress Up* caught them by surprise. It's a smart, fun picture that's hard to argue with. Everyone's talking about it and I've heard plenty over the last couple weeks to make me think this is going to be a big night for us. Of course, I've probably fucked the whole thing up now trying to erase a page from your worry book, but that's my best guess."

Murphy patted Ryan on the shoulder and made off down the hall with his phone glued to his ear.

"Thanks, Murph!"

"OH, HONEY," his mother assured Wyatt, patting his arm as he closed the door behind them, "nothing is wrong."

"You scared the daylights out of me," he joked, only half kidding. "As cool as I'm trying to appear, I'm a loaded powder keg just waiting for someone to light the match."

"Wyatt, your father and I are more proud of you than you could ever know. Oh, shoot, I promised myself I wouldn't cry and if I do, I'm going to mess up my makeup. Give me a second." Mindy took in several deep breaths before she continued. "In our wildest dreams, I never would have envisioned all you have achieved in your young life."

His mother had to pause again as she struggled to keep her emotions in check. Her struggle embarrassed him. He'd always been very sensitive when either of his parents showed any sign of weakness or emotion. *What is she up to?*

"Anyway, we love you so much and no matter what happens tonight, you'll always be a winner in our eyes. We mean that in every sense of the word. This is all so incredible, I feel like I'm in a fairy tale. Dad is planning on talking to you too, but he was in the middle of getting his hair fixed up so we decided I should take advantage of the moment, before… well, you can see how things are going around here. You never know what is going to happen next. Besides, he's so proud of you right now he's about to burst."

Wyatt watched as his mother opened up her twenty-five-hundred-dollar jeweled clutch by Ye Yang and took out a small package.

"Here," she said, handing it to him. Mindy's emotions overtook her and she was forced to blink and fan her face, unaware the mascara the makeup people had used on her was cry-proof.

"What is this, Mother?" Wyatt asked, not sure what he could say at this point that wouldn't contribute to her anxiety.

Mindy was unable to answer, but instead, ventured a break from fanning long enough to gesture down to the package. Wyatt undid the tiny white ribbon, so neatly tied, and carefully removed the silver paper wrapped around the thin, black box. He giggled as he removed the cover. Mindy, who by this point had regained her composure, looked on with her arm locked through his.

"Oh my gosh! Mother, this is beautiful," Wyatt gushed after peeling back the tissue paper. "It's stunning! I love it, I really do." He reached into the box and extracted a very simple brushed silver bracelet inset with a variety of small, colorful gemstones. Wyatt put the bracelet on and held it up for them both to admire. "Where on earth did you find this?"

"It's your lucky charm for tonight, honey. The gems were all your grandmother's."

Wyatt's jaw dropped as he admired the beautiful piece of jewelry. He sat down on the nearest chair and tried it on. Tears welled up when he thought about how special this bracelet was. He had loved his grandmother. She had been his special friend, growing up.

Wyatt felt his mother's comforting hands on his shoulder. "Your dad and I love you so much. We wanted to give you something special. I'm sure if your grandmother were around today, she would be just as proud of you as can be and honored that you have this bracelet."

"Wow, this means so much to me." Wyatt brought his hand to his mouth. When he again found his voice, he said, "It's incredible. I'll never take it off."

"Stay put for a few minutes. I'm going to try and pry your father away from that makeup person before he talks him into false eyelashes."

Wyatt and his mother shared a laugh as she closed the door, leaving him with a few minutes alone. He couldn't take his eyes off the bracelet. It was the finest gift he had ever received.

Once everyone was dressed and ready to go, Murphy began orchestrating the complicated task of getting everyone over to the theater in one piece. The staff had alerted them that there were hordes of fans outside hoping to catch a glimpse of Wyatt and his entourage. It had been leaked by one of the tabloids that he and his family were staying there. These would be hard-core fans who would take anything they could get in the way of an autograph, a picture, or piece of clothing. It didn't matter to them.

In the recent weeks leading up to the ceremony, Wyatt and Ryan had been getting their fair share of press. Wyatt was beginning to understand he wasn't just a director and choreographer from New York any longer. He was now a superstar director of one of the season's most critically successful and highest-grossing films. Life would never be the same, at least not in the very near future. If the movie did well tonight, all bets were off.

Using a service elevator, they headed down into the bowels of the old hotel and climbed into their limousine, which only had to go a block before it was forced to join the slow moving queue of white and black stretch and ultra-stretch limos inching their way up to the theater's entrance. Rows of limousines were backed up as far as the eye could see. One by one they deposited their bejeweled precious human cargo at the beginning of the red carpet.

"Holy shit," Ryan said as he stared out the window in disbelief.

"Holy shit," Mindy repeated, much to their amazement. Wyatt couldn't ever recall hearing his mother swear. Everyone was too overwhelmed by what was going on outside to acknowledge her unassuming entrance into the world of gutter-speak.

The limo was stocked with Wyatt's favorite champagne. They sipped the obligatory glass as they looked back and forth at one another in absolute wonderment. Wyatt, feeling ten years old for some reason, couldn't suppress a giggle as he watched the car in front of them unload a famous starlet and her husband to thunderous applause from the fans in the stands lining the carpet. Looking over at his mother and father, he felt so proud they could be here with him. No matter how the evening turned out as far as awards were concerned, it was already an experience they would cherish for the rest of their lives. His parents would certainly have quite a tale to share with their friends once they returned to their quiet, Midwestern lives.

At last their car rolled to a stop. Tuxedoed, white-gloved attendants opened the passenger doors. Murphy, who had been riding shotgun with the driver in case they ran into any problems, scurried out to mediocre applause from the legions of fans awaiting another A-list celebrity to add to their list. Wyatt could hear more applause as the rest of the car unloaded.

"You ready for this?" he asked, giving Ryan's knee a squeeze. "You're a celebrity too, you know."

"I'm with you, honey," Ryan answered, planting a kiss on Wyatt's lips. "I'm ready for anything. Let's get the party started."

Ryan stepped out of the car and the crowd went wild.

"Ryan! Hey, Ryan! Over here! We love you, Ryan!"

Wyatt stepped out of the limo and was overwhelmed by an explosion of flash from all the cameras.

"Hang on," Ryan said, grabbing Wyatt by the arm. "I've got you covered."

"Wyatt! Hey, Wyatt! Over here! We love you, Wyatt!"

Wyatt put his arm around Ryan, causing a surge of applause. Cameras flashed continuously as the couple inched a few feet away from the car. Smiling from ear to ear and waving with their free hands, they turned to face both sides of the carpet so their fans could get a picture of the two of them together.

Wyatt caught site of Murphy up ahead, who signaled for them to keep on walking. After catching up to the rest of the group. Murphy guided his chicks down the brilliant red carpet, guarding them from the press wolves hoping for one of the much sought after red-carpet exclusives.

The partners had agreed they would make only one stop before entering the theater. Matthew Lyons, saddled with interviewing anyone he could get his hands on for an independent, struggling new gay television network, had been a champion of their projects for years. They strolled down the carpet toward Matt. Wyatt politely waved and smiled past a long line of major network personalities. Murphy, leading the way, made sure they stuck to their plan. They owed Matt their thanks for his support over the years and this was a wonderful way to pay him back.

"Hey, Wyatt," Matt said cheerfully, sticking a microphone in the director's face. "You look devilishly handsome tonight. May I ask who you are wearing?"

"You're so very kind," Wyatt replied. "By the way, you look top-shelf tonight yourself. My tux, Matt, was made by Jake Dennis. But hey, the fashion exclusive you're really going to want is standing next to me. Here's the real diva in the group—Mother?" Wyatt stepped aside to let his mother move up to the microphone. "This is my mother, Mindy Stark. Wait! Let's get Ted up here too." Wyatt took his father by the arm and pulled him forward.

"Mindy, Ted, what an honor it is to meet you. You both look ravishing tonight. Mindy, I absolutely adore those fabulous earrings."

"Well, thank you, honey, you look good too." Mindy was barely able to keep herself together as the camera man behind Matt positioned himself so he could get a full-length shot of her beautiful green gown, and of course, a close-up of those fabulous earrings.

"I have to say, in all honesty, you have one of the most beautiful dresses I have seen all night, and there have been some real winners. Now the audience will want to know, who are *you* wearing tonight?"

Mindy looked at Wyatt in a panic. She had forgotten who she was wearing. Wyatt leaned forward and whispered the name into her ear.

"The gown is by Deonne, and the purse, which I just adore, is by… oh, shoot! Wyatt, I can't remember anything these days." Once again, Wyatt leaned forward and prompted his mother.

"The purse is by Wong… Wang," Mindy corrected herself as she leaned on her son for support.

"Wyatt, I know you have to run, but I have to ask, do you think *Dress Up* is going to take home the big prize tonight?"

Before answering, Wyatt looked over at Murphy, who winked and flashed him a huge smile.

"Matt, honestly, I have no idea. In my mind, we've already won. The movie has done extraordinarily well since its release. I have everyone around me tonight I love. I'm happy no matter what happens. You'll have to believe that, my friend." Wyatt gave a brief wave to an army of bystanders who were shouting for his attention.

"Thank you, Wyatt, and your lovely mother… and your father," Matt quickly added, "for taking the time to chat with us on this incredible night. Your fans are rooting for you and I am too. Have a great evening and good luck."

"Thank you, Matt. Have a great night!" Wyatt shook hands and turned to leave, but before he got more than a foot away, he turned and stepped back to the mike. "Matt, I think we stand a damn good chance of taking home the big prize." Wyatt announced proudly, joining the rest of his party.

Murphy led the way into the theater. They all, as they had been advised, used the restroom before taking their seats, which were amazing. Wyatt and Ryan, as instructed by Murphy, took aisle seats directly behind Lana in the fourth row.

"Hello, darlings," she said, standing and turning to give them each a hug.

"Good luck tonight, Lana," Ryan said, taking his seat.

"Thank you, honey. This is for you," she said, looking back with a smile, holding her fingers up so Wyatt could see they were crossed.

Swiveling his head around to get his bearings, Wyatt glanced back at Murphy and his parents, who were three rows back. He was unable to spot Linda and Sandy, who were on the main floor, but seated even farther past Murphy.

With only minutes to spare, Wyatt fussed with his program and did his best to make himself relax. With a wink and a nervous smile, he took hold of Ryan's hand.

"God, look at the people sitting around us," Ryan said, amused. "There's Jack and Shirley, and… Look at Penelope's date. Argh! Is that her father?"

"Murphy introduced me to him a few months ago. He's her agent. You could weave baskets with all that nose and ear hair," Wyatt whispered while looking around the auditorium, waving back to those mouthing their well-wishes.

"You're not going to believe what's going on behind us," Ryan whispered.

"What?" Wyatt asked, fighting the urge to turn around and see for himself.

"Guess who Mindy is sitting in back of? Come on, guess!"

"Hmmm, is it somebody we know? The seats were empty when I looked back earlier."

There were so many celebrities in such close proximity, Wyatt was flooded with possibilities.

"Meryl. Can you believe it? Your mother is talking to Meryl."

That was more than Wyatt could handle. He had to risk a look for himself. He turned his head as far around as it took for his mother to come into focus. "I hope she doesn't say something I'm going to regret," he thought out loud. He held his gaze for a moment and watched with amusement, and an element of terror. His mother was engaged in a lively and animated conversation with arguably the most talented actress in the history of entertainment. Before he could say another word, the house lights dimmed and the show began.

The night started out with a bang. Wyatt jumped up, unable to contain himself when the supporting actress award went to Lana. Ravishingly beautiful in a long scarlet dress, she was the consummate star, thanking everyone who had ever done anything remotely kind to her along the way. Wyatt felt Ryan grip his hand when she chose him as the subject to end her very moving acceptance speech.

"… in my wildest dreams I never imagined this happening. I wouldn't be standing up here now if it weren't for the incredible guidance and talent of Wyatt Stark. Thank you, Wyatt… so much for one of the greatest experiences of my life. Your work has inspired and will continue to inspire all who come in contact with you. Please let me work with you again," Lana begged as she held her award high in the air and swept off the expansive stage in a fiery ball of red.

Many of the audience, including Ryan and Wyatt, were on their feet applauding wildly as Lana exited. Wyatt blushed and was deeply moved by her generous acknowledgment.

"It's true," Ryan whispered, squeezing Wyatt's leg as they sat back down.

Here we go! I just want this over with! I need a drink! Wyatt tried to look calm, even though his stomach was flapping around like a windup doll that had just tipped over onto Formica.

He sat in awe as he watched his baby pick up the award for best set design, best sound, best song, and of course, best costumes. Dahlia Reynolds, who had created the original costumes for the stage version, had pulled out all the stops for the movie. This was the one award Wyatt would have bet the bank on.

Before Wyatt knew it, the award for best director was upon them. He had tried to do his level best to plan for this moment. Telling himself at every opportunity there was a better than fifty-fifty chance this wasn't going to go his way. Years of experience had taught him anything could happen when you got to this level. The fellow nominees he was included with tonight were among the very best in the industry. Wyatt braced himself. He felt Ryan grab his arm and hold on tight.

"… and the award for best direction goes to…."

Time stopped. Wyatt could feel his heart pounding. The entire audience sat hushed in anticipation.

I can't breathe.

As nonchalantly as he could manage, he gulped for air, fully aware that nine trillion people were watching him to see his reaction when he lost.

"Wyatt Stark!"

"*Wheeeeeeeeeeeee!*"

Was that a police whistle?

People all around him stood and turned in his direction with smiles and waves of congratulations. Lana turned around and planted a huge, wet sloppy on him. Ryan grabbed him by the waist, lifting him a foot off the ground.

Is this fucking really happening?

He turned around to face his parents and Murphy, who, along with Meryl, were jumping up and down like rabbits.

Well-wishers from both sides of the aisle slapped his hands as he bounded up toward the podium.

"We love you, Wyatt," a hysterical fan yelled from the rafters. Grinning from ear to ear, he turned and saluted the balcony before racing up the stairs and onto the stage, where he was greeted by last year's winner for direction.

"Thank you, Clint," Wyatt said as he pumped the hand of the renowned director. A model in a sparkly white dress handed him his Oscar.

"Fuck, this thing is heavy!"

Wyatt prayed he'd said that to himself as the applause seemed to build to an even louder level. He peered out into the audience and struggled to organize his thoughts.

"You know," he started out, gesturing for everyone to sit when his trained ear heard the applause begin to taper, "you can't imagine what this moment means to me."

He paused, taking a moment to examine the gold figure he was holding. "I've been so blessed, in so many ways, part of me wants to scream 'I'm not worthy' and run like hell."

The audience exploded in laughter and applause. Wyatt waited a few seconds before continuing.

"I'm going to take the easy way out tonight. It's the surest route for a scatterbrained dancer and hopefully the least likely to embarrass." Wyatt looked out over the crowd in the huge auditorium. It was surreal to see so many famous faces smiling back at him.

"To all of you who have helped me get here tonight—and I hope I've done a good enough job along the way of thanking you all so you know who you are—from the bottom of my heart, I thank you. I'm tremendously honored by this recognition."

"*Wheeeeeeeeeeeeeee!*"

Wyatt was forced to pause again as the crowd reacted to the loud whistle from an excited fan.

"My mother and father." Wyatt couldn't prevent his eyes from growing moist. "I can't imagine a better mom and dad. Your acceptance, your guidance and encouragement provided the perfect foundation for me to go out there and do what I wanted from my earliest memory... sing and dance. Thank you!"

Wyatt waited patiently for the applause to ebb. *Please don't let the music start. Not yet.*

"Murphy... I know you know I love you... but I wonder if you know just how much." Wyatt couldn't resist making the "itsy bitsy" sign, which sent the audience into fits of laughter.

"Seriously, I can't imagine life without you, my dear friend. Thank you for being there at the best, and worst, of times. I will go to my grave owing you."

Wyatt fought back the familiar trembling that always occurred in his lower lip just prior to the all-out eruption of emotion.

"Listen, before I get the hook...." Taking a deep breath, he forced himself to focus. "I want to thank...."

Goddamn it! Hold it together! You're almost through this!

He was holding on by a string. Closing his eyes for a moment to gather his wits, Wyatt willed himself to go on before he lost complete control of himself.

"My husband, Ryan Taylor!"

"*Wheeeeeeeeeeee!*"

"Oh... God bless you," Wyatt laughed as he gestured up to the heavens, thankful for the comic relief.

"Ryan, I don't know what you saw in me, but I certainly know what I saw in you. You're a kind man, a funny man... you're true-blue... and there's no greater feeling in the world than when you wrap your arms around me. I'm so proud to be yours. Please share this moment with me forever."

Whew! I made it.

Wyatt had always wondered how people got so disorientated after giving an acceptance speech, and now he understood. He gladly accepted the arm of the model who led the way off the stage.

The world was buzzing around him. Everywhere he looked, the stage lights, the technicians, the dancers, as familiar a world as it was to him, tonight was different. Tonight it all seemed so new. Wyatt stood in the wings with his head bowed as the award for best picture of the year began.

"Good luck, Mr. Stark," an eager young man with headphones said, giving him an enthusiastic thumbs-up. More well-wishers from backstage gathered around.

"… and the award for best picture goes to…."

Wyatt closed his eyes. Hands down, this was Murphy's award. *Please… please… please let this one go our way.*

"DRESS UP!"

Thank you!

"Mr. Stark." Wyatt opened his eyes to see the handsome young technician wearing headphones gesture for him to walk back out onto the stage. Still clutching his best director award, Wyatt strolled out to the podium where Murphy waited, laughing wildly, holding his own gold statue.

"We did it," Wyatt squealed, throwing his arms around his partner.

"It's only the beginning, Wy," Murphy whispered in his ear.

As agreed, should they miraculously find themselves in this moment, Wyatt stepped aside while Murphy approached the microphone.

"Hurry," Wyatt joked while Murphy waited for the crowd to calm down.

"Many… many years ago," Murphy began, "I went to the big city with a dream. I wanted to be a great big Broadway star."

Nervous laughter from the audience. Wyatt clutched his Oscar to his chest as he weathered a wave of images from their past.

"Well," Murphy continued, "that wasn't meant to be. But that's okay. It's okay because shortly after arriving in New York, I met up with a dazzling smile who just happened to have two extremely long and talented legs attached to it. I immediately fell in love."

"*Wheeeeeeeeeeee!*"

"Buddy, I've got to tell you, Murphy said, shielding his eyes from the bright lights, "if I'm ever in the market for a whistler, you've got the job."

Wyatt loved how relaxed and casual Murphy was being. How confident and strong he appeared. Looking out over all the faces, he could see how much the audience loved this moment. And Ryan, how adorable he looked sitting at the edge of his seat with his hands clasped tightly together, all smiles. How handsome his man looked tonight in his spiffy tuxedo.

"I'm going to run out of time and I don't want that to happen."

Murphy's voice brought him back into the moment.

"Well, you know the story by now I'm sure. I hooked up with Wyatt and together we gave it our best shot. That's what you can count on when you work with Wyatt, getting his best shot."

Wyatt could feel his face turning red.

"There are so many people to thank, and like my buddy here, I would feel terrible if I left anyone out, so I'm also going to go the lame route and thank everyone… who has ever had a hand in helping me, helping us get here… from the bottom of my heart, I will forever be thankful. Your kindness and generosity has meant so much to me. Part of this is for you." Murphy held his statue high in the air.

"Not the head—you can't have the head, because I love that part the most."

"Murphy," Wyatt scolded in mock dismay. Sensing the moment was right, he took his friend by the arm. Hand in hand, they strolled off the stage to the biggest applause of the night.

Epilogue

RYAN peered out of the porch after two short horn blasts announced the imminent arrival of Dragon Balls, a fully restored 1965 Chris-Craft thirty-six foot Challenger Murphy had recently added to his collection of toys. Ryan and Wyatt, still hesitant to embrace the boat's official name, referred to it as "Murphy's yacht."

Ryan secured the last cluster of balloons to the back of a chair and stepped aside to give the entire room a final once-over. He had spent the better part of the morning cooking and decorating in preparation for today's party. *Perfect!*

Ryan timed the arrival of Murphy's yacht with his own arrival at the end of the dock. He caught the line Rafael tossed to him and lashed it around the cleat.

"You guys look… fabulous," Ryan said, acknowledging the loud, floral-print shirts the two were wearing. "But you must have taken a wrong turn. The Islands are that way."

"Jealousy… can be such a nuisance," Murphy groaned. "Don't go there, my friend. This is a very special occasion so we thought we'd come over looking… what's the right word, Rafael?"

"Festive," Rafael answered with an elaborate flip of his wrist.

"Ah yes… we're appropriately… festive," Murphy agreed, mimicking Rafael's overly festive wrist flip. "Where's Wyatt and Cheeri O?" Murphy asked, jumping off the boat and taking the line from Rafael, joining it together with another already secured to the bow.

"Wyatt and O are working." He hugged Rafael, "Hi, sweetie!"

"You look great," Rafael said as he stepped back to give Ryan the once-over.

"Hey, Skipper," Ryan said, giving Murphy a peck on the cheek and a bear hug.

"Hey, lil' buddy," Murphy said, returning the kiss and hug. "What do you mean, Wyatt and O are working?"

"They won't be long," Ryan said, looking over in the direction of the dance studio attached to the side of the house. "Wyatt's putting some choreography on video to send to Sandy. She's starting to work with dancers for the gay-teen project. He shouldn't be too long. They've been going at it for several hours now. I'll pull the plug if I have to."

"Please... please tell me Wyatt isn't dancing naked," Murphy begged.

"Shouldn't be. O has a tendency to tug on Wyatt's dangly downs when he's naked, so he's been taking precautions and wearing clothes more these days," Ryan joked.

"Okay, but wait a second. Rafael, please grab Ducky."

"Ducky?" Ryan asked quizzically.

Rafael climbed into the boat and hopped back out with an enormous stuffed duck sporting a huge blue ribbon around its neck.

"That's outrageous," Ryan squealed.

"Do you think he'll like it?" Murphy asked.

"Of course he will," Ryan assured, shaking his head in wonderment. "I love it! You guys are crazy!"

"Do you think he'll be scared of it?" Rafael asked, concerned.

"Well, it might take him a few days to warm up to the big guy, but he'll be climbing all over him in no time. Here... I'll run Ducky up to the porch and meet you guys at the studio."

"Got it," Murphy said as Rafael handed over the stuffed duck.

"Whatever you do, don't let them see you, okay?" Ryan hauled Ducky from the dock up to the house, depositing it next to the birthday table, and then sprinted back down to join Rafael and Murphy.

"Are they still working?" Ryan asked, jogging up to meet them at the studio.

"How fucking cute is that?" Murphy giggled as the three of them peered around the corner of the doorway.

Music pulsated throughout the studio. Wyatt, dressed in loose-fitting sweats and a T-shirt, was dancing like a madman in front of a wall of mirrors. Off to the side, several feet away, O was popping up and down in his bouncy seat.

"Meet the next big talent to hit the Great White Way—Oscar Cohen Taylor," Uncle Murphy announced proudly.

"I sure hope you guys have this on film. I can't believe he's already a year old. He's going to be so big and strong," Rafael observed.

"Just as long as he's big where it counts," Murphy commented with a sleazy smile.

"You stop that nasty talk," Ryan scolded, slapping Murphy on the side of his head. "Besides, that won't be a worry, given the fact that…."

"Yeah, right!" Murphy gave Ryan a playful shove back.

"It looks like they're both still into it. Let's go up to the house and grab something cold to drink," Ryan grabbed Rafael by the hand, pulling him away from the doorway.

"So, does O miss the city?" Murphy asked.

"He seems to be adjusting," Ryan answered. "We've been here a couple of weeks already and so far, no problems. I think at first he really missed Linda. We love her dearly, but man, is that woman possessive! When we're in New York, O has three parents, wait… make that four!"

"Four?" Rafael asked, confused.

"Well… there's me and Wyatt, there's Linda, and we certainly can't forget about Sandy. After all, she baked the little nipper."

"Is she still comfortable with the arrangement?" Murphy asked.

"Oh, hell yes! You guys want beer… wine?" Ryan asked.

"Beer, wine," they answered back in unison.

"Gotcha!"

Ryan and Wyatt had worked with Murphy to design the cozy, cottage-style home they had built last year on a cove just a few miles down the shore. It was the perfect design for them. Having the studio here was a godsend, and allowed for much longer stays.

"Sandy is thrilled with the arrangement." Ryan continued, coming back with beverages. "I know this for a fact because, a couple of weeks ago, she stood by me while I changed O's diaper, and trust me... the lady isn't mommy material. Not by a long shot!"

"And Wyatt is...." Murphy asked, raising an inquisitive eyebrow.

"I wasn't sure how this parenthood thing was going to work out," Ryan confessed, "but I have to tell you, Wyatt's been amazing. He's totally into it. Even the diaper-changing. But I have to admit, that took some conditioning."

"Oh, I bet it did," Murphy said, cracking up.

"This is between us... he still wears a nose plug," Ryan gossiped. Rafael and Murphy could hardly contain their amusement.

"I'm serious, he found a cheap, flesh-colored plug at the local drugstore."

"That is so damn funny," Murphy said. He and Rafael were loving this.

"But this is what cracks me up," Ryan went on. "The other day... he came back from changing O's diaper and, in all seriousness, told me that changing O was just like removing the frosting from little cupcakes and replacing it with powdered sugar."

Murphy and Rafael exploded into fits of laughter.

"What's so funny?" Wyatt asked, sweeping onto the porch. "What the hell is that?"

"It's Ducky," Murphy answered, wiping tears from his eyes.

"Hey, O! Look what Uncle Murphy and Uncle Rafael have brought you. It's Ducky!" Cradling his son in his arm, Wyatt strolled slowly around the table so the baby wouldn't be startled by the enormous duck lurking at him from the corner.

Everyone in the room held their breath while Wyatt knelt down so O could be on the same level as the duck's face. A few tense seconds passed before a universal sigh of relief came when the little tot reached out and petted its nose.

"Nice ducky," Wyatt prompted as O continued to pet and explore his new friend.

"Dada," O cooed.

"Everything's Dada these days," Wyatt explained proudly. "Even the gulls!"

"Here!" Ryan pushed another bouncy chair toward Wyatt. "Why don't you put him down, and I'll grab his bottle."

"What a little actor you are," Wyatt said, making a face as he pulled O away. "The duck scared the crap out of him, but who knew? I'll go change him first." Wyatt gave Ryan a smooch on the lips as he passed by.

"Be gentle with those little cupcakes," Murphy barely managed to get out before collapsing into hysterics.

"Well, it's true! They're like stinky little frosted cupcakes," Wyatt chuckled as he carried O back into the house like a squirming football.

"There're some rough spots we have to work on," Ryan joked, "but we're making progress every day."

Ryan drifted up and out of the conversation. He was acutely aware of how fortunate he was. This was the family he had always wanted. Loving and happy. Murphy and Rafael, he hoped they would grow together and continue to enjoy each other's company. He loved them both. He smiled over at Wyatt, such a proud papa. How fortunate they were to have so many loving and supportive people in their lives.

Drifting back into the moment, he settled his gaze on his little guy, whose face was now coated in cracker. One thing was clear: O was the frosting on *their* cupcake.

"What the hell is that?" Wyatt asked, startled. A loud beeping was coming from somewhere under the table.

"Hang on!" Murphy reached into his pocket and pulled out his BlackBerry. "Shit... this isn't good," he said after studying the device for several minutes.

"What isn't good?" Wyatt asked.

"There's a huge band of thunderstorms headed our way."

"Really?" Ryan asked, standing to look out over the cove.

"We should think about getting the boat back and secured before all hell breaks loose." Murphy looked over to Rafael, who nodded back.

"Ah, come on!" Wyatt protested. "We haven't done cake yet."

"I don't think that's going to matter much to O," Ryan said, squeezing Wyatt's arm. Oblivious to the drama unfolding, the baby had fallen asleep.

THE storm was taking its time, but it was getting closer. There were rumbles in the distance when they climbed into bed. Ryan spooned his hubby as they listened to the rain begin.

Wyatt rolled over onto his stomach, stretching out his long frame. Ryan climbed on top and began massaging his back. Leaning forward, he was soon nipping and kissing Wyatt's neck.

You'll always be the hottest man I know.

Ryan slid his body back and forth, each time moving a little farther back until he was where he needed to be. Pushing Wyatt's legs apart, he nestled his face behind his man. Using his hand to force an opening, his tongue began lazy circles, darting back and forth.

"Oh...." Wyatt moaned, arching his backside toward Ryan.

In no rush, Ryan relaxed his body and continued to pleasure Wyatt. With the thunder growing louder, he moved back on top and slowly worked his way deep inside his man.

"Mmm, you're so warm and tight." Ryan paused and resumed his kisses, concentrating on Wyatt's neck and his ears. *He's ready for more, I can sense it.* Hunching back onto his knees, Ryan reached under Wyatt's long body with his strong arms and pulled Wyatt backward, sliding in deeper. He pulled back further yet, until Wyatt was on his knees, stretching his arms high into the air. Ryan's large hands began caressing Wyatt's chest.

The rain increased, and feeling a familiar urgency, Ryan released his grip on Wyatt's torso, allowing him to fall back onto his palms. He began his assault with slow, deliberate thrusts.

"Oh… yes," Wyatt begged as he reached behind, resting his hand on Ryan's hip, riding it as it pumped steadily back and forth.

Repositioning himself, Ryan reached forward, grasping Wyatt's pulsating shaft. His hand glided up and down, pausing along the way to tease and nurture.

"I … I… can't hold back," Wyatt soon cried out.

Ryan pumped harder, his hips bucking. Streams of sweat ran from his forehead down his cheeks. Throwing his head back, he was forced to give in.

"Yes! Yes!" Ryan hollered into the air. Waves of sensation rocked and rolled his body as he released deep into his man. With a final thrust, he collapsed them both back down onto the bed.

Wyatt's powerful body continued to heave up and down. Ryan buried his face into the back of Wyatt's head, gasping for air as he rode Wyatt's body.

The approaching storm was growing impatient. Occasional flashes of light lit up the room, followed by loud rumblings of thunder. Ryan moved off of Wyatt. Lying side by side, they listened to the storm intensify.

"Wyatt," Ryan whispered into his husband's ear.

"I can't… I just can't. Not again. God… not again," Wyatt pleaded. "I'm spent. Do me if you have to… I'll wait here."

"No, it's not that." Ryan engulfed Wyatt in his strong arms and hugged him even tighter. "I'm still savoring the last round. Hon, I want to say something to you."

"What is it, sweetheart?" Wyatt reached behind and ran his hand through Ryan's moist hair.

"Thank you so much for coming after me that day. I know I've thanked you before, but I'm just so... I'm so thankful. I'm so incredibly lucky!"

A loud crack of thunder made the windows above their heads vibrate. "Well, there go any hopes for a good night's sleep." Ryan crawled out of bed and crossed to the door, where he stood motionless, his head cocked as he listened down the hall.

"Did he wake up?" Wyatt asked, sitting up.

The storm was getting closer and an even brighter flash of lightning lit up the room, followed by another loud crack of thunder that rattled the entire house.

"Well, if the one before didn't wake him, that one certainly did the trick."

Ryan left the room and headed down the hall, stopping at the door of the adjacent bedroom. Wyatt followed and was standing beside him.

"Can you believe it," Ryan said in a whisper, "I think he's managed to stay sleeping through all of this."

"Let's take a look," Wyatt whispered back.

They tiptoed into the nursery. Peering over the edge of the crib, they saw that their little one, despite the noisy storm outside, remained in peaceful slumber.

"Isn't he beautiful?" Wyatt asked, pulling the tiny cotton blanket back up and over his boy.

"How could he not be? Look how handsome his daddies are," Ryan whispered. "And mommy Sandy is so... so beautiful. Pa, O's going to have it all going on. I'm tellin' ya."

"I still can't believe she agreed to do this for us. It just made the whole thing all the more special," Wyatt whispered back.

"That it did!" Ryan put his arm around Wyatt. "Okay, that's enough ogling. Let's try and get some sleep while we can. O's going to be a little pistol tomorrow."

"Sure thing, Pop," Wyatt joked, kissing Ryan on the neck.

Back in their warm bed, the thunder rumbled in the distance. Ryan probed and pestered until he had coaxed Wyatt into another round. He was relentless and he knew it. They kissed with increased passion, and when it felt right, Ryan made his entrance. Wyatt nibbled and sucked at Ryan's fingers.

I can't get enough of you, baby!

Taking a cue from the rain, which had started to come down harder than ever, Ryan picked up the pace, matching the intensity of the rain. He moved Wyatt onto his side. Thunder cracked even closer than before and, as if on cue, their bodies tensed as they both were rocked by uncontrollable waves of ecstasy.

"Fuck," Wyatt gasped.

"I know," Ryan said softly, panting and struggling to catch his breath.

"Please stay inside me," Wyatt said. "I love how you feel there."

"Sure. I love being there."

WYATT loved when Ryan buried his face into the crook of his neck. Minutes passed and Ryan began to snore.

Still wound up from their lovemaking, Wyatt pulled away and crawled out of bed. He padded down the hallway to check on his precious, Oscar. The baby had moved, but still continued to sleep. He reached down and stroked the tiny little hand.

Please give me what it takes to be the best daddy I can possibly be. I'll do whatever it takes. And whoever you are out there, please protect my little one and keep him safe. Would you do that for me? For us?

Smiling, Wyatt kissed the tip of his finger and placed it on Oscar's nose. "Good night, son," he whispered.

Satisfied all was well, he returned to bed. Draping his arm across his other man, Wyatt drifted off to sleep as the storm headed out to sea.

JOEL SKELTON is the son of a big-band pianist. Consequently, the arts have always played a prominent role in Joel's life. Sports... not so much. Much to Dad's dismay, piano lessons gave way to the saxophone, which was eventually retired when the stage called out loud and clear. Writing is the latest destination in the author's tour of the arts. Joel, along with his partner and a handful of tropical fish (Bruce, Dottie, Nemo, the Blue Guys, the Joannes, and Bitch) live in the thriving Minnesota arts community commonly referred to as the Twin Cities.

Romance from DREAMSPINNER PRESS

http://www.dreamspinnerpress.com